FOLK LEGENDS OF JAPAN

by RICHARD M. DORSON

Chairman, Folklore Program
Indiana University

illustrated by YOSHIE NOGUCHI

CHARLES E. TUTTLE COMPANY : PUBLISHERS
Rutland, Vermont   Tokyo, Japan

Representatives

For Continental Europe:
BOXERBOOKS, INC., Zurich

For the British Isles:
PRENTICE-HALL INTERNATIONAL, INC., London

For Australasia:
PAUL FLESCH & CO., PTY. LTD., Melbourne

For Canada:
M. G. HURTIG LTD., Edmonton

Published by the Charles E. Tuttle Company, Inc.
of Rutland, Vermont & Tokyo, Japan
with editorial offices at
Suido 1-chome, 2-6, Bunkyo-ku, Tokyo

Copyright in Japan, 1962, by Charles E. Tuttle Company, Inc.
Library of Congress Catalog Card No. 60-11972 — not right

International Standard Book No. 0-8048-0191-6

First edition, 1962
Eighth printing, 1973

0293-000260-4615
Printed in Japan

For TOPPER and REIKO

TABLE OF CONTENTS

PART FIVE. HEROES AND STRONG MEN : *149*

ACKNOWLEDGMENTS

My INITIAL DEBT is to the United States Educational Commission in Japan, which awarded me an appointment as Fulbright Professor of American Studies at the University of Tokyo for the academic year 1956–57 and so made possible the present undertaking. The Commission also provided funds for translation and research assistants.

The Japanese Folklore Institute in Seijo-machi, Tokyo, proved a treasure house for me, and I cannot sufficiently express my gratitude to Kunio Yanagita, its founder, Tokihiko Oto, its director, and Toichi Mabuchi, one of its advisors and Professor of Anthropology at Tokyo Metropolitan University, all of whom extended me every kindness. At the Institute, Miss Yasuyo Ishiwara, a graduate of Tokyo Women's Christian College, spent long hours with me translating Japanese legends and giving me the benefit of her training and knowledge as an assistant to Professor Yanagita. Naofusa Hirai, director of the Institute of Classical Studies at Kokugakuin University, acted as interpreter when I first visited the Institute and proved a friend throughout the year. Also at the Institute I met Fanny Hagin Mayer, who generously allowed me to read her unpublished translation of Professor Yanagita's *Classification of Japanese Folk Tales* (Nippon Mukashi-banashi Meii) and accompanied me on a trip to Niigata. At the KBS Library, curator Makoto Kuwabara aided me in tracking down studies of Japanese folklore in their fine collection of Western-language books and journals on Japan.

My student at Tokyo University, Kayoko Saito, who subsequently studied in the United States on a Fulbright award and is now back at the university as a graduate student, helped me in important ways—by collecting legends from her grandmother, by translating for me, and by introducing me to Professor Masahiro Ikegami, now at Showa Medical University, and interpreting the two private lectures with slides he kindly gave me on the syncretism of folk religion with Buddhism and Shintoism as seen in Japanese mountain religion. Teigo Yoshida, Professor of Sociology at Kyushu University, contributed to my volume a folk legend he had collected during his field work. Authors of collections of Japanese legends who personally or through correspondence have generously granted me permission to publish translations of their texts are Keigo Seki, noted student of the Japanese folk tale; Riboku Dobashi; Kazuo Katsurai; Kiyoshi Mitarai; Chihei Nakamura; and Shogo Nakano; to all of whom I am deeply indebted, as well as to the other authors listed in the sources, who have faithfully recorded Japanese legends. Masaharu Murai generously procured for me a copy of his translation *Legends and Folktales of Shinshu* when I met him in Nagano.

On my return to the United States I was fortunate to meet Ichiro Hori, an outstanding younger Japanese folklore scholar then lecturing at Harvard University and the University of Chicago on popular Buddhism, and Mrs. Hori, the daughter of Professor Yanagita. Professor Hori has graciously read my introduction and given me helpful suggestions. To contributors of the forthcoming *Studies in Japanese Folklore* which I am editing for the Indiana University Folklore Series, I must express gratitude for a preview of their illuminating articles. My deep thanks go to Professor George K. Brady of the University of Kentucky, who has helped make available in English translation important Japanese folklore studies, and who has aided me in personal ways. Indiana University has bountifully provided me with research facilities.

Both Miss Ishiwara and Miss Saito, named above, and Meredith Weatherby of the Tuttle Company have been most helpful in checking my manuscript and straightening out certain perplexing points.

Finally, I must express my pleasure and good fortune to have as publisher an old friend and classmate, Charles E. Tuttle, who has been so active in the publication of "books to span the East and West."

Bloomington, Indiana.   RICHARD M. DORSON

FOLK LEGENDS OF JAPAN

INTRODUCTION

JAPAN POSSESSES more legends than any country in the Western world. So says Professor Kunio Yanagita, who founded the scientific study of folklore in Japan, and who remains today its venerable sage. We cannot say with certainty how many legends a people cherish, but we know that a vast number have been collected from every district in Japan. Even Yanagita-*sensei* is at a loss to explain just why his culture has produced so many legendary traditions. But volume after volume has appeared in the present century setting down village stories connected with mountains and trees and pools and hot springs, with *kappa* and *tengu* and other demonic creatures, with wealthy peasants and doughty samurai, and above all with the grieved and hateful spirits of those who died with anger in their hearts. Altogether some fifty such books of folk legends have been printed in Japan, not to mention the many hundreds of individual legends which have appeared in collections of general folk tales or in topographical and historical works. In the United States not a single book of legends spoken by the folk has ever been published.

The word legend has various meanings in modern usage, and even folklorists disagree on its precise significance. A legend is a particular kind of folk tale, and so belongs to the family of stories passed down by word of mouth over the generations. The best known and most frequently collected type of such stories is the fairy tale, and fairy tales have now been reprinted and rewritten so frequently that they belong to literary as much as to oral tradition. The key difference between fairy tale and legend is that narrator and audience accept the fairy tale

17

as fiction, while they believe the legend describes an actual happening.

The legend is therefore a true story in the minds of the folk who retain it in their memory and pass it along to the next generation. There would be little point, however, in remembering the countless ordinary occurrences of daily life, so the legend is further distinguished by describing an extraordinary event. In some way the incident at its core contains noteworthy, remarkable, astonishing, or otherwise memorable aspects. The presence of a goblin or a giant, a ghost or an apparition, inevitably causes village talk. A strong man may perform some prodigious feat of strength, or a village wag perpetuate some ludicrous prank that endures in local memory. Legends range in length from brief outlines of a dimly recalled event, to a full narrative of strange experiences. Fairy tales, being composed of several adventures arranged in a set pattern and well fixed in the mind of the storyteller, run longer and contain more substance and detail than legends. When the fairy tale becomes anchored in a particular locality, is told as having occurred there, and incorporates the family- and place-names of the neighborhood, it has crossed the line into legendry. More rarely, when a myth of the gods, preserved in an ancient literary manuscript, takes on local coloring and the god is spoken of as having appeared in the vicinity, the myth assumes the form of living legend.

These considerations bring up another point. The legend is believed, it is remarkable, and also it is local. The scene of its action may be the village itself, or some special landmark in the environs. A stunted pine, an ominous cavern, a deep pool, a lofty peak are all customarily endowed with legendary associations. Geographical landmarks keep fresh the memory of events connected with them by power of association, sometimes fixed in the name itself, like "The Mountain of Abandoned Old People" or "The River of Human Sacrifice." Furthermore, since legends, like all other kinds of folklore, are carried from one place to another, they fasten easily onto a similar feature of the landscape in a different part of the country. Man-made structures as well as nature's handiwork become encrusted with traditionary incident over the course of time: bridges, dams, castles, derelict dwellings. In Japan especially, every shrine and temple seems to bear its burden of ancient story. Some dark tragedy of the long ago has caused the erection of yonder Shinto shrine, and the villagers who pass it daily or honor it annually know its message. As legends attach to particular places in the district, so they cling to unusual persons who have lived in or passed through the township. Individuals who stand out from the everyday throng in some peculiar way, because of their physical prowess or roguish humor or occult powers, are talked about by later generations until they take on legendary hues. Or a famous historical figure has traveled briefly through the district, and given rise to a host of apocryphal stories about his actions in the locality. A priest, a saint, a god has performed his miracles and left his traces here. In short, a legend needs anchorage, whether to a person, a place, or an event, or to all three in combination, if it is to persist in the unwritten annals of the community.

The "localness" of legends has a simple explanation. These believed episodes continue to be told by people who find in them a strong personal interest. If interest lags, the legend dies. What maintains interest is the intimate association with family or neighborhood history, or with familiar landmarks. The audience knows the names of the actors, whose descendants live in their midst, and who may indeed include their own ancestors, and they see regularly the sites of the bygone events. While the history of textbooks seems distant and impersonal, the remembered traditions of the community possess the fascination of immediate concern; they happened *here*, to *us*. To the appeal of the unusual and arresting incident is thus added the attraction of local interest. Legends represent the folk's-eye view of history.

As a consequence, local traditions flourish most vigorously in hamlets and villages that have endured with little social change for long reaches of time. In such a society one knows his neighbors and shares their sense of a common past; the community has roots, traditions, almost an independent corporate existence. Legends cannot persevere in the big city, save perhaps in local neighborhoods that manage for a space to preserve a sense of identity before the bulldozers desecrate the old landmarks and new swarms of migrants uproot the established dwellers. Nor will too sparse a settlement nourish the seeds of traditionary tales. Enough of a society must exist to set the stage for action, rumor, the play of fancy, and the bubbling currents of excited talk. It is no accident that in the United States New England, the oldest section of the country, and the one chiefly settled in compact townships, contributes the lion's share of American legends. Scarcely a New England town history but contains one chapter on local traditions: a case of witchcraft; a visit from the Devil, whose footprint remains in solid rock; foibles and antics of eccentric townsfolk; a sighting of the sea serpent off the shore; specters in a haunted house that bears an ineradicable bloodstain.

In closely knit communities a legend lives on through constant repetition. This repeated telling of the legend over the generations insures its folklore quality. For even if a story begins immediately after some remarkable happening, in a form fairly close to the facts, it will assume ever more fantastic hues over the years. The Icelandic sagas were first told in the eleventh century by professional saga-men as factual histories of the great chieftains, but when they were finally written down two centuries later, many floating folklore themes and tales had slipped into the narratives. There is indeed one group of scholars who contend that after 150 years of unbroken oral tradition not a vestige of historical truth remains. In more recent times some check is provided on the fanciful growth of oral legends through printed versions, which help to stabilize their form in a local history or topography, or traveler's report. So long as the legend continues to be told, whether or not it has seeped into print, we can call it a "folk legend." If some scribe wrote down the story in an earlier day with stylistic embellishments, in a manner no longer to be found on the lips of the people, we may call such a form a "literary legend." The classic documents of Japanese historical literature, the Kojiki and the Nihongi, contain literary legends of this sort. Or a contemporary writer may select a legendary theme as a basis for his own inventive additions, and this too is a literary legend. While in Japan I met an English couple who were preparing a book of Japanese "legends" for a series of volumes on legends of all lands being issued by a distinguished publishing house, and they planned to elaborate upon themes in the Kojiki and the Nihongi according to their own imaginative fancy. Such a volume may well prove entertaining, but its contents will bear no resemblance to the word-of-mouth traditions of Japanese villagers.

*   *   *

We may now return to the question of why Japan possesses such an abundance of folk legends. All the elements favoring the creation of folk legendry coalesce in the Land of the Rising Sun. A stationary people have lived in their village communities since the dawn of history. No frontier march has drawn the population toward virgin land, save for the late nineteenth-century push to Hokkaido—and some Japanese today speak slightingly of Hokkaido in contrast to the "real Japan." No colonial empire has sucked out the people to foreign shores, except for the abortive expansion that ended in 1945. For three centuries, by imperial decree, no Japanese could leave nor foreigner enter the homeland. As a national boundary ringed in the islands, so did a village boundary fence in each *mura,* a formidable barrier erected by folk belief, which increased the natural isolation of mountain fastness and sequestered isle. Beyond the village boundary lay an unknown outside world beset with danger and mystery. Each returning villager purified himself with proper ritual when he recrossed the *mura's* edge. Dwellers in each farm village worshiped their own local deity, of whom indeed they all regarded themselves as descendants. Hence each *mura* possessed a powerful sense of its own individuality and tradition. Still, travelers and strangers crossed the boundary from time to time—itinerant monks, singing priestesses, woodworkers, peddlers, performers, blind musicians, tax collectors from the daimyo—bringing with them hearsay and traditions which easily adapted themselves to new homes. In spite of the tight clannish organization of the village society, one can find an identical legend scattered in fifty or a hundred *mura* the length and breadth of Japan.

The rice farmers or deep-sea fishermen and their families, living compactly in each hamlet, furnished the human reservoirs for the storing up of legends. An ancient history extending back into mythical origins presented a panorama of stirring events from which legends sprouted. From southern Kyushu to northern Aomori one hears of settlements founded by the Heike nobles who fled from the battle-fields of the twelfth-century civil wars after their defeat by the Genji, and whose supposed descendants now live on as anonymous peasants. A spectacular landscape honeycombed with mountain ranges, watered with lakes, rivers, hot springs, and quiet pools, and covered with forests and shrubbery invites all manner of legendary association. We have simply to scan the titles of a typical collection of Japanese *densetsu* to see the ties between topography and tradition: "The Waterfall of Seven Pots"; "The Strange Willow Tree of Shigekubo"; "The Pond That Does Not Reflect the Moon"; "The Bridge Where Saigyo Turned Back"; "The Hot Spring Where the Son of a God Took a Bath"; "The Foundation Stone That Shed Blood"; "The Mound of Seizo the Strong Man." Collection after collection rings the changes on these themes, until it would seem that every willow tree, mound, and meadow carries its own special story.

Related to Japan's long history and varied geography, and of primary importance for legend material, is the little-understood folk religion of the land. The formal religions of Shintoism and Buddhism have been carefully described for Western readers, but even the Japanese scholars themselves are only beginning to explore the complicated web of folk ideas that preceded and still underlie the institutional religions. These ideas are expressed in seasonal agricultural ritual, farm-village festivals to honor local deities, household taboos and observances, shamanistic auguries by blind old women, shrine offerings to placate hostile spirits —indeed, scarcely an aspect of rural life but touches in some way on religious folk beliefs. There is a god of the hearth; a god of the privy; a god of the rice fields, who descends from his winter home in the mountains every spring and returns after the harvest in the fall. Hence the importance of mountains in Japanese *minkan shinko* (folk religion); often the mountains are considered as possessing spirits or gods, and woodcutters purify themselves before venturing into the hallowed forests on the mountainside.

This vast body of folk custom and ritual contributed to the growth of legend in various ways. Spirits of the dead who nourished some grievance or hatred toward the living at the time of their deaths must be placated by the erection of shrines. Only if the shrine is regularly attended and annually propitiated will the spirit restrain its power to harm. So the ancient tale of human sacrifice or vengeful murder stays alive in the memory of the kin group obligated to tend the shrine, and of the villagers who daily pass by. The curious feature of this belief, to a Westerner, lies in the veneration of an enemy. Sometimes the enshrined spirit has acted nobly and heroically, as when a young boy allows himself to be buried alive in order to appease the god of the lake and keep its waters from flooding the dam. But in many instances the now-honored person lost his life after an act of treachery or wanton cruelty or hand-to-hand strife on the battlefield. Lafcadio Hearn gives an ironic example of this perverse attitude in his *Kwaidan*, where a dishonest servant is beheaded by his master and dies with a curse on his lips. The other servants in great fright beseech their lord to build a shrine to his spirit, but the lord refuses, finally explaining that all the malice of the spirit was expended when the head rolled on the ground and chewed a stone, to fulfill the servant's dying threat. Customarily, of course, the spirit's venom is never drawn by such last-minute diversions.

Besides the spirits of the long dead, Japanese villagers fear also a host of demons. These odd-appearing and malevolent creatures are thought to be the degenerate corruptions of ancient divinities. By far the best known is the *kappa,* a manlike goblin with a saucer-shaped indentation in the top of its head that holds water; if the water is spilled, the *kappa* loses his power. *Kappa* inhabit rivers and prey on children who swim in their waters or upon horses tethered by the river bank. They enter their victim through the anus and draw forth his intestines. Hence when a drowned person is discovered with a distended anus, a *kappa* is believed to have pulled him under. Recently a Japanese sociologist came upon a village in Kagoshima Prefecture whose people still worship at a *kappa* shrine, a fact supporting the theory that the *kappa* descends from a monkey messenger of a river god. The *tengu* is a winged demon with a long pointed nose who lives in the top of tall pine trees and abducts human beings. Since he is found in mountainous regions, and even on occasion serves as protector of a mountain shrine, some historic connection appears to exist between mountain divinities and *tengu*. Today at Shinto festivals the guide in the procession bearing the portable shrine *(mikoshi)* wears the mask of a *tengu*, representing the Sky World deity Saruta-hiko. Divinity may also lurk behind the *yama-uba*, an ogreish witch whose name itself signifies "old woman of the mountains." Legends arise from the experiences of the villagers with these and other anthropomorphic monstrosities.

In a different though related class fall the animals who enchant and deceive—foxes and badgers and serpents. They assume the guise both of ordinary animals and of human beings. They may marry with humans, haunt families, bring treasure to those who have befriended them, and cause humiliation and death to their enemies. A close link binds the *kitsune*, fox, with Inari, the Rice God, whom he serves as messenger, a vestige perhaps of a primeval era of fox worship. Buddhism has influenced the conception of the badger, who is pictured as a full-bellied Buddhist monk. In folk tales and popular belief the serpent, snake, or dragon often assumes the form of a comely maiden or handsome suitor. In ancient times people considered the serpent a mountain god incarnate. The Japanese mythologist Higo Kazuo has identified the serpent with a pre-Buddhist water god, who demands human sacrifices. Since the serpent always ends up in the bottom of a pond, which is ever after known as his lair, his legendary home is clearly marked. Foxes and badgers are not so closely associated with landmarks, but carry on their mischief in country and even city districts, where their outrageous tricks enter into family and village saga.

Because of this pervasive force of *minkan shinko*, the Japanese idea of *densetsu* means something more than our "legend." *Densetsu* intimately and continuously affect the lives of the farming and fishing families. They are not idle and picturesque legends broadcast by chambers of commerce to lure tourists to scenic spots, but traditions based on ancient beliefs. The word "religion," even coupled with "folk," again clouds the issue, for the tissue of beliefs in *minkan shinko* does not carry the ecclesiastical overtones of formal Christian worship. These taboos, rites, festivals, offerings do not linger underground like the folklore of Christianity, with its hidden Devil and witches, ghosts and charms, but survive openly and publicly. The *densetsu* never move very far from this central core of compulsive and time-honored beliefs that dominate Japanese countrypeople. A tradition about a vengeful s irit is remembered not just for itself, but because a shrine has been built for that spirit, which must be tended and served. A powerful wrestler to whom legendary feats of strength are ascribed is said to have obtained his power from a god. A hunter with marvelous skill received the gift of unerring aim from a goddess of the mountain whom he aided in childbirth. Even tricks of a scapegoat, retold in other countries for their comic sauce, in Japan become involved with *minkan shinko;* the knave deceives the god or impersonates a priest. Legends about *choja,* or rich peasants, are inspired by Buddhist ideas of impermanence and the humbling of the rich and prospering of the poor. Ancestral spirits become village deities, deities degenerate into demons, the old nature-religion endows trees and stones, mountains and rivers with spirit life, the imported Buddhism introduces new gods and saints who perform miracles, and every phase produces its growth of folk legends.

European folklorists of the nineteenth century speculated on the origin of folk tradition which, under the glare of civilization, took on the guise of quaint and curious survivals from a pagan society. European and American legends of haunted houses, spiteful fairies, and shape-changing werewolves do seem anachronistic alongside motorized highways and television sets. But *densetsu* belong to the living folk-culture of Japan, and are supported by the institutions of the culture, like Shinto shrines and national festivals and Kabuki and Noh drama, which honor the old traditions. The intellectuals may not believe in a god of the privy or the transformation of foxes, but they are thoroughly familiar with such ideas and should never regard them as quaint or curious. Families still become fox-possessed, and yet bear scales that testify to snake ancestors. While I was in Japan the newspapers carried a story: "Tokyo Restaurant Cook Haunted by Cat's Ghost" (*Asahi Evening News*, June 19, 1957). The story broke first when a secretary of the Austrian Embassy wrote to the papers exposing an act of cruelty she had witnessed while dining out. A cook in a fit of irritation at a stray cat that had been pestering him threw the animal into a hot oven. The restaurant fired the cook, the police fined him, and the cat too exacted revenge:

> The restaurant cook who hurled a tomcat into a roaring oven in a fiery rage told police today the animal's ghost has begun to haunt him.
>
> The cook, Koji Hayama, said every night since Saturday when the cat was roasted to death in the oven of Tokyo Kaikan's Grill Rossini, he has been suffering pains in his legs and hips and has been sleeping fitfully.
>
> According to Japanese superstition, anyone killing a cat will be haunted by the animal's ghost.

*   *   *

The accurate collecting of Japanese legends began only in the present century. Indeed the science of folklore in Japan is no longer than the life of eighty-four-year-old Kunio Yanagita, whose duties as a young man in the agricultural branch of the government brought him in contact with farmers in the rice paddies, and eventually directed his energies toward rural folk-culture. His own enormous labors and wide influence brought about the precise recording of village customs and tales, including the *densetsu* found so abundantly in every village. The first serious attention to legends was given by Toshio Takagi in a work entitled *Nihon Densetsu Shu* (Collection of Japanese Legends), published in Tokyo in 1913. Takagi was a disciple of Yanagita, and with him co-editor of the first Japanese folklore journal, *Kyodo Kenkyu,* founded in 1913. A student of German literature and mythology, Takagi conceived the idea of assembling Japanese traditions from the people, much as the Grimms had done in Germany, and advertised for them through the pages of the *Asahi* newspaper. From the considerable number of replies he selected two hundred and fifty legends, sent in from all over the country, classified them according to their principal element, and published them in simplified form. Some of his twenty-three divisions merely suggest general subjects ("Legends of Trees," "Legends of Stones"), but others pin down variations on a single legendary theme ("The Curse of the Golden Cock," "Legends of Stone Potatoes and Waterless Rivers").

Kunio Yanagita himself devoted considerable attention to legends in several books and in 1950 published an extensive classification, *Nihon Densetsu Meii* (Index of Japanese Legends). He sought to study *densetsu* by the comparative method and to explain the changes they underwent in different localities. Also he sharpened the concept of *densetsu,* pointing out differences from the fairy tale *(mukashi-banashi)*, such as the simpler structure of the *densetsu;* its flexible length, depending on the individual narrator; and its attachment to an "immovable evidence."

The bibliography in the *Nihon Densetsu Meii* reveals the forward strides in the field collecting of folk legends from the 1920's on. Nearly fifty volumes exclusively devoted to *densetsu* are listed by Yanagita, and since his index appeared they have continued to be published at the rate of two or three a year. Many of the collections were undertaken as cooperative projects by local high schools and educational societies. Others were compiled by enthusiastic amateurs. A postmaster in Yamanashi Prefecture, Riboku Dobashi, has issued two collections in the last four years. When I visited Kumamoto City in April, 1957, I learned of four local collectors of *densetsu,* including a newspaper reporter, a radio script-writer, and a professor of folklore at a junior college. A collection represented in the present book, from Niigata and Sado, was undertaken by a local political party official whom I met in Niigata. A good portion of such volumes are locally published (one in Miyazaki was subsidized by a bank); but they are published in small editions, and are difficult to come by. Because these are largely amateur productions, they do not satisfy all the demands of professional folklorists, who wish to see every text documented with the name of the storyteller and the date of the narration. Sometimes such information is given, but more often it is withheld. Nevertheless, these local groups and individuals have performed invaluable service by bringing together the oral legends of their localities which the handful of professional folklorists, concentrated in Tokyo, attached to universities, and studying many aspects of folklore besides *densetsu,* could never have procured. Some local pride and boosterism for special legends can be observed in different regions, which are in any case vain of their products and attractions. Throughout the southern island of Kyushu one encounters in the shops carved figures of *kappa* in endless variety, for Kyushu is reputedly its original home. On Sado Island, off the northwestern coast of Honshu, a spot frequented by Japanese tourists but rarely penetrated by Westerners, I kept seeing the image of a lovely dancing girl with a sweeping long-brimmed hat nearly hiding her features, displayed in dolls, etched on lacquer ware, painted in pictures. This was the likeness of Okesa, who danced as a geisha to make money for a needy old couple on Sado after they befriended a stray cat. To help them out, this cat took the form of a lovely girl and entertained. The memory of her dance and costume stays green and even Tokyo geisha perform the Okesa dance.

Apart from these rare exceptions, the mass of Japanese folk legends remains still the exclusive property of the village communities. None have been widely reprinted and translated as have certain fairy tales, like "Momotaro" (The Peach Boy). The Western world indeed knows very little about these *densetsu.* Early translators concerned themselves chiefly with the *mukashi-banashi,* and only Lafcadio Hearn gave serious attention to the legendary traditions that permeated the land he cherished. *Kwaidan* is entirely devoted to somber traditionary tales, but they recur throughout *Glimpses of Unfamiliar Japan, Kotto, In Ghostly Japan, Kokoro,* and his other books. Hearn tells us that he heard some from a young acolyte he met in a Buddhist temple, while others he took from esoteric Japanese writings. Hearn did not of course have access to field collections of *densetsu,* and his own literary instinct and religious bent turned him to educated priestly informants and to poetic treatments. Nor did he intend any systematic description of Japanese folklore. Still, he provides a trustworthy guide into unfamiliar corridors of Japanese folk ideas, and those who dismiss Hearn as a dewy-eyed romancer should consider his grisly and macabre legends.

The present book is intended to bring a representative selection of Japanese folk legends to Western readers. During the ten months I spent in Japan, from October, 1956, to August, 1957, as a Fulbright lecturer at the University of Tokyo, I had the good fortune to live close by the Japanese Folklore Institute in Seijo-machi. There I met Professor Yanagita and his associates, and there I spent many hours with Miss Yasuyo Ishiwara, who made literal translations for most of the legends printed here. Miss Ishiwara had served as principal assistant to Mr. Yanagita in the work on his *Nihon Densetsu Meii,* and was admirably fitted to steer me through the unfamiliar bibliography and acquaint me with characteristic legends. The Institute closed in May, 1957, for lack of funds, a tragic blow indeed to Japanese folklore studies. Other translations were made by a talented student of mine at Tokyo University, Miss Kayoko Saito, who in addition obtained a number of *densetsu* directly from her grandmother. When I met the grandmother, a wholesome, rotund woman of surprising girth for Japan, she told me—through Kayoko—of hearing village tales from her own grandmother on the southerly island of Shikoku; she could even remember the exact year of her childhood when she first heard a particular story.

In making selections for this volume I have attempted to represent major themes, different geographical areas, and important collections of Japanese oral legends.

PART ONE

PRIESTS, TEMPLES, AND SHRINES

IN JAPAN the religion and lore of the folk merge in a common realm of popular beliefs. The development of Shintoism from primitive nature worship, and the sixth-century importation of Buddhism from China via Korea, merely increased the variety of religious legends circulating among the villagers. Shintoism contributed the veneration of departed spirits, particularly of angry ones, and Shinto shrines proliferated endlessly with each new passionate or noble death. Hence legendary traditions gathered about each shrine, no matter how tiny or humble, for each embalmed a story. Most of the hundred thousand shrines belong to the folk, in distinction to large famous shrines, which employ salaried priests and hold colorful festivals. Buddhism too, while introducing a subtle philosophy with complex ritual, at the folk level scattered miraculous tales about Buddhist priests and statues. The images of Buddha were said to whine and writhe if robbers carried them off. A mass of legends clustered around Kobo Daishi, or St. Kobo (774–835), founder of the Shingon sect of Buddhism, whose esoteric formulas appealed to the magic-minded common people. In the guise of a wandering beggar Kobo Daishi rewarded the generous and punished the greedy, much like St. Peter in Christian legend. Numerous, devoutly believed stories tell of Buddhist priests laying troubled spirits. East or West, the folk mind shuns abstract doctrine for the vivid, concrete tale dramatizing the supernatural power of gods and priests. In Japan, such legendary histories cling to shrine and temple, and are even dispensed by the priestly class, proud of the individual acts of faith and sacrifice connected with their particular sanctuaries.

SAINT KOBO'S WELL

This and the following four legends deal with the miracles of Kobo Daishi. The present one, where he brings forth a well with his cane or staff, is widely told. See Japanese Folklore Dictionary, "Koboshimizu" (Kobo's well); Yanagita, Mountain Village Life, ch. 59, p. 420 (where the miracle is also credited to St. Rennyo). On pp. 432–33 a story is told of a man in Takaoka-mura who prayed at a temple to be cured of eye trouble, and was told by a god in a dream to dig under a certain Japanese cedar tree by the temple, where he would find a well dug by St. Kobo; he washed his eyes in the well water and was cured. Suzuki, pp. 16–17, "The Well that Kobo Daishi Dug," gives an extra twist to the usual form by having St. Kobo's bamboo stick fly three miles away and take root upside down.

For Christian counterparts of this legend see Motif F933.1, "Miraculous spring bursts forth for holy person." The Kobo Daishi legends belong under the general motif Q1.1, "Saints in disguise reward hospitality and punish inhospitality."

General accounts of Kobo Daishi can be found in Anesaki, pp. 251–53: U. A. Casal, "The Saintly Kobo Daishi in Popular Lore (A. D. 774–835)," Folklore Studies, XVIII (Tokyo, 1959), pp. 95–144; Hearn, V, ch. 2, "The Writings of Kobodaishi"; Ikeda, II, pp. 209–11; Joly, pp. 183–84, "Kobodaishi"; Mock Joya, IV, pp. 21–22, "Kobo Daishi"; de Visser, The Dragon in China and Japan, pp. 162–64, 202, 206; de Visser, "The Fox and Badger in Japanese Folklore," pp. 112–13, 136–37.

Text from Kunio Yanagita, "Folk Tales from Hachinoe," in Mukashi-banashi Kenkyu, II (Tokyo, 1937), p. 288. Collected by Kimura, 1936.

THERE IS a spring by the name of St. Kobo's Well in the village of Muramatsu, Ninohe-gun. The following story concerning this well is told in this district. A girl was once weaving alone at her home. An old man, staggering, came by there and asked her for a cup of water. She walked over the hill more than a thousand yards away and brought back water for the visitor. The old man was pleased with her kindness and said that he would make her free from such painful labor. After saying this, he struck the ground with his cane. While he was striking, water sprang forth from the point struck by his cane. That spring was called St. Kobo's Well.

The old man who could do such a miraculous deed was thought to be St. Kobo, however poor and weak he might look.

THE WILLOW WELL OF KOBO

A variant of the above. Text from Edo no Kohi to Densetsu, no. 17, p. 45.
Note: Kashima, a large shrine where warriors prayed before going into battle.

THERE IS a well in the compound of Zempuku-ji in Azabu. In ancient times while Kobo Daishi was staying in this temple, in order to get the water for offering to the Buddha, he put his staff into the ground, praying to the god of the Kashima Shrine. Then clear water gushed forth. Later Kobo Daishi planted a willow tree by the well to commemorate it forever. So it is called the Willow Well.

THE KOBO CHESTNUT TREES

Ikeda refers to this legend and assigns it Type 750 B, "Hospitality Rewarded."
Text from Aichi-ken Densetsu Shu, p. 223.

IN THE mountains around Fukiage Pass in Nagura-mura, Kita Shidara-gun, grow chestnut trees called Kobo chestnuts. Those trees bear fruit very young, even when they are only three feet high.

Hundreds of years ago there was a big chestnut tree on this pass. Boys would rush to climb it to pick the chestnuts, but little children could not climb the tree. One day while they were weeping, a traveling priest passed by, saw the little children crying, and said: "Well, you shall be able to pick the chestnuts from next year on."

The next year every small young chestnut tree bore fruit so that the little children could pick them easily. The villagers thought that the traveling priest must have been St. Kobo, and since then they have called these the Kobo chestnut trees.

THE WATERLESS RIVER IN TAKIO

In some variants potatoes grow hard as stones after they are refused to Kobo. A story from Mimino-mura, in Yanagita, Mountain Village Life, p. 407 (in ch. 56, "Curses of the Gods"), tells of a river turning dry after a man refused a beggar a piece of radish he was washing. Elisséeff, pp. 287–88, reviewing Otari Kohishu by Naotaro Koike, summarizes a legend of greedy fishermen who refuse fish to a begging bonze; he throws a sheet of paper into the water, and thenceforth the fish disappear from the river. Ikeda, pp. 210–11, analyzes the tale under Type 751, "The Greedy Peasant Woman." An unusual variant in Murai, pp. 68–69, "Maidenhair Tree of Yoshida," tells of a woman who refused a night's lodging to a traveler; he says that leaves and snow will fall; after the snow falls, his footprints remain in the drifts; it was St. Kobo. Since then people believe a heavy snow follows the falling of leaves.

Text from Bungo Densetsu Shu, p. 28. Told by Mitsuko Shikishima.

A LONG TIME AGO a farmer's wife was washing sweet potatoes in a stream near Ikarijima. A poor, dirty-looking priest came from somewhere and asked her: "Please give me a potato. I am too hungry to walk on."

But the woman refused him, saying: "I have no potatoes to give you."

The priest, feeble and low of spirit, went along. Strange to say, the waters of the stream disappeared at that moment and never ran again. Since then the villagers have suffered much for lack of water. The upper and lower reaches of the river have water, and only the part that runs through that village is dry.

The people say that this was done by St. Kobo in order to reprove the woman for her unkindness.

THE STREAM WHERE KOBO WASHED HIS GARMENT

Text from Shimane-ken Kohi Densetsu Shu, Mino-gun no. 7, pp. 5–6.

LONG AGO Kobo Daishi went on a pilgrimage throughout the country. He came to Momotomataga in Toyoda-mura, and he took off his dirty clothes. He washed them in the Hinomoto River. The villagers who saw him did not know that he was a virtuous priest, and criticized him for washing dirty clothes. St. Kobo went away without saying anything. He went to Takatsu-mura, and he washed his clothes on the bank in Suko. For this reason, in Momotomataga the river dries up in summer and people often suffer from lack of water. On the other hand, in Suko, through the mercy of the priest, no one has drowned in the river.

At present almost every year the water is dried up in Hinomoto and gushes out in Kadoi.

THE PRIEST'S TOWEL

Motif Q1.1, "Saints in disguise reward hospitality and punish inhospitality," also applies here. A Korean legend of Merciful Buddha disguised as a beggar, which fits into the pattern of this and the preceding tales, is in Zong In-Sob, Folk Tales from Korea (London, 1952), no. 27, pp. 45–46, "The Lake of Zangje." Chinese legendary tales of Lu Tung-pin appearing as a beggar to test mortals are in Wolfram Eberhard, Chinese Fairy Tales and Folk Tales (New York, 1938), nos. 74, 76, 77, pp. 220–21, 222–24.

Text from Kunio Yanagita, "Folk Tales from Hachinohe," Mukashi-banashi Kenkyu, II (Tokyo, 1937), pp. 329–30. Collected by Ishiyama.

Notes: Tenugui, *a Japanese-style towel or face-cloth (see Mock Joya, II, pp. 72–73).* Mochi, *cakes made from pounded, glutinous rice.*

THE YOUNG WIFE of a household kindly gave a piece of *mochi* to a traveling priest who came by the door. Afterwards, her mother-in-law counted the pieces of *mochi* and realized that the young wife had given one to the priest. She scolded the young wife and sent her to regain the *mochi* from the priest. When the priest heard the young wife's honest plea, he not only returned to her the *mochi*, but also gave her a *tenugui*, praising her gentleness.

Acting on his suggestion, the young wife wiped her face with that *tenugui* every day. Then her face became extremely beautiful. The mother-in-law envied her and borrowed her *tenugui* to use it herself. However, the mother-in-law's face gradually became horselike and at last it turned into a horse's face.

The daughter-in-law felt very sorry for her and went to the priest and begged him to turn the mother's face back to normal. The priest said that when a greedy woman wiped her face with the *tenugui*, her face would turn into a horse's face, and he instructed her to tell the mother-in-law to rub her face with the reverse side of the *tenugui*. The young wife hastily went home and relayed the instructions to her mother-in-law. When the mother did as she was told, her face became as it had been before.

And thereafter she turned into a goodhearted woman and loved her daughter-in-law.

THE KANNON WHO SUBSTITUTED

The theme of the Buddhist deity assuming the guise of a pious worshiper to ward off injury or death to the mortal occurs frequently in Japanese religious legends. Suzuki, pp. 65–68, "The Living Headless Priest," has a clay image of Kannon take the form of Priest Baizan to save him from the murderous sword strokes of his host. Murai, p. 10, "Six Jizo," tells of an image of Jizo that bears a sword scar meant for a boy. In the Japan Times for February 23, 1957, Mock Joya recounts the legend of "One-Eyed Emma," the statue enshrined at Genkaku-ji, Hatsune-cho, Bunkyo-ku, Tokyo, which gouged out its own eye to save the sight of a poor old lady bringing her offerings. Under "Weeping Buddha" in the Japan Times of March 9, 1957, Mock Joya tells how the painting of Fudo, the God of Fire, shed bloody tears and took to itself the sickness of his young worshiper Shoku, in the thirteenth century; the painting with its bloodstained tears was later placed in Mii-dera, Otsu, Shiga-ken.

Text from Bungo Densetsu Shu, p. 110.

Note: Kannon, a Buddhist bodhisattva, commonly known as the Goddess of Mercy.

LOOKING UP from a small village nestled at the foot of a certain mountain, one can see a little shrine of Kannon on the very top. A young couple used to live in that village. The wife, for all her youth, believed in Kannon with utmost sincerity. Every night, after she had finished her daily housework she visited the shrine to worship the image. Her husband did not know the reason for her going and became suspicious of the wife who went out and returned to the house every night at the same time. One day he finally lost patience with his wife and determined to kill her. So he hid in the dark woods by the roadside and waited for his wife to come back. At the usual time she returned. The husband watched her coming near and, carefully aiming at her shoulder, swung down his sword askance. At this moment the wife felt her blood run cold throughout her body.

The husband wiped the blood from his sword and put the sword back in its sheath. When he returned to his home, he was astonished to see his wife, whom he thought he had slashed to death. He marveled, and went back to see the place where he had struck his wife. Sure enough, there were the dots of blood on the ground. He retraced his steps homeward, and asked his wife: "Didn't you feel something strange at such and such a time in such and such a place?" Then the wife answered: "Just at that time something made my blood run cold." The husband could not but confess all that had happened.

The next morning he awakened early and was surprised to see blood dotted all the way from the entrance of his house to the shrine on top of the mountain. When he looked at the statue of Kannon, he was again surprised to see a scar on the statue's shoulder, on the place where he had struck his wife the night before.

Now this Kannon is still popular in the neighboring villages, and they celebrate a festival for her on January 24 every year.

THE STATUE OF BUDDHA AT SAIHO-JI

To the theme of the substituting Buddha are joined here motifs that fall under "Magic Statue" (D1268) and "Images" (V120), and the specific miracle of D1551, "Waters magically divide and close."

Text from Shimane-ken Kohi Densetsu Shu, *Ohara-gun, pp. 8–9.*

THE PRINCIPAL IMAGE of Saiho-ji at Iida, Sase-mura, Ohara-gun, is the seated statue of Amida Buddha, almost three feet in height. It has a burn on its left cheek. The following story tells the reason why.

A maidservant who worked in the house by the gate of this temple worshiped the image every morning and evening within the temple. For many years she had never failed to do this. Every time she cooked rice, in the morning and in the evening, she took some rice out of the pot and offered it to the image of Buddha. At last this became known to the mistress of the house, who grew enraged and pressed a heated iron rod on the pretty cheek of the maid. With a scream, the poor maid ran out of the house.

That night the master of the house had a strange dream. The shining golden Buddha stood by his pillow and spoke to him: "Your maid has been very pious and worshiped me for a long time. Therefore I substituted myself for her in the time of her disaster." As the master looked at the face of the Buddha, he saw blood running down his left cheek. As soon as he awakened from the vision, he arose and went to the temple. There he was astonished to see the appearance of the image, for blood was running down its cheek. Struck with awe, he returned home and talked with his wife. Greatly disturbed, they looked at the face of the maid, but it was as pretty as before, and bore no trace of injury. They asked her about the event of the previous day, but she answered that she knew nothing of it. At her words the master and the mistress realized that the image of Buddha was really injured in place of the pious maid. The mistress repented of her deed. People who heard of the occurrence were deeply moved by the grace of Buddha and worshiped the image more sincerely than ever.

In later days Lord Matsudaira of this province worshiped this image at Saiho-ji very earnestly. He decided to move the image to the newly built temple of Gessho-ji. According to his order, the holy statue was carried away by forty strong men. On the way they stopped over at Shigaraki Temple. While the image was resting there, it spoke to the priest in a dream: "I want to go back to Saiho-ji." And it shone brightly every night. All the priests thought this strange and reported the matter to the lord. Then the lord issued an order: "Have the sculptor make a statue just like that image and install it in Gessho-ji. As for that image, carry it back to Saiho-ji."

So the people started to take it back to Saiho-ji. Strangely, this time the holy statue became very light and was easily carried by only five or six porters. When they came to the river called Aka-kawa, a storm suddenly arose, and the skies began thundering and hailing. Rapidly the river rose to a great height and was soon impossible to cross. But the porters of the holy image boldly plunged into the water, firm in their belief that the image would protect them from drowning. Indeed, the angry waves immediately subsided and lowered to a heel's height. The porters could easily cross to the other side. But when the other travelers followed the porters and attempted to wade the river, the waters rose up again, and the raging waves overflowed the river banks.

People were filled with awe and spoke to one another about this miracle of Buddha, who, they thought, had subdued the dragon underneath the water.

THE EARLESS JIZO OF SENDATSUNO

The collector points out that Hearn published a similar legend under the title "Mimi-nashi Hoichi" in Kwaidan *in 1904, taken from an old Japanese storybook* Gayu Kidan *(Strange Stories Told While Resting). In Hearn's tale the ghosts of the Heike listen to biwa music in places famed for Heike legends, and at the tomb of the Emperor Antoku.*

The small village of Sendatsuno was named for Heike refugees fleeing from the Genji disguised as sendatsu, *or guides for mountain pilgrims. The Heike are said to have turned on and killed their pursuers. Many families in the village claim to be Heike descendants. Tombs of the Emperor Antoku and his followers are on nearby hills, and none can approach unless they are barefooted.*

Text from Tosa no Densetsu, II, *pp. 8–13.*

Notes: Jizo, *a Buddhist bodhisattva, the guardian deity of children.* Biwa, *a four-stringed Japanese lute.* Heike Monogatari, *the tale of the Taira family (Heike) in their bitter struggles with the Minamoto family (Genji).*

SOME STORIES MAKE such an impression that, once heard, they can never be forgotten. Such a tale is this.

There is a place called Sendatsuno in the suburbs of Ochi-machi, Takaoka-gun. It is on the way to Matsuyama, over the Ohashi bridge, along the Niyodo River. Long ago an earless Jizo by the name of Mimi-nashi Jizo [Earless Jizo] stood there. This is the legend concerning it.

Once on a time there came wandering into Ochi-machi from the direction of Matsuyama in Iyo a blind *biwa*-player named Joryo. In those days, that district of Ochi-machi was called Mio-mura, and it was far more lonely than it is today. The chief priest, Senei, lived at that time in the temple Yokokura-ji. He called Joryo to his temple and let him stay there. He asked him to play his *biwa* before the tablets of the deceased to console their spirits, and sometimes it pleased him to listen to the music himself.

Gradually, however, one of the young priests of the temple became aware of a strange, repeated occurrence. Every night Joryo stole out of the temple on tiptoe and came back at dawn. A priest-official, hearing of this, summoned Joryo and asked why he went out nightly. Joryo said: "I am strictly forbidden to speak about this, but since you are a man of the temple from which I receive such great favors, I cannot but tell you the reason."

And he began to talk as follows:

"Every night, at the time of the *ne* (nowadays 12 midnight), a warrior who seems to be a messenger from a man of high rank comes to this temple to fetch me. As I follow him, we come to a house on a hill. This house is like a court, with long corridors and a wide inner

42

room where there are many women who seem to be court ladies. I am led into this inner room, where I play the *biwa* and sing for them the *Heike Monogatari*. But, strangely, I must not utter a word about the Genji. I am told that the site of the court is Mariganaro."

The priest-official was excited to hear this and told the details of the story to the chief priest, Senei. Senei wondered greatly, murmuring: " 'Tis a strange story, indeed. In Mariganaro lies the tomb of the Emperor Antoku, who, while very young, sank with the last of the Heike into the sea. To be invited there is truly an honor, but when a man of this world mingles with men from the other world, he is sure, in the end, to become one of them."

Senei sat for a long time before the tablets of the deceased and recited sutras. Then he called Joryo to him and said: "You still belong to this world, certainly. I should like to save your life, so I shall sever your relationship with the other world." And he spread scented water for incantation all over Joryo's body; then he strictly forbade him to go out that night, telling him not to move when the warrior-messenger arrived.

Next morning, the chief priest and the priest-official hurried to Joryo's room to see how he had fared. To their surprise, they found him lying face down, in a faint, with his ears cut off. At once the chief priest realized that he had forgotten to spread the scented incantation water on the blind musician's ears. The priest felt deeply sorry for the deformed blind man who must now go earless through life. He invited him to stay on at the temple as long as he wished, and he took care of him with great kindness.

Thus several years passed. At last the poor blind *biwa*-player set out alone from the temple for his final trip to the other world. The people of the temple buried his body carefully at Sendatsuno, north of the temple, and set up there an earless Jizo in his honor.

And it is told that, since that faraway time, the worshipers at this shrine have always called the statue the Earless Jizo of Sendatsuno.

THE RED NOSE OF THE IMAGE

This legend has been studied by Kunio Yanagita in a translated article, "The Japanese Atlantis," Contemporary Japan, III (June, 1934), pp. 34–39. However, he associates it not with Uryu Island, as in the text below, but with the island of Korai west of the Goto Archipelago in northwestern Kyushu, and with one of the Koshiki islands off the coast of Satsuma. In both cases the face of the image was painted red by wiseacres and doom followed, fulfilling the prophecy. In literary form the tale appears in two masterpieces of the Heian period (794–1185), Konjaku Monogatari and Uji Shui Monogatari, which show influences from China or India.

Text from Bungo Densetsu Shu, p. 110; collected by Takako Tanabe in Haya-mi-gun.

HIGH PRIEST BEACH takes its name from High Priest Ippen, who lived there in olden days. One day he called the villagers together and said to them: "My last moment is drawing near. I am going to die now, but my spirit will remain in the image carved on that rock. If ever a calamity is destined to occur in this district, the nose of that image will become red."

At that time Uryu and Kuko islands were in Beppu Bay, and the scenery was as beautiful as a picture. Uryu Island possessed a fine harbor, and the islands flourished as pleasure resorts, attracting many visitors to their numerous hot springs and handsome buildings.

A day came in the second year of Keicho [1597] when the nose of the image on the rock suddenly turned red. The news spread rapidly from mouth to mouth throughout the village. When the people heard it they were filled with fear, and made ready to escape. Before they could do so, with a tremendous sound there occurred a great eruption, an opening up of the earth, a landslide of the mountains, and a tidal wave, all at the same time. Not only were all the houses with their inhabitants and animals destroyed, but the islands vanished into the sea.

Hundreds of years have passed since that cataclysm. Now the fishermen of this district say that when they row their boats into the open sea on quiet days, they can see a stone pavement at the bottom of the sea, and this they believe to be Uryu Island.

THE PRIEST WHO ATE THE CORPSE

A similar tradition from India is cited under Motif G36.2, "Human blood (flesh) accidentally tasted: brings desire for human flesh." Hearn's grisly story "Jikininki" in Kwaidan (XI, pp. 198–204) tells of a priest in a mountain district condemned for impiety to assume monstrous shape and feed on corpses of deceased villagers.

Text from Edo no Kohi to Densetsu, *no. 58, pp. 125–26.*

Notes: Ombo, a person whose trade is dealing with dead bodies; regarded as very mean and low. Kasha, a specter which bears away dead bodies, sometimes coming to a funeral and taking coffin and all.

FORMERLY there was a temple called Tokusu-in at the southern side of Anyo-in in Shiba Park. A man who lived in Hiroo asked the Tokusu-in to perform the necessary rituals for a certain dead man. The temple accepted the request and sent a hanger-on priest to the house of the dead. By mistake that priest cut off about one inch of the dead man's head when he shaved his hair. As he thought he could not make proper apologies for his error, he put the piece of flesh into his mouth. To his surprise it tasted very good. After that he could not forget that taste. He wished to eat such flesh once more. So one night he secretly dug up the corpse and cut it into pieces to eat. This time the flesh tasted more delicious than the flesh of the head. He wanted to try once more.

Soon after that a new corpse was buried in the grave. The priest thought it a good opportunity. He stole into the graveyard in the dead of night and dug up the corpse and ate it up. Thus again and again he dug up the grave whenever a new corpse was buried. At first the chief priest of the temple thought that some dogs or foxes had done these things. But as the matter became more and more horrible he grew suspicious. Other people, too, grew curious about the affair. One night when the priest was at last caught on the spot, he had to confess all about eating the corpses. He was exiled and driven away. After he had wandered through many places, he came back to Edo again and became an *ombo*. When he was about to eat, suddenly a *kasha* appeared on a dark cloud and took the priest up in the sky, tore his body into pieces, and disappeared.

It is not clear when this event happened but it is said that during the era of Kansei [1789–1800] there was in Edo a priest who ate men.

THE MONK AND THE MAID

Anesaki, in his chapter on "Local Legends and Communal Cults," relates this story of the "Hira hurricane" that occurs annually since the death of the hapless maiden (pp. 254–55). In his version the monk is replaced by a lighthouse keeper, and the girl deliberately jumps into the lake when the light fails to appear, praying that a storm destroy the lighthouse; her dying curse is fulfilled.

Text from Nihon Densetsu Shu, *pp. 162–63, under "Legends of Ferries." Told by Hiroshi Morita.*

IN AND AROUND Otsu in Omi Province, they are sure to have stormy weather at the end of March every year. They call that time *Hira no hachiare*. By that they seem to mean that Mt. Hira rages for eight days.

At a little distance to the west of Yoshinaka Temple, which stands at the east gate of Otsu, there is a ferry called Ishiba. There was an inn named Harimaya beside that ferry. It still exists today. In former days a young Buddhist monk spent a night there. A pretty maid of the inn fell in love with him at first sight. Unable to suppress the passion flaming in her heart, she stole into the monk's room late at night. Needless to say, she poured out all her longings for him and tried to win his affection. But the monk was a man of such strict morality that he would not be moved. However, he must have felt sympathy for the extent of the woman's love for him, for he told her that he was a hermit at the foot of Mt. Hira beyond the lake, that she should row in a big washtub from Ishiba to his place one hundred nights continuously if her longing for him were strong enough, and that he would fulfil her desire if she could accomplish the feat.

It was a very difficult task, and one by which he aimed to evade her once and forever. When the night came and the bells of Mii Temple rang out, however, she started from Ishiba in the tub and, passing the shore off Karasaki and Katada, reached a place from where she could see the light of the hermitage at the foot of Mt. Hira. After gazing at it for a while, she returned home. She continued this for ninety-nine nights. The hundredth night came. The maid was cheered by the thought of attaining her purpose at last. She rode over miles of waves and came to the place which commanded the view of the light. But what was the matter? There was no light, but only sheer darkness. She must have been cheated, she thought. At that moment, a storm came down from Mt. Hira and overturned the woman's tub in an instant. In great agony and chagrin, she was drawn to the bottom of deep water as if she had been a leaf of seaweed.

It was on March 20 that she was lost. Because of her passion, they say, the lake rages around that date, even now.

47

THE SHRINE OF THE VENGEFUL SPIRIT

This legend is a good example of the goryo, *the spirit that harbors a curse at the time of its unnatural bodily death and hence must be enshrined. A comparable tradition in Yanagita,* Mountain Village Life, *pp. 390–94, tells of a refugee warrior in Kita-mura who hid himself in a hollow tree and was betrayed by a girl signaling with her eyes to the enemy; they pierced his chest with an arrow, but from his dying curse the girl's family suffered chest ailments. The refugee is now deified as a local god. Similarly in Yanagita,* Fishing Village Life, *pp. 110–11, an account is given of Engen-sama, a refugee betrayed in Okinoshima-mura by the Matsuuras, who now worship him to deflect his curse that their children would die young. The general motif is M460, "Curses on families."*

Text from Bungo Densetsu Shu, *pp. 58–59, from Kita Amabe-gun.*

IN THE THICK WOODS at Yamada there is a small shrine by a little stream. A long time ago a young sister and brother fled to this village in order to hide from their pursuers. They found a cave called Komoridan and there they lived. One day a woodcutter who passed by the cave saw them and took pity on them. He decided to give them a cup of rice every day. The mother of the woodcutter became curious about her son's doings and asked him what he was up to. He told her about the sister and brother, begging her not to tell the other people about them. The old woman promised not to tell.

One day as the old woman was washing clothes in the river, the men who were chasing the brother and sister came to her and said: "If you tell us where the young people are, we will give you a reward." The greedy old woman was tempted to tell about them, but she remembered her promise to her son, so she did not tell them openly but turned her head in the direction of the mountain where the two young people were hiding. As soon as the pursuers saw that, they hastened to the mountain to search for the fugitives. Finally the pair was caught, and they were about to be killed under a big pine. Then the head man of the pursuing party took pity on the sister and brother and made a sign, shaking a baton in his hand. However, the men took it to be the sign to kill the two and they cut off their heads.

From that moment on, the old woman's head curved to one side and never regained its normal position. And her descendants all suffered from sore eyes. Moreover, an epidemic spread throughout this village. Therefore the villagers, fearing the curse of the two young people, enshrined the brother's spirit at Yamada and the sister's in the neighboring village of Kazamashi. This is said to be the origin of the Goryo Jinja [Shrine of the Vengeful Spirit].

THE SHRINE BUILT BY STRAW DOLLS

Hearn speaks of the belief in dolls coming alive and refers to a legend of a doll running out of a burning house (V, pp. 309–10). The present tale may belong to a cycle about the legendary carpenter Hida-no-takumi (the skilled worker of Hida). The pertinent motif is F675, "Ingenious carpenter."

Text from Katsuhiko Imamura, "Folktales from Bizen" (present Okayama-ken), in Tabi to Densetsu, V (August, 1932), p. 579.

A LONG TIME AGO a feudal lord searched for a skillful carpenter in order to have a shrine built on the borders of Bizen and Bitchu provinces. But he could not find one. One day a carpenter came traveling from a distant province. The lord wondered why he came alone, because all the carpenters who had come before had had many apprentices. So he asked the carpenter: "Can you build a shrine all by yourself?" Then the carpenter answered: "Yes, I can. I will take it on my own responsibility if you give me the job." The lord granted his request, as he thought he was a rather unusual carpenter. All the people had a great interest in this carpenter. He told everybody not to come to the place where he was working until the building was completed.

The lord and all his servants were anxious to see the carpenter's work, but they let him work alone. The carpenter made rapid progress. In the daytime he worked alone, but by next morning he had done a great deal. The lord was curious about this and one night he secretly looked into the carpenter's working place. To his surprise he saw thirty or fifty carpenters identical with the original carpenter, all working busily. He tried to tell which was the true carpenter, but he couldn't. They were working hard in silence.

The days passed, and the shrine was about completed. The lord went there to give a reward to the carpenter, but he could not tell which one was the real carpenter. He asked the one beside him, who answered: "It is the one who has a mole near his eye." So the lord looked for the carpenter with a mole near his eye and gave him the reward. When the shrine was entirely constructed, that carpenter went away before anyone knew about it, and all the other carpenters fell down into the valley and died. People found many straw dolls down in the valley afterwards.

It is told that there was a small shrine where the straw dolls were found, and this shrine is the present Kibitsu Shrine.

VISIT TO ZENKO-JI DRIVEN BY A COW

This famous legend has become proverbial. Murai gives a Buddhist tradition on "The Origin of Zenko-ji Temple," pp. 57–61, and a variant of the present text on pp. 49–51, "An Old Woman at Nunobiki." His rendering of the verses traced from the cow's slobber is this:

> *Do not regard the fact,*
> *As a mere ox's freak;*
> *'Twas mercy of Buddha*
> *To lead thee to righteousness!*

The lines refer to a woman's cloth carried off on an ox's horn to a statue of Buddha. When in Nagano, I duly saw the grand Zenko-ji and was startled to come suddenly upon a frieze below a small altar showing the farmwife running frantically after the cow and her cloth, past astonished bystanders. The shrine on the mountainside at this old woman's village can be seen at the fourth station beyond the famed summer resort of Karuizawa. The story says that the old woman ran all the way from her village to Nagano, a distance ordinarily requiring ten hours to walk. A lovely illustrated four-page leaflet carrying a version of the legend has been issued by Zenko-ji Temple, written by Priest Junsho Hayashi, and captioned "Pilgrimage to Zenko-ji Temple led by an Ox." Priest Hayashi interprets this title, which is used proverbially, in the sense of "entering the religious life led by grief," because ox is "ushi" in Japanese and "ushi" literally means grief.

Text from Masao Koyama, Chiisagata-gun Mintan Shu *(Tokyo, 1933), p. 76.*

Note: A temple often has two names, the first referring to the mountain on which it is built. Thus, for example, we have rendered Nunobiki-yama Shason-ji as "Shason-ji on Nunobiki-yama."

LONG AGO there was an old couple in Chiisagata-gun. They were bad-hearted and did not believe in any god or in Buddha. One day the old woman was bleaching cloth under the eaves. Suddenly a cow came there and, catching the cloth on its horn, ran away. The old woman became very angry and ran after it to get back the cloth, but the cow ran away somewhere and the day grew dark. The old woman looked around and found herself in front of the temple of Zenko-ji in Nagano. She could see the slobber of the cow by the light of the Buddha's statue. She read it as follows: "Don't complain about the god. It is from yourself that you find the way to a religious haven."

At these words the old woman immediately recovered a good heart and worshiped the Buddha. She went home with a clean, pious heart.

One day when she was going to pay homage to the Kannon of her village, the wind blew in and carried the cloth away to the mountainside. This remains now as the Cloth Rock of Saku. When the old woman arrived at the Kannon shrine, she found the cloth was hanging on the head of the Kannon's statue. So she came to believe in Buddha still more sincerely and she lived there as a nun.

This story may mean that Kannon, disguised as a cow, guided the old woman's fate. The Kannon is said to be the Kannon of Shason-ji on Nunobiki-yama [Mt. Pulling-the-Cloth].

THE TEMPLE OF RAIKYU GONGEN

*Hito-dama, literally "human spirit" but more commonly rendered as "death fire,"
is described in the Minzokugaku Jiten as a yellowish flame with a long tail which
comes out of the body just before death. In some places people say that a death fire
has a face and speaks. This belief appears in the following legend, along with the
idea of goryo.*

*Text from Densetsu no Echigo to Sado, I, pp. 88–90. Collected in Hojo-mura,
Karina-gun, Niigata-ken.*

IN ANCIENT TIMES castles stood on Mt. Hachikoku and in Hojo-mura.
Mori Tamanosuke was the lord of the castle on Mt. Hachikoku and
Hojo Tango was the lord of the castle in Hojo-mura. Being at odds
with each other, they often had quarrels and sometimes fought battles.
But Mori excelled his enemy in wisdom and valor. Moreover, he was
a young and handsome warrior.

Lord Hojo had a daughter whose beauty surpassed that of the pret-
tiest flower. The father married his daughter to Mori, and by so doing
he outwardly pretended to become friendly with Mori, while secretly
planning his destruction. Friendship now took the place of hostility
between the two lords. The young couple lived happily for half a year.

It was one summer day that Hojo determined to carry out his plan
to ruin Mori. He sent a messenger for Mori. Unsuspecting, Mori readily
accepted his father-in-law's invitation and immediately made ready to
go. But his wife, feeling uneasy about her husband for some reason,
advised him not to go that day. The husband departed nevertheless,
saying with a smile that there was nothing to be afraid of.

When he arrived at Hojo's castle, he was at once guided to the bath
to wash off his sweat. But the bathroom turned out to be a hell for
him. When he was about to be steamed to death in the locked bath
room, he realized for the first time his father-in-law's cowardly trick. He
was furious but helpless. He regretted that he had not followed his
wife's advice.

After her husband's death, the wife killed herself by thrusting a knife
into her throat. Mori's castle on Mt. Hachikoku was soon reduced by
Hojo. After that, a strange fire often appeared on Mt. Hachikoku.

It always floated to Hojo-mura. When people saw it, they shivered with fear and prayed for the disappearance of the fire, but it grew brighter.

The fire was seen especially on summer evenings and it continued to burn all night long. It was said that the fire was the spirit of Mori's wife.

The priest of Fuko-ji Temple tried to subdue the fire. He built a temple called Gongen-do for the souls of Mori and his wife, and recited sutras for twenty-one days. Thereafter the fire never appeared again on Mt. Hachikoku.

THE ORIGIN OF ENOO-JI

In Hearn's similar legend of "Oshidori" in Kwaidan *(XI, 176–78), the mate of the mandarin duck killed by a hunter upbraids him in a dream, and next day kills herself before his eyes. Anesaki, pp. 320–22, has, however, a happy ending to a tale of mandarin-duck lovers; the one freed by a servant rejoins its mate and assists both mate and servant.*

Text from Aichi Densetsu Shu, *p. 318.*

A PATHETIC STORY is told concerning the bridge called Shiraki-bashi [White Wood Bridge] in Haruki-mura, Nishi Kasugai-gun. Once when Lord Todo of Tsu Castle crossed this bridge, he saw a pair of mandarin ducks swimming congenially on the water. For mere pleasure the lord shot one of them with a bow and arrow of white wood. One night soon after that he had a dream in which a pretty woman appeared and expressed her lamentation over the death of her husband, who had been shot to death by the lord.

The next year the lord passed across the same bridge again and this time also shot several mandarin ducks. When he picked up one of them casually, he saw that the bird had the head of the mandarin duck which he had killed there the year before.

"Then is this the female mandarin duck that lamented over the death of her mate in my dream last year?" thought Lord Todo. He felt pity for the birds and established a temple for the repose of the souls of the two mandarin ducks and called it Hakkyu-zan [Mt. White Bow] Enoo-ji [Mandarin Duck Temple]. The white-wood bow was kept in that temp'e.

The temple fell into decay afterwards and there are no traces of it now, but Shiraki Bridge still remains.

THE ORIGIN OF KAZO-JI ON MT. WOODEN PILLOW

This kind of religious legend explaining the origin of a temple or shrine is called an engi. *Hearn relates temple legends in the chapter "A Pilgrimage to Enoshima" in* Glimpses of Unfamiliar Japan *(V, ch. 4), saying: "In nearly every celebrated temple little Japanese prints are sold, containing the history of the shrine, and its miraculous legends" (p. 78).*

Text from Shimane-ken Kohi Densetsu Shu, *Yatsuka-gun, pp. 18–21.*

THE PRIEST WHO FOUNDED the temple of Kazo-ji on Makuragi-yama [Mt. Wooden Pillow] was High Priest Chigen. His former name was Mita Genta. He belonged to a family branch of Emperor Kammu but he was exiled to Oki Island. Then he wandered around many places and also went across to China. On the return voyage from China, his boat was attacked by a sudden storm. Then a dark cloud covered all the sea and nothing was visible except an object like a mountain at the edge of the cloud. Genta prayed to the god: "If there is a god in the

mountain, may he guide this boat to the foot of the mountain. If this transpires, I will be converted and become a bonze."

Very strangely, a faint light began to glimmer in the direction of Kasaura. Genta thought this must be the sign of the god's mercy and he encouraged the boatmen to row as hard as possible to the light. So the boat arrived at Kasaura.

That night Genta climbed up the mountain, treading on the rocks and making his way through thorns. When he got to the top of the mountain, day began to dawn. He saw a pond on the mountain. As he was standing by the pond, a young woman appeared. Genta asked her: "Is there any god or man living on this mountain?" The girl answered: "Since ancient times no one has ever climbed this mountain. You are such a pious person that I have come here to ask you something."

Just then a young man suddenly appeared. This man and woman were the god and goddess of the mountain. The god lived in this pond and the goddess lived in another pond. But in the valley of this mountain lived the Buddha Yakushi, who should rightfully hold a higher place than these gods. So the gods said to Genta: "Please take Yakushi to the top of the mountain." And they took Genta to Yakushi and explained to him that Yakushi was formerly on the rock in the valley with the bodhisattva Miroku, but that Miroku was gone up to heaven. Genta

asked them: "Where shall I install Yakushi?" "On the pond," said the gods. "But one cannot build a temple on a pond." "It does not matter, for we can make flat ground," answered the gods.

Just then a white bird flew away. They followed the bird down the valley. There stood a big rock on which was the statue of Yakushi. After Genta worshiped it, he went up the mountain again, carrying the statue. When he came to the pond, suddenly a thunderstorm broke out and the mountain peak collapsed and filled up the pond. Then the mountain gods appeared again and said: "This pond is called Daio-ike [Great King Pond] and the pond at the back of this mountain is Ryuo-ike [Dragon King Pond]. Now Daio-ike has been made into a flat ground, but Ryuo-ike will remain forever. If you suffer from the drought, pray for rain to this stone."

As soon as they finished these words, the two mountain gods disappeared.

Struck by a strange feeling, Genta was going to set the statue of Yakushi on the ground. The left knee of the statue was broken. Genta could not find anything to support the statue. He remembered the wooden pillow he always carried with him. He took it out and put it under the statue. Strange to say, it turned into a leg of the statue. As he was planting a sacred tree, the same white bird came flying there with ropes in its mouth, holding grasses in its claws. The bird placed these things before Genta. He made a hut with them.

Soon afterwards Genta went to Kyoto and visited St. Dengyo on Mt. Hiei to tell the whole story. Dengyo was moved by it; he gave him the name of High Priest Chigen and made him the founder of the temple.

PART TWO

MONSTERS

THE DEMONS of the Western world have by now become tame household possessions. We think of giants and ogres, goblins and sprites, and possibly unicorns and centaurs, as stock literary characters to entertain children. But in Japan the demons are still seen and talked about in the villages, and they take forms astonishing to the Western mind. The kappa appears ridiculous rather than monstrous, with his boyish form and saucer head, but his actions are far too lethal for comedy. The kappa has penetrated deeply into Japanese literature, art, and popular culture. The brilliant novelist Ryunosuke Akutagawa wrote a mordant satire, Kappa, in 1927, the year he committed suicide, about a man captured by and forced to live with kappa. Another distinguished writer, Ashihei Hino, launched his career by winning the Akutagawa Prize and has published a voluminous miscellany of kappa stories, Kappa Mandara, grafting modern personalities onto the goblin. A comic cartoon series by Kon Shimizu in the Asahi Weekly depicts a naked kangaroo type kappa of lecherous and unseemly behavior. Coffeehouses portray kappa on their checks, and craftsmen shape him into wooden dolls. Almost equally infamous is the flying tengu, a beaked and winged old man, haunting the mountains as kappa infest the rivers, and abducting humans in the Noh and Kabuki of dramatists and monogatari of story-writers, as well as in the legends of the people. Kappa and tengu are not all bad and can teach healing and swordplay to human benefactors.

The oni is an ogre of Chinese origin, usually pictured with horns and fangs and a loincloth of tiger's fur. But to the primitive Japanese he was a friendly mountain giant who requited hospitality with faggots and stamped his footprints in mountain hollows. Other eerie monsters are found all over Japan, wild men of the mountains, apes in the sea, mischievous imps in the house, garden spiders that grow gigantic at night. And they are really seen, for the demons of Japan have not yet escaped from the folk to the pages of nursery books.

THE KAPPA OF FUKIURA

"The kappa is a fabulous creature of the rivers, ponds, lakes, and the sea," writes Shiojiri in his introduction to his translation of Akutagawa's Kappa. Shiojiri goes on to quote from dictionaries and travel books of the eighteenth and nineteenth centuries which describe the kappa as an ugly child with greenish-yellow skin, webbed fingers and toes, resembling a monkey with his long nose and round eyes, wearing a shell like a tortoise, fishy smelling, naked. He is said to live in the water and come out evenings to steal melons and cucumbers. He likes to wrestle, will rape women, sucks the blood of cows and horses through their anuses, and drags men and women into the water to pluck out their livers through their anuses. The trick on meeting a kappa is to make him spill the water in his concave head, whereupon he loses his strength.

Typical kappa legends, like the present one, deal with the creature's attempt to drag a cow or horse into a river. A comparative ethnological study of this theme showing similar accounts of water monsters in Asia and Europe, by Eiichiro Ishida, has been translated into English as "The Kappa Legend," Folklore Studies (Peking, 1950), IX, pp. 1–152. The Minzokugaku Jiten, Joly (p. 161) and Mock Joya (I, pp. 196–98), all discuss kappa. Joly writes (p. 22) that kappa are usually propitiated by throwing cucumbers bearing the names and ages of one's family into the river. The contemporary vogue of kappa was described briefly by Lewis Bush in the Asahi Evening News, Tokyo, May 29, 1957, "The 'Kappa'— Japan's Goblin."

Ikeda, p. 43, suggests Type 47–C, "Water-monster captured, dragged by a horse," for the kappa traditions, and on the basis of her index Thompson has added Motif K1022.2.1, "Water-monster, trying to pull horse into water, is dragged to house where he begs for his life and is spared." Ikeda says that the affidavit given by the kappa, promising to do no more mischief, is treasured in some families.

Text from Bungo Densetsu Shu, pp. 76–77. Collected by Shizuka Otome.

IN FORMER DAYS a *kappa* often appeared to trouble the villagers of Fukiura.

in Nishi Nakaura-mura. One time the *kappa* came out of the river to the beach where a cow was tied to a tree. The *kappa* tried to insert his hand into the cow's anus and draw out its tongue. This startled the cow, which started to run round and round the tree, and in so doing caused its rope to wind round and round the *kappa*'s arm. A farmer working in a nearby rice field noticed the *kappa*'s plight and came running to the spot. Afraid of being caught by the farmer, the *kappa* tried to escape in such desperate haste that his arm, around which the rope was tightly wound, was pulled from his shoulder and fell to the ground. The farmer picked it up and carried it home.

That night the *kappa* called at the farmer's house and said: "Please give me back my arm that you took today. If you do not let me have it within the next three days, I cannot join it again to my shoulder." After imploring the farmer in this fashion he went away. The next night he came again, and the third night he appeared once more and repeated the same petition so piteously, with tears in his eyes, that the farmer felt sorry for him. He said: "Will you promise us that you will never do harm to the villagers, either the children or the adults? I will give you back your arm if you will keep your promise until the buttocks of the stone Jizo over there rot away."

The *kappa* made this promise to the farmer, and in consequence was able to depart with his arm. After that he went to the stone Jizo every night and examined its buttocks to see if they were rotted, but they showed no sign of going bad. He sprinkled excrement on the Jizo, but still it failed to rot, and the *kappa* at last grew disappointed and gave up all further attempts.

Even today people in summertime sometimes hear the voice of the *kappa* from the sea, saying: "Don't let the children go out to the beach, for the guest is coming." By the guest he means the *kappa* from Kawajiri. As the *kappa* from this other village is not bound by the promise of the *kappa* who lost his arm in Fukiura, the latter warns against the coming of the former.

So it is said that children have never been injured in the river or at the seashore of this village.

THE KAPPA OF KODA POND

The legend of the wooden-bowl lender is described in the Minzokugaku Jiten *under "Wankashi densetsu" as extending all over Japan from southern Kyushu to northern Tohoku. Some families even claim descent from the dishonest man who refused to return the bowls to the* kappa *and say they still have those bowls (zenwan). The article cites a Chinese legend of borrowing bowls from a mountain fox, and a French story of borrowing a pan from a mound. Kitami Toshio has analyzed 150 such legends in Japan, finding them concentrated near important rivers (Folklore Studies, XIV, Tokyo, 1955, pp. 258–59).*

In Murai, pp. 11–12, "Kappa Who Repaid Kindness," the story begins like the present one but the kappa *leaves his liberator fish rather than bowls. In Yanagita-Mayer, Japanese Folk Tales, no. 54, pp. 155–57, "Mototori (Clearing-the-Old-Score) Mountain," a greedy farmer keeps tray sets borrowed from a mountain cave; his six-year-old son cannot walk, until one day he stands up and carries two rice bags back to the cave as compensation.*

Text from Chiisagata-gun Mintan Shu, pp. 61–62.

THERE WAS a *kappa* in Koda Pond in Junin-mura. Saito Bunji of that village tied his horse to a tree by that pond. The *kappa* came out of the pond and took the reins and began to pull the horse into the pond. The frightened horse jumped up and ran back home and entered the stable. As the water in the *kappa*'s head had been spilled, the *kappa* lost his strength and was dragged by the horse into the stable. When Bunji came to see the horse, the *kappa* made apologies to him and said: "Please forgive me. If you prepare a feast in your home, I will certainly lend you necessary bowls." So Bunji forgave him.

From then on, any time he held a feast, the bowls were prepared in the yard the night before. After he had used them, he put them in the yard and they disappeared during the night. However, one time a neighbor hid a set of the bowls when the rest were being returned to the *kappa*. The *kappa* took them during the night, but he never again lent bowls to Bunji.

THE KAPPA WHO PLAYED "PULL-FINGER"

The kappa *is seen here in two more of his favorite roles, an evil water creature who devours humans, and a helpful one who sets their broken bones.*
    Text from Chiisagata-gun Mintan Shu, *pp. 10–11.*

THERE IS a pond called Akanuma-ike at the foot of Mt. Tateshina, and near the pond there is a big stone called Kagihiki-ishi [Pull-Finger Stone]. Once a child used to stand on that stone and called to the passers-by: "Let's play Pull-finger." The passers-by would stop and play Pull-finger for fun. Then the child would pull them into the pond and eat them up. Many people were killed in that way. At last the people decided that the child must be a *kappa* who lived in the pond.

A man named Tachiki from Suwa said: "I will destroy the *kappa*." He asked his lord if he could borrow a good horse. Then he rode by this stone, and as he expected, the child asked him to play Pull-finger. He answered the child: "All right." And they locked fingers. No sooner had they locked fingers than he whipped the horse and rode as fast as he could. The child could not bear to be dragged by the horse. He said: "Please excuse me, I am really the *kappa* of Akanuma Pond. Please don't kill me. Then I will teach you the secret of bonesetting." And the man said: "Then teach me that secret."

The *kappa* taught him in detail. "Because you've taught me the secret of bonesetting, I will set you free. But if you continue to live in this place, you might have the desire to eat people again. So go somewhere else tonight," said the man. So the *kappa* went away to the pond of Wada-mura and he has been living there quietly.

And this Tachiki is said to be the founder of the family line of the famous surgeon Tachiki.

THE KAPPA BONESETTER

The kappa's occult bonesetting powers are further described here. Ikeda, p. 43, speaks of a certain salve as reputedly the kappa's secret. Such a tradition is related by Shiojiri, pp. 18–19, going back to the early eighteenth century, and told on an old family in Himeji. The kappa asked the samurai to give him back the right arm he had cut off, saying he could reset it with a special medicine. In return for the favor he gave the samurai the formula for the salve.

Text from Sempo Nakata, "Kappa's Medicine," in Tabi to Densetsu, I (February, 1928), pp. 5–6. From a larger selection entitled "The Story of Unsho-an Takatori, a Bonesetter at Hakata in Chikuzen," pp. 1–9.

IT WAS during the Genroku period [1688–1703] that a bonesetter named Takatori Unsho-an lived at Hakata in the province of Chikuzen. His wife was a daughter of Miyake Kakusuke, a masterless samurai in Higo. She was noted not only for her surpassing beauty but also for her accomplishments.

Late one night it happened that while she was in the toilet, she felt some strange hand touch her buttock. As she was a stout-hearted woman she did not become too upset but shouted: "Rascal!" Then she saw in the moonlight a strange, shaggy little man running away toward the river side. Nothing else happened that night. The next night the wife went to the toilet with her precious short sword. While she was in the toilet the strange creature appeared and repeated his action of the night before. The wife cried out: "Rascal!" and she cut off its hand with one stroke of the sword. The strange creature ran away shrieking with pain. The next morning the wife told her husband all about what had happened and showed him the creature's hand she had cut off. It was webbed and looked something like a snapping-turtle's foot.

After examining it carefully, Unsho-an said to his wife: "Fine, fine! It's a wonderful thing. This is a *kappa*'s hand. A *kappa* must have fallen for you. Anyway you did very well. A *kappa*'s hand is a rare thing."

"How disagreeable to think of being loved by a *kappa!* Don't say such a thing," said the wife, giving a scowl at the husband. But soon she softened her countenance and asked: "Is it really a *kappa's* hand?"

That night a voice was heard by the head of Unsho-an's bed. It said: "Give me back my hand." Unsho-an was not a mere doctor, but a samurai who attended the feudal lord. He took up his bow from the *tokonoma* and plucked the string. Then the voice stopped. The next night and the next, the same voice was heard. By the third night Unsho-an was tired of hearing it, so he spoke to it saying: "What can you want with your hand which was cut off a few days ago?"

"Your question is reasonable in the human world, but it is different with us. We *kappa* can join a hand to the arm however cold it may become, and when we join it, it will perform just as well as it ever did. So please give it back to me, I pray you," said the *kappa,* showing himself before Unsho-an and bowing down his head. On hearing this, Unsho-an thought to himself: "He speaks pleasingly. I will see how he sets bones." So then he said to the *kappa:* "In truth, I determined to kill such a rascal as you on the spot with my sword the moment I saw you. But now I will return your hand to you, provided you show me how you set broken bones."

"That is an easy thing," said the *kappa,* and on receiving his dead-cold hand, joined it skillfully to his arm before Unsho-an's eyes. The samurai watched the *kappa's* action with keen interest, murmuring: "That's good, that's good." Then the *kappa* thanked him and disappeared.

The next day there were two big fish on the fence of Unsho-an's garden. He knew that the *kappa* had brought them out of gratitude, and he enjoyed eating them with his wife. From that time on he practised the method of bonesetting which he had learned from the *kappa*, and gradually he became a famous bonesetter. His family prospered for a long time and this method of bonesetting was transmitted from generation to generation.

A GRATEFUL KAPPA

Chihei Nakamura, who wrote the present story, is a well-known Japanese author. I met him in his native town of Miyazaki in southern Kyushu, where he showed me his considerable collection of kappa figurines. This account shows signs of literary style, for instance in the use of dialogue, although it is clearly in a genuine tradition.
Text from Hyuga Minwa Shu, pp. 68–71.

IN THE NORTHERN DISTRICT of Miyazaki Prefecture, they sometimes call the *kappa* "*hyosubo*." There are not a few stories concerning the *hyosubo*. The following is one of these stories which has been handed down in this district.

Once upon a time, at Nakayama Shrine in the present Kadokawa-machi (in Higashi Usuki-gun), there lived a Shinto priest called Kimmaru. Although a priest, he was very good at fencing and was renowned for his bravery throughout the neighborhood.

One fine day, he was rambling in the village at random and he came to the foot of an earthen bridge. Suddenly he felt that something was there and stopped walking. A *kappa* peeped out from under the bridge.

"Is that you, *Hyosubo*? Don't be too mischievous." Throwing out these words at the *kappa*, the priest was about to pass by when the *kappa*'s voice hastily beseeched him from behind.

"Mr. Priest, Mr. Priest, please listen to my story." The *kappa*'s voice sounded very sorrowful. The priest turned round and even saw tears in the eyes of the *kappa*.

"Mr. Priest, I used to have many children—my treasures. But a tremendously big snake which dwells in this river appeared every night and swallowed my dear children one by one. I have now only one child left. I hear that you are very expert in fencing, so please do away with the snake by dint of your sword."

"I am sorry to hear that. I'll kill the snake for you."

Kimmaru thus promised the *kappa,* and he stood under the bridge that night carefully prepared for battle. When he had made ready to attack the snake, the creature appeared to swallow down the surviving child of the *kappa*. Kimmaru lost no time in slashing at the snake with his sword. He was so skillful and speedy that the enormous snake was cut into two and died instantly.

When Kimmaru put up his sword and stood upon the bridge, the *kappa* appeared before him.

"Thank you very much, Mr. Priest. From now on, we can sleep in peace. I'd like to repay your kindness. Don't you have any wish? If you have, please tell it to me."

Kimmaru was reminded of the pranks that *kappa* sometimes played upon the village children. "Then, will you promise me that you will never play tricks on my offspring, for instance, by pulling them into the water?"

"Certainly I will, Mr. Priest. I will never be mischievous towards your offspring. So please be assured on this point." So promising, the *kappa* disappeared again into the night-darkened river.

Even today, children of that town will loudly recite the following words before they plunge into the water to swim:

"Mr. Hyosubo, we belong to the family of Kimmaru. Don't play pranks on us."

This custom is said to have originated since that time.

WRESTLING A KAPPA

The similarity between Goro and his rice and Popeye and his spinach will strike American readers.

This story was collected by Professor Teigo Yoshida while doing field work in a mountainous farm village, Nao, Yamato-mura, Saga-gun, Saga-ken, in 1955. He heard it from Zengo Morita, then about seventy years old. Professor Yoshida has given me other information about kappa beliefs in Kyushu, which I have included in the introduction to this chapter.

ONCE UPON A TIME there was a strong man named Goro. Walking along a stream, he met a *kappa* and wrestled with the creature. At the outset the *kappa* was so much stronger that Goro was almost defeated. Then he said to the *kappa*: "Since I have become hungry, I want to eat some rice. After taking it, I shall continue wrestling. Would you mind waiting a little while? I'll come back soon."

The *kappa* consented to wait, and Goro went back but could not find any rice in his house. Then he went to a Buddhist temple and found rice offered to an image there. After eating the rice, he immediately returned to the stream to continue wrestling with the *kappa*. The *kappa* was still waiting for him. As soon as the wrestling began, Goro proved much stronger than the monster. As he laid down the *kappa,* the water contained in the saucer on the *kappa*'s head spilled out completely. As a result, the *kappa* lost his power and Goro was the final victor.

MEMORIES OF KAPPA

Told by Mrs. Hitoshi Kawashima, 69, to her granddaughter, Kayoko Saito, in Tokyo, April 8, 1957. Mrs. Kawashima was born in what is now Nishi Hama, Aki-shi, Kochi-ken, Shikoku.

WHEN I WAS but a small child, I often went to a nearby river with my friends to bathe and swim. There was a place in the river where the water made a deep, green pool. We were forbidden to go swim there because, it was said, a *kappa* would catch us and pull us into the water.

One day a friend of mine who was swimming in the river was suddenly somehow lost in the river, and was found dead in that deep, green pool. The village people made much ado about this loss of the child and believed that she had been taken by a *kappa* because her anus was removed exactly in the way the *kappa* was believed to do.

As little children, we believed naively in the existence of *kappa*.

When we had to go along the grassy path on the bank of the river, we went hopping in great haste lest the *kappa* should catch our feet.

Such were my simple and innocent childhood days.

TALES OF TENGU

General discussions of the tengu can be found in Anesaki, pp. 287–88; Minzoku-gaku Jiten, *"Tengu";* Mock Joya, *II, pp. 133–34, "Tengu";* De Visser, "The Tengu" *25–99 (a detailed account of the tengu from the eighth to the nineteenth centuries, surmising that in old Japan the Buddhist devil was grafted onto the tengu).*

Mock Joya describes the tengu as human in form, but winged, with long sharp nails on fingers and toes, and carrying a fan, a stick, and a sword, all of good size. Sometimes he is depicted with a long nose, and this is the more powerful tengu, and at other times with a pointed bill. Mountain people still claim to hear tengu felling trees and laughing in the woods.

Professor Ichiro Hori, Japan's eminent scholar of folk Buddhism, has graciously furnished me with the following information about tengu. In the course of time, representations of tengu have altered. At first he appeared to manifest the crow, and was beaked. A Buddhist painter, in his "Tengu Soshi" (Painting Scroll of the Tengu) satirized vain Tendai monks of the Heian period (794–1185) who had lapsed into secularism with this crowlike figure. In medieval times haughty and insincere Buddhist monks were believed to be reborn as tengu after death. However, an influence from Shinto mythology caused a shift from a birdlike to a more human appearance, and the beak of tengu became a large, round, red nose. Currently the tengu mask worn in Shinto festival processions represents the god Saruta-hiko, who guided the descent of the Sun Goddess from the Sky World to govern the Central Land of the Reed.

The brief texts below are typical of local allusions to the presence of tengu. They come from Aichi-Ken Densetsu Shu *pp. 72, 242–43.*

1. THE STONE OF THE TENGU'S HEEL. Near the top of Mt. Shira at Inaba, Asahi-mura, Higashi Kasugai-gun, there is an old stone about three feet in diameter. It is called *Tengu no Kakato Iwa* [The Stone of the Tengu's Heel]. On the surface of the stone there is a hollow in the shape of a heel of a big foot facing the east. It is said that the *tengu* who lived in this mountain in ancient days, intending to go one night to Mt. Saru-nage on an errand, stepped on this stone and jumped a big jump eastward, leaving his footprint on the stone. People say that there is a *tengu*

still living on Mt. Shira and that the *tengu*'s fire is sometimes seen on dark, rainy nights.

2. THE TENGU'S FIRE. There is a big pine tree at Kita Takai in Yamato-mura, Nakajima-gun. It is said that Yamato Takeru-no-Mikoto (a hero of mythological history) once put his sedge hat on this tree. The villagers often see a strange fire moving between this tree and the old cedar tree at Kumano Shrine in Kita Takai. This is said to be caused by the *tengu* who has his residence on the tops of these two trees and comes and goes between them.

3. THE TENGU'S PINE. There was a big pine tree in the precincts of Shimmei Shrine at Kanesato, Tomita-mura. A *tengu* had lived there since ancient times. When he was in good humor, his laughter was heard throughout the village and the village was left in peace. But when he was offended, he did violence and frightened the villagers. This tree fell down in the severe storm of 1921.

THE TENGU PINE AND TAKEGORO

This legend describes a customary tengu practice of kami-kakushi, divine kidnaping. De Visser, op. cit., dates in the fourteenth century (p. 74) the first instance of a person abducted by a tengu falling from the sky and writes: "Even nowadays the country people beat drums when a child is lost, and call upon the tengu to bring it back" (p. 76).

Text from Shimane-ken Kohi Densetsu Shu, Yatsuka-gun, pp. 3–5.

THERE IS an old pine tree which stands as a mark for boatmen sailing in Lake Shinji. As eight branches issue forth from its trunk, it is sometimes called the Eight-Branch Pine. People say that if a man cuts off a small twig it will shed red blood and the whole mountain will rumble and the man will be divided into eight pieces on the spot. Therefore no one dares touch it with cutlery.

In olden times a small shrine stood beneath that tree, though now nothing of the sort remains. Evenings when the white waterfall of Mt. Mitaki was colored crimson by the setting sun, the young *tengu,* fatigued from play, used to come back to that pine tree. The old *tengu* flew down from the mountain to take them back. In the morning the old *tengu* came down again with the little *tengu* to let them play by themselves.

An honest man named Takegoro who lived near the pine tree was wont from his youth to see those *tengu* who came every morning and returned every evening. One night it happened that he disappeared on the way back from the village meeting. The neighbors thought he might have been taken away by the god. They searched for him, ringing the bell and beating the drum, for three days and nights, though all in vain. But on the fifth evening he came back from somewhere with his clothes torn to pieces. His face was pale and his eyes glittered strangely. He had a stick in his hand, which thenceforth he always kept beside him.

From that time on, every day when the old *tengu* sent the little *tengu* off, Takegoro emerged from his house and, looking up at the sky and shaking the stick heavenwards, cried out: "Wait a minute, wait a minute!" In response, a voice from the sky rumbled: "Hoh." The next moment Takegoro would disappear, and his voice would be heard from the top of the pine tree talking with the old *tengu*. After a while Takegoro appeared in the sky flying around here and there. Since he had been once abducted by the *tengu,* thenceforth he must fly with the *tengu* every day. In addition Takegoro was often threatened by the *tengu* that at his slightest disobedient deed he would be thrown down into the stormy sea or dashed upon the cruel rocks.

Sometimes they held feasts on the *tengu* pine. On such occasions the *tengu* would say, pointing to a wealthy *sake*-brewer's house below the river: "Let's burn that house and drink *sake* while viewing the house in flames." Only with great pains could Takegoro check the *tengu* from carrying out this design.

Takegoro served the *tengu* in that fashion for more than twenty years. When he became old it grew burdensome to him to fly with the *tengu*. So he asked to be relieved from the service. Then the *tengu* said: "There is no one so honest and attractive as you. But now I cannot deny your request to take leave of me. I know of another man in Hikawa. I shall make him my servant from now on."

Even after that, however, the *tengu* sometimes visited Takegoro. Once when his wife was weaving, a wind from the *tengu* suddenly blew into the house, and the sound of clink, clink was heard inside. As Takegoro touched the spot with his stick, there came into view many coins. When he was making a mortar from a log, the edge of his hatchet was blunted from coins within the log. Takegoro often met with such happenings, and by and by he became quite rich. While he was supervising workers in making a road, he struck a stick he was holding against the stones which had been picked up from the river for the road bed. The stones split in two, and glittering gold coins dropped out. He paid the workers with those coins, and moreover he entertained them with *sake*. The villagers admired him greatly, calling him "Old Father Luck." After he retired from work, he often invited the *tengu* to his home as a precious guest and feasted him. Until the feast ended and the *tengu* left, no other members of the house could enter the room.

BURNED TO DEATH BY A TENGU

The theory that the tengu is a degenerate mountain divinity finds support in legends such as this.

Text from Shintatsu Mintan Shu, pp. 37-75.
Note: Akiba—see pp. 139-40, "The God Akiba Revealed as a Beggar."

A MAN NAMED MOTOJI lived at Ishimoda in Fujita-machi, Date-gun. He was a rascal and indulged in drinking and gambling. He did not attend to business at home, but he robbed wayfarers at Kunimi Pass, or he burglarized, or he killed the horses of other people, or he set houses on fire. Early one New Year's morning he stopped in front of a mountain shrine with a gun. He built a fire and he smoked tobacco. As the shrine was in the thick wood and the sun had not risen, it was quite dark. Then a strange bird's cry was heard on top of a tree. Motoji looked up and saw a big long-tailed bird on the treetop. He shot his gun, but the bird still sat on the tree without moving, and Motoji thought he had missed his aim. So he shot again, but the bird still did not move. He shot three or four times continuously. Then the bird uttered a horrible cry and fell down before Motoji.

The moment he thought he had got the bird, the bird stood up before him and turned into a *tengu*. The *tengu* caught him and said: "How did you dare to hit me?" And he took burning wood and touched Motoji with it. Motoji's body was burned. He cried for help. The

villagers heard him. When they came there, his body was all black and only his eyes were shining. Motoji told the whole story to the astonished villagers and confessed all his sins. The villagers carried him home, but he soon died. People said to each other that he had been punished by the gods.

The place where Motoji was burned to death is called Ohayashi in Okido-mura. There is a little shrine there to the god Akiba. It is in the middle of a thick wood and it is feared by the people because the *tengu* is said to be living there. If someone cuts the trees of that wood, there is always a fire in the village. Recently there occurred three big fires, and all the houses were burned. The fires are said to have resulted from the curse against cutting down the trees in that wood.

THE TENGU OF KOMINE SHRINE

The association made here between a shrine and a tengu *follows the belief that* tengu *often served shrines on holy mountains. In this legend the* tengu *behaves like a European poltergeist.*

Text from Shintatsu Mintan Shu, *pp. 70–73.*

IN THE EARLY YEARS of Meiji [late nineteenth century] there was a doctor named Kumagaya Genyo at Datesaki-mura, Date-gun. His foster-father Hambei had an imposing look and was skillful in fishing. When he set his eyes upon a fish, it could not move. In his house a strange apparition appeared. Sometimes it made a great noise suddenly at midnight, and sometimes it spoke in the air or sang beautiful songs from the ceiling.

One morning the maid got up early, opened the front gate, and saw a little man wearing a short black hunting coat and breeches, his cheeks covered with a towel, going out singing a song. But the fearless Hambei said that such a foolish thing could not be. One night when Hambei was drinking *sake* the cup stuck to his cheeks and he could not pull the cup away. But when he bowed down and made apologies to the apparition, he could easily remove the cup. From that time on he set up a shelf for the god and offered *sake* and rice. Then the apparition not only did no further mischief to him but brought him something to eat and some money for *sake*. So the old man respected the apparition and called it his guest.

A gambler named Kintaro one night came to the old man's home to lay the ghost but he was treated badly and went away. One New Year's Day a doctor of Yasuhara-machi named Takagi Kenko visited the old man and was entertained with *sake*. On that occasion, when the conversation turned to the apparition, young Takagi boasted that he would cut it down with one stroke if it appeared there. Just at that time the maid was mashing yams in an earthenware bowl, and the bowl flew up into the air and turned a somersault above the old man. So the yams dropped down on his head. Mr. Takagi felt uneasy, hastily said farewell, and went out. As he hastened away to the ferry of the Abukuma River, the sword which he wore came out of its sheath and floated before his face, so he could neither step forward nor go backward, because the sword moved around behind him. He was really frightened and knelt on the ground, and bowing his head, he made apologies for his harsh words. Then the sword dropped before him, and without encountering any more mysterious happenings, he returned home safely. He told later that he had never had such a fearful experience.

Once Mr. Kumagaya, the old man, tried to subdue the apparition, and he asked the mountain priest to pray for that purpose. Then some invisible thing read sutras aloud behind the mountain priest. So the mountain priest was frightened.

Similar strange occurrences continued for several years. Sometimes there was a fire in the chest of drawers, so the clothes were burned. Or sometimes there were swords lost and later found in ditches. When someone asked the gods for an explanation of such mysteries, the gods replied that it was a *tengu*'s doing. They said that the house of the old doctor was formerly the residence of Ozaki Daihachiro. Daihachiro liked to arrest people. When there was a person whom he thought a little suspicious, he took him to his office and subjected him to the most severe punishment. The ghosts of such people haunted him often. Sometimes a little man who covered his cheeks with a towel loitered around his house. Some men who saw this thought it must be a fox's or a badger's doing. This ghost haunted Daihachiro. He had nightmares every night, so he asked the Komine Shrine in Shimotsuke to send him a *tengu* to guard his house.

After that no more ghosts appeared, but Daihachiro suffered from fever and talked deliriously, then died. During the Meiji era, his house was offered for sale, and Mr. Kumagaya bought it for his residence. The *tengu* could not return to Komine Shrine, and it stayed on in the house. It was that *tengu* who did so many mischievous things.

Mr. Kihei Kumagaya, who is a doctor now living in Fujita-machi, Date-gun, is a grandson of this Kumagaya Genyo.

THE TENGU'S SWORD

There is a tradition in Yanagita, Mountain Village Life, p. 408, of a family in Higashi Kawa-mura that owns an old sword which they keep in the tokonoma (alcove), for if it is moved, sickness comes to the valley. No tengu is mentioned, but Anesaki, pp. 309–10, relates how the young hero Yoshitsune learned from tengu swordsmanship which subsequently brought him victory over the famed warrior Benkei. The ninjitsu magicians referred to below are still the subject of legends among Nisei in California (Marvin K. Opler, pp. 391–92, "Perceptive Swordsmen and Sorcerer's Apprentices").

This story was told to me in Kanazawa on July 11, 1957, by Masaaki Miyazaki, a robust young man of poetic talent on the staff of the American Cultural Center at Kanazawa. He spoke fair English. His father, who was a second son, had migrated to Hokkaido in 1923, where Masaaki was born near Ikeda in 1933. Masaaki returned to Kanazawa in 1949.

Note: Koku, a rice measure, about five bushels.

THIS TALE WAS TOLD by my grandfather in Kanazawa about fifteen years ago, when he was ninety years old. He had been a retainer of Lord Maeda, one of the most important daimyo of the Tokugawa period. (The red gate now in front of Tokyo University marks the site of Lord Maeda's Tokyo residence.)

In those days all the daimyo had to spend some time each year in Edo [Tokyo] in attendance upon the Shogunate. This lord for whom my grandfather was a retainer was a one-million-*koku* daimyo. My grandfather was a two-hundred-*koku* retainer. (After the Meiji Restoration he changed his occupation and became a rice dealer. My father was his second son.)

The story I am going to tell here was told me by my father who heard it directly from my grandfather. But my father said he was not sure how many generations ago all this happened.

It seems that one of our ancestors had learned a special kind of magic called *ninjitsu* from a *tengu* (a long-nosed goblin) in the woods around Kanazawa. This *ninjitsu* was a popular kind of magic in the Tokugawa period, and those who mastered it could make themselves vanish simply by saying some magic words. For instance, one who knew *ninjitsu* could dive under water and stay there an hour, or could run as fast as a horse. It was the custom in those days to show respect by giving a sword, so when my ancestor had learned *ninjitsu*, the *tengu* gave him a sword. It was a very special sword. (I never saw it, but my father says he did, in the house at Kanazawa in the mountains, and it had about one inch of the tip broken off.) After my forebear received that sword he could do whatever he wanted to, then hide himself behind a stone. As time went on, he committed some very wicked deeds, stealing money, even killing people. His bad behavior continued for a long time.

Then one day when he was working alone in the mountains, my ancestor found a farmer, dressed in a humble kimono, walking in front of him as if to block his way. After a bit, my relative became angry and took his sword to try to kill this impudent farmer. He drew his sword from its sheath to cut off the farmer's head. But, when he thought he had finished the deed, the farmer suddenly disappeared from the spot. Just as suddenly, my ancestor heard laughter in the tree just above his head. Then he glanced down and saw that the tip of his sword was broken off. From that moment on, he was unable to use *ninjitsu* at all. A little later, he was captured by priests, sent to Osaka, and hanged.

The farmer was probably the *tengu*.

THE TENGU WHO MADE RICE CAKES

According to the Minzokugaku Jiten, the long nose, the strolling monk's garb, and the feather fan of the tengu, as described below, are late additions to tengu beliefs.

This story also was told to me by Masaaki Miyazaki in Kanazawa on July 11, 1957.

Note: Ankoro, a kind of mochi or rice cake.

MY FATHER also told me this tale.

There is a small town called Matsuto near Kanazawa, and in this town there is a store that sells *ankoro*. My father told me that some hundred years ago a *tengu* told a very poor man living there how to make rice cakes. (This *tengu* was very sympathetic and democratic.) Although that man was very poor, he then became rich and spent the rest of his life in comfort.

Every year, even now, the *tengu* comes once to that house. The family members make special cakes for him, and the *tengu* comes to the house to eat the cakes. My father said there is a miniature shrine near the shop, and there the family makes a special offering for the *tengu*.

Rice cakes are made of rice and beans and sugar, but in this special kind the beans are outside and the rice inside. Someone in this family always learns the recipe from a member of the older generation.

Whenever I go to that town I eat those rice cakes. You can get them at the station for thirty yen. Ten little rice cakes come wrapped in little pieces of bamboo leaf, with a paper which tells how old the tradition is. A picture of a fan also accompanies the rice cakes, because the *tengu*, which has red skin and a long nose, always carries a fan made of feathers.

Ankoro is a special name. Sometimes it is called *ankoro mochi*. Rice cakes somewhat like these are sold in other little towns, but they are only imitations.

THE DEMONS' CAVE

The oni (demons) of this and the following legend are often pictured as hideous, horned, nearly naked giants, with three eyes, three fingers, and three toes. Still, as

Anesaki points out (p. 283), they are frequently subjects of comic tales that revolve around their stupidity. Hence they are kin to the stupid ogre and devil of European stories. Motifs G303.9.1, "The devil as a builder," and G303.16.19.5, "Man imitates cock crowing; devil is deceived," occur in both legends. The present tradition has the characteristic Japanese trait of a task failing fulfillment on the one hundredth repetition, as in "The Monk and the Maid," pp. 46–47.

Text from Bungo Densetsu Shu, pp. 99–100. From Hayami-gun.

AT KAMEKAWA SHRINE there is a stone staircase made of big stones awkwardly piled up. Long ago in a place called Ishigaki in the suburbs of Beppu-shi a demon couple lived. The caves they inhabited were only six feet square. The roof stone of one cave is lifted up a little to make the sun shine into the cave. This was done by the female demon in order to brighten up the room for her weaving.

This couple came to the village every day to catch human beings and eat them. The god of the shrine in Kamekawa, Chinzei-hachiro Tametomo, took pity on the villagers and decided to give some tasks to the demons for the purpose of making them stop eating people. So one day he disguised himself as a plain man and called on the demons. He said to them: "If you two can make a hundred stone steps at the shrine tomorrow night, I will give you one man daily and you will not need to go out to catch them."

This was a very difficult task, but the demon couple willingly undertook it. The next night the female demon threw big stones from Ishigaki and the male demon in Kamekawa caught them and piled them at good speed. In a short time ninety-nine steps were finished. Tametomo was surprised to see this, and thought he had to do something. He took two pot lids and, beating them, imitated a cock's crow with his voice. Thus he signaled the dawn of the day two or three times, because he could not bear to see people sacrificed to the demons. The demons heard this, and went back to their caves discouraged. "What a pity! Only one more step."

After that they kept their promise to Tametomo and gave up eating the people. Now only the demons' caves remain to tell their interesting story.

THE TOOTH-MARKED STONE

Two variants are here given of a demon legend which is a variation of the preceding story. The first uses Motif G303.9.1.1, "Devil as a builder of bridges," and the second, which brings in Kobo Daishi to outwit the demon, employs Motif K218, "Devil cheated by religious or magic means."

Texts from Bungo Densetsu Shu, *p. 42. The first version was told by Tadako Saito, the second by Masa Komera.*

Note: Tatami, *a floor mat measuring approximately six by three feet.*

VERSION I. At the right side of the front hall of Nishi Sawada Shrine in Ueda-mura, Oita-gun, there is a big mossy stone about the size of one *tatami*. It seems to have been there for hundreds of years. In ancient times the god of Mt. Hongu, which rises high up side by side with Mt. Rei, had trouble coming and going from Hongu-zan to Rei-zan because of a valley between those two mountains. So he commanded a demon to build a stone bridge over the valley. He promised the demon to let him eat a man as a prize if the demon could build the bridge before the first crow of the cock.

The demon was very glad to hear this and worked hard, carrying great stones in his mouth. He was about to carry the last stone when the god saw him and thought to himself: "The demon is about to finish the work, yet the cock does not crow. If it doesn't crow now, I have to let him eat a man. It's a pity for them." And the god loudly imitated a cock's crow. The demon heard it and was greatly disappointed at missing the prize within his easy reach. He was so much vexed at his loss that he threw away all the stones which he had piled up, into the valley of the Oka River down below.

All those stones were marked with the demon's teeth. The villagers took one of the stones that bore the demon's tooth prints and placed it in the precincts of Nishi Sawada Shrine. It remains there today and shows the clear mark of something like a tooth of three or four inches.

VERSION 2. The demon who lived on Mt. Rei begged St. Kobo to give him a man once a year. Kobo accepted this request on condition that the demon should make a thousand valleys in one day and one night.

The demon had just finished that task when Kobo caused one of the valleys to vanish. The demon counted the valleys over and over again and could number only 999 of them. He was very much vexed at that. He held up one big stone in his mouth and threw it away.

That stone is said to be the same one that is now called "The Tooth-Marked Stone."

GREAT KING WITH EIGHT FACES

Another version is given in Murai, no. 8, pp, 32–37, "Copper Pheasant's Arrow." Yasuke, the old man in the text below, in Murai's story is the son of an herb-gatherer kidnaped by the demon Hachimen Daio. Yasuke rescues a copper pheasant from a trap; she reappears as a beautiful young maid who weds him, while here she becomes Yasuke's adopted daughter. Then, as in the present tale, she gives him a copper pheasant's jointed tail to enable him to kill the demon. But as it was the seat of her soul, she had to leave Yasuke. A simplified account for children is in Yanagita-Mayer, Japanese Folk Tales, pp. 175–77, "Yasuke of Yamura."

   Text from Nihon Densetsu Shu, 2nd ed., pp. 153–55.

   Note: Shinano, now Nagano Prefecture.

A LONG TIME AGO a kindhearted old couple lived in Ariake-mura, Minami Azumi-gun, in the province of Shinano. One day, while on his way to the town to buy rice, the old man found a bird dying in a trap. He felt sorry for the bird, so he bought it from the hunter and set it free in the mountains. The next day a strange girl visited the old couple and asked them to adopt her as their daughter. But they replied that they were too poor to let her live with them. Then the girl said: "Don't worry about such things. I will work and earn money for you." So at last the old couple granted the girl's request.

Every day the girl wove or did other work to get money to help the old couple. In those days a demon called Hachimen Daio [Great King with Eight Faces] lived on Mt. Ariake and troubled the people. The emperor heard of this and sent Sakanoue Tamuramaro as a general to destroy the demon. The demon, who knew of the coming of Tamura Shogun, darkened the sky and dropped big stones down to the foot of the mountain. So the attacking force could not proceed. Tamura Shogun tried to shoot arrows at the glittering demon's eyes, but none of the arrows hit. Finally Tamura Shogun exhausted all possible stratagems and decided he must ask for help from the gods. He prayed to Kiyomizu Kannon at Mizusawa, promising that if Kannon would help him destroy the demon, he would make a thousand worshipers visit the shrine every day. Then, on the final night, Kannon appeared in his dream and told him that if he shot the demon with the arrows made of a copper pheasant's tail plume with thirteen joints, the sky would become clear at the first shot, the demon would be killed by the second arrow, and all the creatures around the demon would be destroyed by the third arrow.

Tamura Shogun was glad to hear this and announced to the villagers that he would give a big reward to a person who would bring him a copper pheasant's tail with thirteen joints. The girl in the old couple's house brought such a plume from somewhere to the old people, saying: "I am the copper pheasant that you rescued. I was waiting for the chance to repay you for your kindness. Now I have brought to you this tail plume, which you may offer to Tamura Shogun."

She handed them the plume and went away. The old couple lived the rest of their life happily as a result of the reward. Tamura Shogun had the arrows made from the copper pheasant's tail plume and shot them. The sky cleared up at the first arrow, the demon was shot to death by the second arrow, and all the creatures were dispersed by the third arrow.

So Tamura Shogun succeeded in destroying the demon. He fulfilled his promise to Kannon by constructing a shrine in Kyoto, which is the famous temple of Kiyomizu Kannon on Higashi-yama.

The demon's corpse was said to return to life if it was buried in one place, so he cut the corpse into pieces and buried them separately. There is a shrine called Daio Shrine built on the place where the demon's head was buried, and the hill called Mimi-zuka [Ear Mound] is the place where his ears were buried. The big stones scattered around Ariake-mura and Nishi Hodaka are the stones that the demons threw. The old

man was given the name Yasuke Yamura by Tamura Shogun and his house continued long afterwards, even up to the present time.

MOUNTAIN GIANTS

Joly, pp. 16–17, writes: "Yama Uba the mountain muse is another female goblin, occasionally described as having a mouth under her hair, the locks of which transform themselves into serpents, or catch small children, upon whom the Yama Uba feeds." Anesaki gives an idealized account of the yama-uba from a lyric drama, portraying her as "a personification of the clouds and mists" (pp. 290–92). In Yanagita-Mayer, Japanese Folk Tales, nos. 32–33, pp. 98–105, the yama-uba appears as a stupid ogre and a child-eating demon ("The Ox-Driver and the Yama-uba"; "O Sun, The Iron Chain!"); but in no. 58, pp. 168–170, the yama-uba befriends a lost young girl, giving her a treasure coat ("The Magic Straw Cloak of the Yama-uba").

The present tale is of the stupid-ogre type. However, additional densetsu from the same source show the yama-uba in a favorable light, making thread from vines to weave cloth, acting as midwife (samba), and killing troublesome wild boars by throwing stones at them from the mountain top. The yama-uba is particularly well known in Shizuoka Prefecture.

Text from Shizuoka-ken Densetsu Meguri, II, pp. 72–75.

Notes: Yama-otoko and yama-uba, literally, "mountain men" and "mountain old women." Soba-dango, buckwheat cakes.

It is said that in the mountains of Yamaka-mura and Tatsuyama-mura in Iwata-gun, the mountainous region of Enshu [Shizuoka-ken], there lived giants in ancient times. The males were called *yama-otoko* and the females, *yama-uba*. They were more than six meters tall and ran around barefooted in the mountains more swiftly than they traversed the plain, speeding by like the wind. They lived near the rocks or under the trees, feeding themselves with wild fruits and smaller animals and such. On the one hand, they committed evil deeds such as eating human babies and doing harm to the crops; but on the other, they performed with their supernatural power wonderful works beyond the power of human beings. As a matter of fact, most of them were deified, since the people feared their awful strength. However, being sometimes more dull-witted than human beings, they often acted in a stupid way.

Long ago, at Fukuzawa in Yamaka-mura, there was a house called by the name of Hinata. A *yama-uba* often visited this house. She tended the baby and looked after the house while the people were busy outside. So they thought well of her and thanked her for her help. One day, however, she ate the baby.

"Oh, dear! How terrible!" The people of the family were frightened and saddened. "What a pity! We will by any means get even with Yama-uba for our poor baby. We must see that such things never happen again," they thought, and they talked over a plan to carry out.

One day later, the *yama-uba* visited the house again. The people offered her a dish of several hot-baked *soba-dango,* saying with an innocent look: "Please, will you take one?" Inside the *dango* they had put heated stones. The *yama-uba,* not knowing this, said: "Oh, thank you," and swallowed up all the *dango.* Then her stomach became very hot with the heated stones and she could not stand the pain.

"Hot, hot! Give me some water, water," she cried in agony.

"Here is water." The people gave her oil instead of water. The *yama-uba* drank it, and it gave her awful pains. She ran out of the house groaning and got to the bank of the Tenryu River at the place called Ochii, about four kilometers away. Trying to drink water, she fell into the river and drowned.

"We have taken our revenge at last," said the people in satisfaction. But they feared the *yama-uba* would put a curse on them; so they built a little shrine for the spirit of that *yama-uba*. This shrine still remains today, called by the name of Samba-sama.

THE MOUNTAIN MAN OF MT. MITSUBUSHI

Another legend dealing with a mountain-man monster is in Murai, typescript, p. 14, "Mountain Man of Shiro-uma-ga-take (Mount White Horse)." The creature terrifies woodsmen who attempt to cut down a zelkova tree, and dismembers a boastful hunter. The hunter's son finally kills the monster.

Text from Tosa Fuzoku to Densetsu, *p. 60.*

FUKUJI WAS a hunter who lived a great many years ago at Matobushi in Kagami-mura, Tosa-gun. One cold, snowy day he went out hunting on the mountain called Kasamatsu-mine. (This is a very steep peak that rises in the same range with Mt. Sekko.) He found there strange footprints, in no wise resembling a wild boar's. Thinking they might be a big beast's footmarks, he put his gun in a tree nearby, fastened a string to the trigger, and stretched the string along the ground. Thus having set the gun so as to make it fire when an animal passed by, he went down the mountain and stayed the night in a straw hut, where he had in the past stayed overnight when he hunted wild boar in the mountain in winter.

The next morning Fukuji went to see the place where he had set his gun. He found the string rolled up and hung on a branch of the tree. Thinking it very strange, he fastened the string again in the same way, but this time he tied two strings together. He spent the night again in the hut. At midnight he heard a sharp report of a gun which echoed back with a terrible sound.

Fukuji arose early the next morning and went up the mountain. On the summit he saw blood drops. Wishing to find out where they led, he followed the drops, on and on, passing through hills and valleys, until he came to the depths of Mt. Mitsubushi. A little valley lies there, on one side of which rests a great rock. He saw a queerly formed cave in the rock, and at the mouth of the cave he beheld a creature about six feet in length lying dead, facing south and with hands folded. It was a mountain man with long, thick whiskers, half human and half animal.

Fukuji was astonished at the sight of this mountain man. He made apologies saying: "Please excuse me. If I had known that it was you, I would not have shot you." He offered his gun before the dead body of the mountain man and went down the mountain, when suddenly a terrible storm overtook him. He reached his home after barely escaping with his life. But he suffered from fever from that night on and died not long afterwards.

THE FLUTE PLAYER AND THE SHOJO

Anesaki writes, pp. 273–74: "Another fairy-like being of marine origin is the Shojo; though he does not actually belong to the sea but is believed to come across it to Japan. Probably he is an idealized personification of the orang-outang. . . . The Shojo is a merry embodiment of Epicureanism, who, deriving his chief pleasure from perpetual drinking, is therefore regarded as the genius of sake-beer. His face is red or scarlet and boyish in appearance. His long red hair hangs down nearly to his feet; he has a dipper for ladling sake, wears gaudy dresses of red and gold, and dances a sort of bacchanalian dance."

Text from Muro Kohi Shu, p. 78.

ONCE THERE WAS a young man whose parents had died and who had neither wife nor child. He had a special skill in playing the flute and used to take much pleasure in this.

One day when he was playing his flute on the beach at Tenjin-saki, Motomachi, in Tanabe-machi, a pretty young woman appeared beside him, listening to his flute in ecstasy. The young man, however, did not notice her and continued playing. When he had finished several melodies, the woman said to him: "Please play one more tune for me." But as the young man seemed suspicious of the strange woman, she added: "I am a female *shojo* who lives in the sea. Charmed by the tune of your flute, I have come here in the form of a woman." Thereupon the young man played a tune as he was requested. The *shojo* was very much pleased with it and said: "I shall offer you fishing implements in return for your kindness. With this you can catch any fish you want, without bait."

She pulled out a hair from her own head and gave it, together with a fishhook, to the young man. Then she disappeared. Although the young man was suspicious of what she had told him, he tried fishing with that hook and line from the beach. And he was able to catch whatever kind of fish he wanted, such as mackerel and sea-bream and bonito.

Nowadays at Tenjin Point there is a fishing site called Shojo. This is said to be the place where the young man fished for the first time. Afterwards he moved to Katada Inlet at Nishi Tomita-mura, and he offered his fishing tithes to Hachiman Shrine in the village there. So there is also a place called Shojo Point at Katada Inlet. A house called Shojo Hut is at Hosono in Nishi Tomita-mura.

According to the tradition, a *shojo* came up from the sea in olden times. By the order of the feudal lord, the villagers caught him in this house through making him drunk with three pints of strong *sake* made by boiling down three times that much ordinary *sake*. The *shojo's* hair that they use in the festival rituals at Hachiman Shrine there is said to be the hair of this same *shojo*.

SPIDER POOL

The spider is a prominent demon figure in Japanese densetsu. Yanagita discusses spider legends in his Nippon Mukashi-banashi Meii (tr. Mayer, vol. 2, pp. 385–87). Hearn speaks of the common belief that spiders turn into goblins after dark (VI, pp. 40–41). Yanagita-Mayer in Japanese Folk Tales, no. 23, p. 77, "The Water Spider," follows the present tale in having the fisherman tie the spider's thread to a tree, but adds that the fish in his basket jumped out when a voice called from the pond. In Murai typescript, p. 4, "Spectre Spider," a Shinto priest helps an old woman and her son kill a tormenting spider.

Text from Zoku Kai Mukashi-banashi Shu, p. 124.

ZENEMON, who lived at Yasaka, Shimo Kuisshiki-mura, was an old woodcutter. One day he was working by a stream up in the mountains. There the stream flowed evenly from far within the mountains, forming itself into a deep pool on both sides of which trees grew so thickly that it was quite dark there even in the daytime. The old man, after working a while, grew tired and sleepy, leaned against a tree on the bank, and took a nap. Then a big spider came out of the pool, wound its thread around the old man's foot, and then went back into the pool. Thus did the spider rise up again and again, repeating the same action. Then the old man woke up and noticed the spider.

"That is strange," he thought. Pretending to be asleep, he opened his eyes slightly and watched the spider. In the meantime, the spider repeatedly came out of the pool, wound the thread around the old man's foot, and returned to the pool. At last the threads made a rope. When the spider had gone back once again into the pool, the old man took the thread off his foot and quickly wound it around the root of a big tree nearby. Just at that moment the thread was pulled toward the pool with a loud shout: "Yo-o-i sho!" from the bottom of the pool. The old man was astonished to see the big tree trembling and shaking and at last being uprooted. It was pulled harder and harder until at last it toppled into the pool. The frightened old man said to himself: "Oh, I have escaped from a great danger!"

From that time on that pool has been called Kumo-buchi [Spider Pool].

THE BODYLESS HORSE

"Revenant as headless horse," Motif E423.1.3.3, is indicated here. This is another reminiscence from her childhood days told by Mrs. Hitoshi K. Saito to her grand-daughter, my student Kayoko Saito, in Tokyo, May 8, 1957.

IN ORDER TO GO to Doi Village from the town where I lived [Aki-machi, Aki-gun, Kochi-ken], we had to pass across an open field. In the midst of the field was a spring which was dammed up for irrigation. When we would pass by the dam, we were told that since olden days something there came after people with the noise "Chan-chara, chan-chara." That's the bodyless horse with small tinklers around its neck, making the sound with those tinklers. If you hear the sound, don't walk straight ahead, but clear the way for the horse. Then you will hear the sound no more. If you do not leave the way open, the bodyless horse will lean over you.

One day, a man turned round when he heard that sound and saw a horse's head, just like one you might see in a toy store in those days, coming after him, shaking up and down as if it were walking, and making the sound with the tinklers around its neck.

I myself have never seen that horse. But when I was walking by there in my childhood I was very scared from anticipation that the bodyless horse might come after me, "Chan-chara, chan-chara." I was especially frightened in the evening when it was getting dark.

TALES OF ZASHIKI-BOKKO

The Minzokugaku Jiten *describes the* zashiki-warashi *as a house spirit. Zashiki is a room with* tatami *mats used for a parlor;* warashi *is a term for "boy," and* bokko *is its dialect equivalent in northeastern Japan. Yanagita,* Mountain Village Life, *p. 58, no. 12, says that in the northeastern parts of Japan a spirit in the form of a boyish figure is believed to dwell with old families and to indulge in much harmless mischief, such as upsetting a bed with someone lying in it. The same work reports a tradition from Yamagata-mura, Iwate-ken, that the decline of a family inevitably follows when the* zashiki-warashi *leaves the house.*

Texts from Miyazawa Kenji Meisaku Sen, 7th ed., pp. 43–48. Translated by Kayoko Saito, whose grandfather came from the northeast and knew of the zashiki-bokko; *she said her grandfather knew there were many Saitos living in the Saraki of the last story. One sees here the deft handling of folk traditions by a professional writer.*

Note: Hakama, *a man's divided skirt for formal wear over kimono.*

THE FOLLOWING are tales about *zashiki-bokko* that are told in our district [northeastern Japan]:

1. One bright day everyone had gone to the mountain to work, leaving behind only two children, who were playing in the yard. As there was nobody in the big house, a deep silence reigned all around them.

Suddenly, from somewhere inside the house, there came the sound of a broom sweeping the mats: "Zawatt, zawatt."

Throwing their arms around each other's shoulders, the children tiptoed inside to see who had made the sound. But they found not a soul in any room. They noticed only that the sword-box in one room was lying there silently and that, outside, the hedge of ground cypress looked greener than ever. Not another soul was to be seen anywhere, neither inside nor outside.

"Zawatt, zawatt" came the sound of the broom again.

Was it the voice of some distant shrike; was it the murmur of the Kitakami River; or was it the sound of beans being sifted? The two children wondered and wondered while they listened quietly to the sound. But they could think of no explanation for it.

They were sure that, from somewhere, they had heard the sound of a broom going "Zawatt, zawatt."

Once again, stealthily, they peeped inside, but still there was no one in any of the rooms. There was nothing to be seen but the bright sunshine filling the air.

Such is the story of the *zashiki-bokko.*

2. "Here we go along the highway! Here we go along the highway!" Shouting these words at the tops of their voices, ten children had made a circle with their hands and were going round and round in the *zashiki.* They had been invited to the house for a feast.

Round and round they went in a circle. And then suddenly, without anyone's knowing when or how, there were eleven children in the circle.

There was no unfamiliar face among them, nor was any face repeated twice. And still, no matter how they counted themselves, there were always eleven of them.

A man came in and said: "The extra person must surely be the *zashiki-bokko*."

But which one of them was it? Each child sat there looking innocent as though declaring that the *zashiki-bokko* was anyone but himself.

Such is the story of the *zashiki-bokko*.

3. There is another story.

The main household of a certain family made it a custom to invite the children of its cadet branches to celebrate the festival of Nyorai Buddha at the main house during the beginning of each old-calendar August. One year, one of the cadet children had the measles and was confined to bed.

"I want to go to the festival of Nyorai-san. I want to go to the festival of Nyorai-san," the boy kept saying every day as he lay in his bed.

The grandmother of the main household came to visit him. She patted him on his head and said: "I'll put off the festival until you can come. So hurry and get well."

The boy finally got well in September, and all the children were invited to the main house for the festival. But the other children were spiteful: not only had the festival been postponed for the sick boy, but they had had to give up their favorite toys—a lead rabbit here and some other wonderful plaything there—so the boy would have something to play with while he was in bed.

"We've paid dearly for his being sick," they said among themselves. And they promised each other: "We won't play with him when he comes to the festival today."

While they were playing in the *zashiki* one of them suddenly cried: "Oh, here he comes, here he comes."

"All right, let's hide." And with these words they all went running into the next room.

But look! There, in the center of the next room, was the boy who had had the measles and whom they had seen just approaching the house. He was sitting there politely with a new toy bear on his lap. He was gaunt and pale and seemed on the point of weeping.

"It's the *zashiki-bokko!*" one of the children cried and ran out of the room. The others ran out after him, shouting.

The *zashiki-bokko* sat in the middle of the room weeping.

Such is the story of the *zashiki-bokko*.

4. Once the ferryman at the Romeiji Crossing of the Kitakami River told me this tale:

"Once on the night of August 17 of the old calendar I had been drinking *sake* and went to bed earlier than usual. Then someone called me from the opposite bank: 'O-o-i! O-o-i!' I got out of bed and went outside. The moon was high in the sky. I rowed quickly to the opposite bank, and there I found a pretty boy wearing a crested coat and a *hakama,* with a sword at his side. He was all alone and wore white-strapped sandals. 'Do you want to be ferried across?' I asked, and he answered: 'Yes.'

"As I rowed him along, I watched the boy on the sly. He sat with his hands folded tightly on his lap and looked at the sky. I asked: 'Where are you going? Where do you come from?' The boy answered in a melodious voice: 'I stayed at the Sasadas' for a fairly long time, but I got tired of them, so I'm going some other place.' 'Why are you tired of them?' I asked, but he only smiled and didn't answer. So I asked again: 'Where are you going?' Then he said: 'I'll go to the Saitos' at Saraki.'

"When we reached the other bank, the boy had already disappeared from the boat and there I could see myself sitting at the door of my cottage. I don't know whether this was a dream or not. But it must have been true, because about that time the fortunes of the Sasada family rapidly declined, while at the Saito house in Saraki their invalid got well almost at once, their son graduated from a university, and the family has prospered greatly."

Such is the *zashiki-bokko*.

FOR THIRTY-THREE YEARS *after bodily death, the* reikon *(spirit, soul) of a deceased person hovers about its lifetime residence. In this state it can inflict powerful curses on the living; after that period, however, it becomes a general ancestral spirit. Death is therefore regarded as a great pollution in the folk religion of the common people, who insist that the bereaved family live in isolation and cleanse themselves with purification rites. Formerly a widespread custom of double graves separated the body and spirit of deceased persons. According to the researches of Takayoshi Mogami, the common people of Japan buried a corpse in an* ume-baka, *but after the expiration of the mourning period they visited and held memorial services at a* maeri-baka, *where the spirit of the departed one rested in peace and purity. In the* ume-baka, *the spirit was contaminated from the presence of its corpse, and of fresh corpses deposited in the communal cemetery.*

Under extreme circumstances the spirit can leave the flesh even before death. If death occurs when the shirei *(spirit) is troubled, inflamed, resentful, or in any way disturbed, that angry spirit presents a fearful danger to any human being it encounters, and may indeed enter and possess that person. Hence the reason for* goryo shinko, *the honoring of a revengeful spirit with a special shrine and a summer festival and noisy pageant, quite at variance with the gravity of the winter festival for tutelary shrines. Goryo shinko began under imperial auspices in 863 to placate the spirits of grudge-bearing warriors be-lieved to ravage cities with epidemics, but eventually the practice spread to the peasantry. The goryo shrines subordinate embittered spirits to more powerful ones, who control their passions. If a person dies suddenly, without opportunity for proper death rites, say by drowning at sea, that spirit* (yurei) *also grieves and is tormented. In paintings and drawings the spirit-ghost appears without feet, clad in a flowing garment.*

All spirits are on their way to becoming kami, *who might roughly be described as ancestral or tutelary deities. The social structure of farm-village life, based on a kinship group called* dozoku, *increases the veneration toward the common ancestral* kami *of the villagers, who are all his descendants and worshipers. From the viewpoint of legend, it is the vengeful spirit which inter-ests us most, because a story lies behind his hostility and is written into the* goryo *shrine.*

THE GHOST THAT CARED FOR A CHILD

A closely parallel story is in Hearn, Glimpses of Unfamiliar Japan *(V, ch. 7, p. 192). A pale woman buys a* mizu-ame *at a shop and is followed by the ame-seller to a tomb, where he finds a live child beside her corpse. There are world-wide references under Motif E323.1.1, "Dead mother returns to suckle child."*

Text from Shintetsu Mintan Shu, *pp. 61–63. Collected in Yasuhara-machi, Date-gun, Fukushima-ken.*

Note: Ame, *a caramel-like candy made of wheat or rice gluten.*

A LONG TIME AGO someone knocked feebly at the door of a certain confectionery shop at Yasuhara-machi, Date-gun. It was midnight. When the shopkeeper got up and opened the door, a woman slipped into the house. It was a young woman but her hair was disheveled and she wore white clothes. She had a newborn baby in her arms. Nervously putting up her frowzy, loose-hanging hair with her fingers, she said that she wanted some *ame,* and handed a penny to the shopkeeper. He felt suspicious, but put some *ame* on a stick and gave it to the woman. She thanked him and went out of the shop.

Next night and the following nights she visited the shop at the same time and with the same appearance and each time bought a penny's worth of *ame.* The shopkeeper thought it very strange. One day when he met a painter who was an old acquaintance, he told him about the woman. The painter also had suspicions. He asked the shopkeeper for his permission to stay at his house that night and observe the woman. The shopkeeper agreed.

That evening the painter visited the shop with drawing paper and brush, bringing along *sake* and some food. He spent hours talking and drinking *sake* with the shopkeeper until midnight. Then there was heard the same knock at the door as on the previous nights. The shopkeeper opened the door, winking at the painter, and the woman slipped in and demanded a penny's worth of *ame*. While the shopkeeper was intentionally taking time putting the *ame* on a stick, the painter who had hidden himself in the rear of the shop, drew a portrait of the woman.

A young man of Hashira-mura, sobering up from the effects of *sake* that he had drunk at a wineshop, was walking homeward along a lonely, drizzly path one midnight, murmuring a little song. Suddenly he heard a baby's cry behind him. He stood still to listen to it. Who on earth was coming that way with a crying baby at the dead of night? He thought he would wait for the person and walk with him. So he remained by the wayside. As the baby's cry came closer, he looked in the direction of the sound. There was a woman, in white clothes with disheveled hair, coming toward him with a crying baby in her arms. She hardly seemed to be a woman of this world. The young man was astonished.

Soon the strange woman slipped past him and went toward Hashira-mura. The young man, as soon as he came to himself, followed after her from curiosity. Or he might have been bewitched by the woman. When she came to the graveyard of Toko-ji at Hashira-mura, she turned back and smiled at the young man. No sooner did she do so than a fiery host set the night ablaze, and she disappeared in the smoke. The young man lost his senses on the spot. Next morning the priest of the temple cared for him and sent him back home.

The wife of a certain farmer at Hashira-mura, who was in her last month of pregnancy, died of a sudden illness. On the forty-ninth night after her death, the forty-nine rice cakes that had been offered before the tablet of the deceased in the temple disappeared. People grew suspicious and examined the graveyard, finding a big hole dug beside a new grave. The relatives talked over the matter and decided to open the tomb in the presence of the village officials. When they dug up the coffin and opened it, they saw that the corpse looked as if death had just occurred. Still more strange to say, it embraced a baby in the sleeves of its shroud, and the baby had grown fat and was licking a piece of rice cake which he was holding in his hands. All the people were astounded at the sight. The child had been born alive in the coffin after the funeral ceremony had been performed.

The people tried to separate the child from the dead mother, but they could not, because she would not loosen her arms. After consultation, they took a woman who had a newborn baby to the corpse and had her show her breast and speak to the dead one, saying that she would give milk to the baby and that the other need have no worry if she entrusted the child to their care. Then the dead woman loosened her embrace and let the baby be taken from her arms.

The rice cakes that had vanished from the temple and six *ame* sticks were found inside the coffin.

THE GHOST OF THE FIRST WIFE

The theme of a dead wife's revenant twice intrigued Hearn. The Izumo legend in A Japanese Miscellany, "Of a Promise Broken" (X, pp. 199–207), gives a cruel climax to the idea treated below; the ghost of the dead wife terrifies and then de-capitates the samurai's second wife. In "The Story of O-Kame" in Kotto (XI, pp. 25–29), a husband again promises his dying wife he will not remarry; her spirit haunts him, until a priest opens her grave and traces holy words on her warm limbs.

John Greenleaf Whittier based his poem "The New Wife and the Old" on a New Hampshire ghost legend of the dead first wife plaguing her husband's second bride.

Text from Shimane-ken Kohi Densetsu Shu, *pp. 46–47.*

Notes: Kotatsu, a quilt-covered frame over a charcoal brazier to provide winter warmth for feet and legs. Futon, a heavily padded quilt.

THERE WAS A CERTAIN handsome man among the samurai that served the feudal lord of Matsue. His wife was also very beautiful, and they loved each other. All the people talked of them favorably. However, Fortune did not smile on them, and the wife fell sick. No medicine or treatment was effective and she became seriously ill. One day the wife took the husband's hand and said: "If I die, you will marry again. I am sad to think of it." The husband answered: "I will never marry again if such a thing comes to pass. So don't worry about that."

The wife was glad to hear his words, and she died with a smile. The husband in his grief buried her reverently. A year passed. The husband's friends advised him to marry again, but he did not accept their advice because of the promise he had made to his wife. However, he became lonely and gradually the memory of his wife faded. At last he married a new wife.

The days passed peacefully for some time. One day the husband went away on business and did not return home that night. The wife, being lonely, went to bed early. Then a woman sat at her bedside looking as hazy as a cloud of smoke. "What a beautiful lady you are! Your husband ought to love you," she said, and touched the wife's face with her hand. Her hand was as cold as ice. The wife thought it must be the ghost of the first wife. But she spoke no words. Afterwards, whenever the husband was not at home the ghost would appear at night and worry the wife. At last the wife could bear it no longer and went back to her family's house and stayed there.

The husband held a ceremony on the anniversary of his first wife's death. That night, after the guests had gone away, the sister of the first wife was resting at the *kotatsu*. A strange drowsiness overcame her. Then the candlelight on the family altar flickered, and the first wife appeared like a cloud of smoke from the altar. She came to the *kotatsu* and sat on it. "Dear sister, I am glad to meet you," she said and embraced her sister's shoulder. The sister cried out and called for someone to come. The ghost disappeared immediately, but the *futon* on the *kotatsu* was wet with water.

THE MIRROR GIVEN BY THE GHOST

The idea of goryo *is clearly presented here. The general Motif E710, "External soul," also appears, although a mirror as a specific location is not represented in the Motif-Index. There are many references for "Magic clairvoyant mirror," Motif D1323.1.*

Text from Shimane-ken Kohi Densetsu Shu, *pp. 33–35.*

THERE WAS A YOUNG MAN named Hayasuke in the house of Matsumoto, who served the feudal lord of Matsue as instructor in the art of the spear. Being an honest man, Hayasuke was loved by his master. He possessed a special skill in flute playing, which he displayed during his leisure.

Hayasuke always had a small box with him which he kept carefully locked. When people asked him about it, he explained no more than to say that it contained a precious object, nor did he ever show it to anyone. The young samurai of the Matsue clan who customarily assembled to perform spear exercises in Matsumoto's exercise hall were all very curious about the box. Several of them conferred together about the matter and one day opened the box secretly while Hayasuke was taking a nap. To their disappointment, however, they found only a little mirror in the box. When Hayasuke awoke from his nap and learned what they had done, he took great offense. He accused them of doing a dishonest deed unworthy of samurai. The young men made apologies for their error, saying: "We were wrong." Then they asked him: "Why do you guard that mirror so carefully and so secretly?"

Hayasuke answered: "Up till now I have kept this mirror in secret, but now that it is discovered, there is no further use to maintain secrecy. I will tell you everything." So he told them the story of the mirror.

In his younger days Hayasuke was greatly enamored of flute playing. One night he ascended Mt. Seikoin with his friend, playing on flutes under the moonlight. It was already late autumn. They wandered around the dewy hillside among the bare trees. Hayasuke was so much absorbed in playing the flute that he paid no heed when his friend said: "Let's go back now." As Hayasuke did not stop his flute playing, the friend said: "I'm going," and went away.

Then suddenly Hayasuke felt someone hold fast to his legs and pull at them with hands as cold as ice. He was startled and turned around. A beautiful woman sat on the ground. She was clad in a white dress, her hair hung in loose tresses down to her shoulders, and her pale face wore a wistful look.

"Who are you?" asked Hayasuke.

"I am a ghost," the woman answered.

Being of stout heart, Hayasuke did not fear and asked the woman to tell all about herself. The woman said: "I am the wife of a merchant in the city of Matsue. But my husband is a loose man and he has indulged in dissipation. He brought his sweetheart home and let her live with us. She was evil-hearted and hated me. One day when I was at the well drawing water, she pushed me down into the well. After she had killed me in this way, she reported to the police that I had committed suicide, and soon she became the legal wife of my husband. Oh, please just think of my bitter resentment! Some day I shall possess her and wreak vengeance upon her. But the difficulty is that I cannot get into their house, because she had a charm pasted on the door which drives away ghosts. I want somebody to take the charm away. Many men have I accosted and tried to ask them to undertake that task, but there has never been a one who did not run away from me. It is very fortunate that I met you tonight. I pray you to grant my request.

"My husband's house is at Odamaki-cho in Suetsugi and his name is such-and-such. As a proof of my trustworthiness I will give you this

mirror. I used it whenever I blackened my teeth, and it contains my soul." So saying, she handed him a small mirror.

With some suspicion Hayasuke said: "I will do as you want." Thereupon the strange woman disappeared.

Hayasuke went down the mountain, passed Nakahara and Dote, and came to Odamaki-cho. He examined each house and finally found the one with the charm on the door. He reached out and took the charm down. He had walked on about ten yards, when there arose a sudden clamor in that house, and a man rushed out in great haste.

"What's the matter?" asked Hayasuke.

"The mistress is suddenly taken ill. I'm going for the doctor," answered the man, running.

Afterwards the neighbors of this house told Hayasuke, when he made inquiry about the episode, that the mistress of the house died of a strange disease. She had struggled furiously as if she were being choked and crushed on her breast by some apparition. She refused to take any medicine and died crying: "I was wrong. Forgive me!"

Hayasuke finished his story and added these words: "I understand that a person will be rewarded according to the way he treats others. Ever since, this mirror has warned me against doing any evil deed."

THE DISH MANSION IN UNSHU

In his article on bakemono *(ghostly goblins), Joly speaks of the dramatized legend of Okiku, the Well Ghost (p. 15). His version varies from the text below in having a samurai break one of his precious plates in order to fasten blame on the maid Okiku, whom he then propositions. When she refuses his advances, she kills herself and her ghost haunts the well. Joly refers to a print by Hokusai and a tale by Mitford on the legend (in "The Ghost of Sakura," p. 186; in Mitford's rendition the servant-girl breaks the plate and then commits suicide). Hokusai's sketch is reproduced in James A. Michener's* The Hokusai Sketchbooks *(Rutland, Vermont, 1958), p. 205.*

Text from Shimane-ken Kohi Densetsu Shu, *pp. 4–5.*

DURING THE SHOHO ERA [1644–48] a certain samurai who served the feudal lord of Matsue treasured ten china dishes. His wife was an evil-hearted woman who always treated the maidservant cruelly. The wife broke one of the precious dishes and dropped the pieces down the well, after which she declared that the maid had stolen the dish. The maid was given a severe whipping. Having no way to plead her innocence, she hung herself by the well.

After that her ghost appeared every night by the well and counted the number of dishes: "One, two, three . . ." in a sad voice. When she had counted up to nine she burst out crying without saying " ten." This strange occurrence took place night after night and became known to all the other samurai. The master of the house worried greatly over the matter. One of his friends, who was a steady, clever man, said: "I will get rid of the ghost for you."

So one night he hid himself near the well to wait for the ghost. At midnight the ghost of the young woman came out and began to count: "One, two, three . . ." As soon as she uttered "nine" the samurai said "ten." At that instant the ghost-woman vanished from sight.

Since then the ghost has never been seen.

FISH SALAD MINGLED WITH BLOOD

The general Motif M460, "Curses on families," applies here. A similar curse occurs in "Blood-Red Pool," p. 235–36, where rice is mixed with blood.
    Text from Bungo Densetsu Shu, *p. 47. Collected by Ume Namba.*
    Note: Namasu, a kind of fish salad.

THIS IS A STORY told at Kawazoko in Toji-machi. Long ago the village headman's household was very busy preparing food for New Year's Eve. There was an old dish that had been carefully kept in this house from past generations. On this occasion they put *namasu* in this dish, and a maid broke it by mistake. The master of the house grew very angry and roared at her. The maid worried herself so much that she threw herself down the well.

After that time on every New Year's Eve the *namasu* served in this house was mingled with blood. Therefore the family decided never to make *namasu* in that house on New Year's Eve.

WHITE RICE ON THE POT

Text from Shimane-ken Kohi Densetsu Shu, p. 6, from Naka-gun.

DURING THE SHOTOKU ERA [1711–15], a man named Ichijiro in charge of the rice storehouse of the feudal lord lost one of the straw bags of rice while carrying them to Tanojiri. Ichijiro was tried and sentenced to death. This cruel punishment rendered his mind distraught and led him to commit violence on different occasions. The people of his family sought to restrain him, but he broke free from their confinement and killed himself beside the rice pot over the fire.

It is said that every year after that, on the anniversary of his death, one or two cupfuls of rice would appear on the lid of the pot. In fact, later on, during the Ansei era [1854–59] in the time of Zenemon, the latter one morning found a handful of rice on the pot. He removed it, but soon another handful of rice appeared on the same spot. Thinking that this strange event was caused by the dead soul of Ichijiro, Zenemon had a memorial service held for Ichijiro's soul by the priest of Eisho-ji.

Thereafter nothing strange occurred any more.

THE SEVEN BLIND MINSTRELS

Motif M411.3, "Dying man's curse," and M442.1, "Curse: descendants to be unshapely," are present. Mitford writes: "The belief in curses hanging over families for generations is as common as that in ghosts and supernatural apparitions" (p. 187). He then relates a tradition of a curse visited on the house of Asai by a concubine cruelly beaten by her lord, who put out her left eye with a candlestick and then killed her. He and his descendants lost their left eyes at forty and soon after died.

Text from Kotaro Hayakawa, Tabi to Densetsu, I (October, 1928), p. 25.

AT THE BORDER of Shimo Tsugu-mura, Kita Shidara-gun, Aichi-ken, alongside the road leading to Futto of Furikusa-mura, there stand seven round stones in a row which are called the tombs of Shichinin Zato [Seven Blind Minstrels]. As one goes on and passes those tombs, the road slopes down. This slope is called Sando-no-saka [Blind Minstrels' Slope].

Long ago seven blind minstrels who traveled together lost their way at this slope. They asked the road of a man who was cutting the grass nearby. He told them the wrong way on purpose. So the blind men lost their way in the mountains. When they reached the top of the slope and came to the pool now called Biwa-buchi [Pool of the Lute], they could go neither forward nor back, and all seven fell down together into the pool and died.

Thereafter, because of the curse of these blind minstrels, the family of the man who gave them the wrong directions has suffered from sore eyes in each generation up to the present day. Once a member of the family had eyes carved on the tombstones of the blind men, perhaps because he thought he could console their spirits that way. So now all those stones have eyes carved upon them.

It is told, however, that this had no effect.

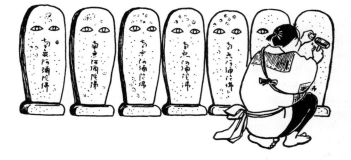

THE REVENGEFUL SPIRIT OF MASAKADO

"Dying man's curse," Motif M411.3, also occurs here. Onryo is the term here translated as "revengeful spirit."

Text from Edo no Kohi to Densetsu, pp. 6–8.

Notes: Kanda Myojin, one of Tokyo's major Shinto shrines; within its precincts is a shrine to Taira no Masakado, leader of the unsuccessful Tenkei Rebellion, during which he declared himself emperor of eastern Japan. Yujoya, a pleasure house, courtesan house. Musashi Province included what is now Tokyo.

MASAKADO FOUGHT against Hidesato at Nakano-ga-hara in Musashi Province in the third year of Tenkei [940]. He was shot in the shoulder by Taira Sadamori and grappled down by Fujiwara Chiharu, and his head was cut off. Thereafter Masakado's spirit remained on the field of Nakano and caused suffering to the people of the vicinity in many ways. In the eastern districts of Japan Masakado's spirit effected various miracles, but to the people who had some blood connection with Hidesato, his spirit caused fierce spells. Especially in the Sano family it was forbidden to go to the Kanda Myojin Shrine, because the Sano were the descendants of Hidesato. The Sano house at Ogawa-machi in Kanda was very near the Kanda Myojin, so on the festival day at this shrine the gate of the house was not opened to anyone; on ordinary days every person of the Sano house was forbidden to walk in front of the shrine.

During the Anei era [1770–80], a samurai named Kanda Oribe lived at Kobinatadai-machi. This man was a descendant of Masakado and wore his crest. His close companion Sano Goemon lived at Yushima. One day Sano dropped in at Kanda's on his way back from his official duties, as they were intimate friends. They had a good time together, and after a while Kanda said: "I shall take you to a fine place." And he took Sano to a *yujoya* named Kashiwaya, near Akagi Shrine.

At the time Sano had been wearing ceremonial dress. But it was ridiculous to go to a *yujoya* dressed thus, so Kanda lent Sano an informal cloak with the Masakado crest on it.

While they were making merry at the *yujoya,* Sano's face suddenly turned pale, sweat poured from his brow, and he fainted in agony. In a moment the circumstances were entirely changed. In confusion, they called for doctors and medicine. Kanda hired a sedan chair and sent Sano to his home.

Kanda was so anxious about his friend that he hurried over early next morning to see him. However, Sano came briskly out of his room and said: "Last night I shivered and fainted. After shivering and fainting I fell unconscious until they took off that cloak of yours I was wearing. When I went into bed, I immediately recovered. And now I feel just as well as usual. This probably happened because I borrowed your cloak with your crest on it. Maybe Masakado's spirit put a spell on me."

So Kanda was also convinced of the power of his ancestor's spell, and he apologized to Sano for his carelessness.

THE EVIL SPIRIT OF FUSATARO

The term mamono *which is translated here as "evil spirit" contains also the idea of magic (ma). Motif D1840.1, "Magic invulnerability of saints," appears.*
Text from Densetsu no Echigo to Sado, *II, pp. 129–32.*

IT WAS DURING the Enryaku era [782–806]. The district now called Kari-ha-gun was then called the province of Samizu and was governed by Kiemon of Sekiya. One evening a fine-looking boy came from somewhere and called at Kiemon's house. He asked Kiemon to let him stay as a servant. Kiemon felt a little suspicious, but the boy, with his fine features and good manners, did not seem to be a vulgar country lad. Moreover, he was young and his request was so earnest that Kiemon granted it and let him enter the house. The boy called himself Fusataro. As he was amiable, he attracted everybody in the house. He spent some years in Kiemon's house, loved by everybody. However, there was one strange thing about Fusataro. Every night he went away somewhere. Where did he go, and for what business? All the people of the house talked it over. Someone followed after him one night but he lost Fusataro's trail on the way. It was reported the next morning that a traveler had been killed at Sekiya, and a dead body was carried away.

Once, in those days, St. Dengyo came to preach in the province of Echigo and stayed one night at Sekiya. It was a very warm summer night. He was in bed half-awake and half-sleeping. A warm wind blew in, and in an instant a specter holding a big sword in his hand appeared by the pillow. Just at the moment that the sword touched the saint's neck, the saint turned aside, held up his scepter, and struck off the specter's arm with it. The specter picked up his arm and disappeared.

The next morning the saint found many bloodstains here and there in the room. He followed the bloodstains. The bloodstains led him to

Kiemon's house. The saint met Kiemon and told him all about the event of the night before. Kiemon guessed that it was Fusataro's doing and searched for Fusataro, but he was not to be found anywhere. But they found the bloodstains continuing from Kiemon's house up to the nearby mountain. Following the bloodstains, they came to a rock cave. Kiemon called out loudly: "Fusataro, Fusataro." Instantly the door of the cave was opened. Inside the cave was a bloody Fusataro, standing like a demon. "Fusataro, you are really a specter!"

No sooner had Kiemon spoken these words than Fusataro's knife gouged out Kiemon's left eye. Then immediately St. Dengyo, through his religious powers, seized Fusataro and cut his body in three parts. He buried the parts on a mountain that marked the border of Samizu, and built a temple for Fusataro's soul there.

Now it is said that there are still three mounds on that mountain, called Kubi-zuka [Head Mound], Hara-zuka [Torso Mound], and Ashi-zuka [Leg Mound].

THE WEAVING SOUND IN THE WATER

The Minzokugaku Jiten *under* "Hataori Fuchi" *(Weaver's Pool Legend), comments on the connection between this* densetsu *and ancient festivals in which a village maiden weaves cloth, in a sacred cottage by a holy pond, for the robe of a god who comes from the sea or river. Mock Joya, IV, pp. 32–33, "River Bottom Weaver," says: "Tales of the sound of weaving looms being heard from the bottom of streams*

or ponds are told in many parts of the country. This type of legend is said to have developed from the ancient custom of weaving and sewing new clothes for the local kami for the annual festival." He then gives two examples, one of human sacrifice and one of suicide. In Yanagita, Mountain Village Life, p. 398, the weaving lady is reported from the bottom of a waterfall basin in Kameyama-mura.

Text from Tosa no Fusoku to Densetsu, p. 77.

A LONG TIME AGO there was a woman named Osen at Otochi, Maki-yama-mura, Kami-gun. She was about twenty-five years old. Though not particularly pretty, she was gentle and kindhearted, and so she was loved by her neighbors. Now in Otochi there was a famous vine bridge. Its length was thirty-six yards and it also hung at a height of thirty-six yards above the river. When a person walked on this bridge it rocked so much that even those who got used to it were sometimes afraid to pass over it.

One day Osen crossed this bridge carrying a loom on her head. When she came to the middle of the bridge, she missed her footing and tumbled into the water. It was a pity that she fell into such a fathomless pool and was drowned with no one to give her succor. Strangely, both her dead body and the loom sank into the water and did not come to the surface again.

After that people who passed on this bridge at night often heard a woman's voice along with the sound of weaving.

It is also told that there was a woman who saw a long sash in the water under the bridge and fainted with surprise.

THE PHANTOM BOAT

Funa-yurei, *"phantom boat,"* is described in the Minzokugaku Jiten. *"Every village investigated has a story of a ghost boat,"* reports Yanagita, Fishing Village Life, *and mentions this tradition from Shigaura-mura: "When the south wind blows and it is raining, a ghost boat is apt to appear all of a sudden before their boat, against which it seems to collide and then it disappears. It is good to try to urinate on it"* (pp. 188–89). Hearn heard a sailor on the coastal sea tell of two ghost ships, a junk and a steamer. *"As long as they come behind you, you need never be afraid. But if you see a ship of that sort running before you, against the wind, that is very bad! It means that all on board will be drowned."* (VI, ch. 23, *"From Hoki to Oki,"* pp. 261–62.) Motif D1812.5.1.10, *"Sight of phantom ship a bad omen,"* is pertinent.

Text from Keigo Seki, Tabi to Densetsu, I (April, 1928), pp. 100–01.

"IT WAS a mild autumn evening. A gentle west wind was blowing. Although our boat was under full sail, it did not move so swiftly as to prevent our being at ease while steering. We were homeward bound from the sea of Satsuma, where we had been engaged in fishing. Our craft was sailing between Amakusa Island and Chijiiwa Bay. Mt. Unzen hove in sight, and we expected to reach shore by daybreak. The boatmen were all asleep. Only I was awake, steering the boat.

"It was perhaps a little after midnight when I became drowsy. I was about to smoke tobacco. Then I heard the sound of a boat moving on our left. Wonderingly I looked up. I saw a sailing ship going ahead at great speed against the wind. It was indeed strange. But I hesitated to wake up the other men, who were sleeping peacefully, so I watched the mysterious vessel with close attention. The ship was drawing near. Although it was still at some distance, I could see the ship so clearly that if some acquaintance had been on board I could have recognized him. The ship had only one side. The yard was just set on the mast without braces. Yet the ship was sailing safely in the face of the wind. The people on board were crying out, but I could not hear them well.

"It is a custom at sea that if we are spoken to by another ship, we are obliged to answer them. But if we know that it is not an ordinary ship, then we should not answer. I hear that the people on such boats often demand that we lend them a pail to bail water out of their boat. Then we must lend them a bottomless pail. Otherwise they will pour water into our boat with that pail and make us sink into the sea.

"I answered the ship as usual. Then the boat came nearer and nearer. I saw some pale men standing in a row and crying aloud. For the first time in my life I saw with my own eyes what I had been told about by other people. It was the so-called 'phantom-boat.' So close had it already approached that there seemed to be no way to avoid a collision. Without any forethought, I called out to my mates at that moment. I thought the ship struck against our boat, and I lost my senses. I remained senseless until I was awakened by my mates some time afterwards. Then I learned from them that the ghost ship had attacked us once more that night.

"I was only twenty years old at the time. Shocked by the horror of it all, I lay on the bottom of our boat and had a nightmare every night for a week. Even now, when I think of that I feel my hair stand erect with fright. I have had similar experiences several times since then."

An old fisherman told me this story.

ONE HUNDRED RECITED TALES

This story about storytelling illustrates the belief that a group of people reciting monogatari *expect something evil to happen. Mock Joya, II, pp. 146–49, speaks of "Ghost Stories," and the custom of holding* obake *storytelling sessions on summer evenings in eerie surroundings. Mitford sets down several weird tales of "Ghostly apparitions, related one cold night in Edo by Japanese friends huddled around the brazier" (in "The Ghost of Sakura," pp. 185–87).*

Text from Chiisagata-gun Mintan Shu, *pp. 270–71.*

A YOUNG NOVICE of a temple invited his friends over and they decided to tell one hundred tales. So they put up one hundred lighted candles in the hall of the temple. When one person finished a story in the other room, he was to come to the hall and blow out one candle. The most timid person was to begin, and the bravest one was to go last. Finally this novice and the son of the village headman remained as the last ones. Only two candles were left lighted. Then these were blown out too. Having finished the hundred stories, most of the boys went home. It was very late.

Two boys stayed in the temple with the novice. Two of the three went to sleep, but the son of the village headman stayed awake. He heard something in the room. He looked around. There appeared a ghost who picked up the novice in his quilts and carried him away. After a while the ghost came again and this time carried away the son of the sword dealer. The headman's son called out the names of the two boys, but no answer came. "They must have died. My turn will come next."

While he was thus affrighted, the first morning cock crowed. So he rose and went home. He visited the shrine to pray that such a fearful thing would never happen again.

Every time he visited the shrine he met the same girl on his way back. Gradually they became intimate, and finally they married. One evening his wife stayed in the kitchen for such a long time that the husband peeped in. The wife was blowing the fire with a hollow length of bamboo, and her face looked just like that of the ghost he had seen in the temple. Fearfully, he remembered the night just a year ago when they had recited tales. He cried out. His wife immediately ran to him and blew a breath in his face.

The husband died on the spot from that breath.

ONE COMMON THEME in Japanese legendry is the changing of shape by supernatural beings. In English folklore the witch customarily shifts her form for purposes of enchantment and bedevilment, taking a variety of animal guises. This situation is doubly reversed in Japan, where beasts, primarily serpents and foxes, take on the appearance of beautiful maidens, to seduce and even mate with mortals. Sometimes in the legends the serpent comes as a man, and sometimes a seemingly normal human being is transformed into a snake and consigned to the bottom of a pond. Serpents are usually involved in tragic romances, while foxes carry on a good deal of mischievous activity, of which seduction forms but one aspect. Badgers are also much given to illusory impersonations, although on the whole they are less feared than foxes and seem more easily apprehended. The anthropomorphic as well as the animal deities too take on human forms, appearing as beggars or forlorn women to test the piety of the folk. If aggrieved, they can permanently transform the impious mortals they meet into rocks or rats. The world revealed in these transformation legends suggests the universe of the North American Indians, whose tales describe courtships between warriors and deer-maidens and the adventures of a trickster culture-hero who assumes chameleon shapes. But the Indian legends are set in the depths of the forest, while the Japanese densetsu take place in towns and castles and even in the modern metropolis.

THE SERPENT SUITOR

This is one of the most popular of all Japanese tales, occurring both as fiction and as legend. Ikeda reports ninety-seven versions collected from all over Japan, besides appearances in literary classics such as the Kojiki and Shaku Nihongi, and instances from Korea, China, and Formosa (pp. 125–26). She identifies it as Type 425C ("The Girl as the Bear's Wife") calling it "Snake Husband." Thompson has the pertinent Motif T475.1, "Unknown paramour discovered by string clue," with solely Japanese references. Ikeda reports that the legendary form is attached to important local families who claim to be descendants of snakes.

Legends of a threaded needle used to detect a serpent-lover appear in W. Alexander, "Legends of Shikoku," New Japan, V (1952), pp. 566, 579, "Dragon Spawn"; De Visser, "The Snake in Japanese Superstition," pp. 277–78; Murai, pp. 62–67, "Huge Serpent of Nameri Pond"; Suzuki, pp. 51–52, "The Serpent Grove." The lasciviousness of the serpent is mentioned by Anesaki, p. 332. Under "Irui Kyukontan" (Tales of Marriage between Humans and Non-human Creatures), the Minzokugaku Jiten classifies four forms of snake-bridegroom tales. The present story falls into the so-called spool type.

ONCE THERE LIVED a village headman named Shiohara in Aikawa-mura, Ono-gun. He had a lovely daughter. Every night a nobleman visited the daughter, but she knew neither his name nor whence he came. She asked him his name, but he never told her about himself. At length the girl asked her nurse what to do. The nurse said: "When he comes next time, prick a needle with a thread through his skirt, and follow after him as the thread will lead you. Then you will find his home."

The next day the girl put a needle in the suitor's skirt. When he departed, the girl and the nurse followed him as the thread led them. They passed through steep hills and valleys and came to the foot of Mt. Uba, where there was a big rock cave. As the thread led inside, the girl timidly entered the cave. She heard a groaning voice from the interior. The nurse lighted a torch and also went into the cave. She peered within and saw a great serpent, bigger than one could possibly imagine. It was groaning and writhing in agony. She looked at the serpent carefully, and she noticed that the needle which the girl had put in her lover's skirt was thrust into the serpent's throat.

The girl was frightened and ran out of the cave, while the nurse fainted and died on the spot. The serpent also died soon. The nurse was enshrined in Uba-dake Shrine at the foot of Mt. Uba, and the cave of the serpent is also worshiped as Anamori-sama.

If a man enters this cave with something made of metal, or if many people go into the cave at the same time, the spirit of the cave becomes offended and causes a storm.

THE BLIND SERPENT-WIFE

"We have several legends told about snakes sacrificing one or both eyes for the benefit of unhappy human beings," writes Suzuki, p. 91, and gives two examples ("The Blind Serpent," pp. 91–95). The first seems based on the same outline as the text below, and this is also true for Yanagita-Mayer, Japanese Folk Tales, no. 62, pp. 180–82, "The Blind Water Spirit." De Visser reports a separate treatment of the theme in "The Snake in Japanese Superstition," p. 306, where an ugly younger

sister drowns herself, becomes a serpent, and gives her eyeballs to a friendly maid, who must yield them to the headman; this is from Kiuchi Sekitei, Unkonshi Zempen, 1772.

Text from Shimabara-hanto Minwa Shu, *pp. 131–33. Told by Hiroshi Ejima in Minami Arima-mura.*

A YOUNG DOCTOR lived at Fukae-mura with his mother. One summer day when it began showering a beautiful girl took shelter under the eaves of the village headman's house. Although she expected that the shower would soon be over, the weather did not clear up, and by and by it began raining heavily. Meanwhile the sun was going down in the west. The people of the headman's house took pity on the poor strange girl who was standing under the eaves of their house and they kindly induced her to come inside and wait till the weather cleared. Through conversations with the girl, the headman came to know something about her: that she was a maiden and came from Higo, and so forth. Since he had been asked by the doctor's mother to find a bride for her son, he thought this girl might be appropriate. So he acted as go-between, and everything went smoothly. The girl from Higo became the wife of the doctor of Fukae, and a child was born in due time.

One day when the doctor's mother opened the door into the wife's room, she was astonished to see a big serpent sleeping in the center of the room, coiled around the child and snoring. When he came home from a patient's house, the doctor saw his mother looking very pale,

and he was so anxious to know the reason that his mother told him about his wife. He could not believe her story that his wife was a serpent. But the next day when he peeped into the wife's room, he saw exactly the same sight that his mother had described to him.

At last he determined to divorce his wife. She said in her grief: "I was rescued by you at the beach some years ago. In return for your kindness I came here in the form of a woman to serve you. I am a serpent in the pond on Mt. Fugen. If you cannot find a good nurse for the baby, please come to Fugen Pond." And she left him.

The doctor remembered that some years before he had rescued a white eel which the village children had been teasing. Maybe this serpent was that eel.

He searched for a nurse, but he could not find anyone. So he went to Fugen Pond with the baby, according to the wife's instructions. When he arrived at the pond, the wife appeared in the form of a woman and gouged out one of her own eyeballs. She handed it to the husband and he gave it to the child who licked it, and strange to say, milk came out of it. The doctor was pleased at this. He started back home with the baby on his back and the eyeball in his bosom. It was a dark night. The doctor met a few patrolling samurai on his way through the mountain. They became suspicious on seeing the doctor's bosom swelled up with the eyeball, so they examined him and found a fine jewel ball. The doctor was robbed of the precious eyeball by those men.

The following day the child wept so bitterly that the father had no recourse but to go to Fugen Pond again. Then the woman, now with only one eye, appeared again and said: "I shall be blind if I give you another eyeball. But I dare do so for my child's sake." She gouged out her other eyeball, weeping. The husband returned with that eyeball.

The jewel eyeball which the patrols had taken away from the doctor was presented to the feudal lord. It was so beautiful that the lord thought that if he presented it together with another eyeball to the shogun in Edo, he would be rewarded. So he sent his officers to Mt. Fugen in search of another eyeball. The unfortunate doctor met them again on his way home and was robbed of the second eyeball. In the utmost distress, he turned back again to the pond to tell the story to his wife. Her rage was beyond description.

It is said that soon afterwards a great earthquake occurred in those parts.

THE SERPENT GODDESS OF AMO-GA-IKE

"Of all the animals in Japanese folklore, the serpent plays perhaps the greatest part, and superstitious ideas concerning the 'walking rope' are still widely held by the people. . . . A jealous woman is likened to, or said to turn herself into, a serpent." So writes Anesaki, p. 331. The idea of human descendants of snakes is mentioned by De Visser, "The Snake in Japanese Superstition," pp. 312–13, who says the inhabitants of Manako-mura, Hidaka-gun, Kii province, made such a claim. He describes graphically the scaly appearance of a woman of snake ancestry.

The Motif B656.2, "Marriage to serpent in human form," has been reported from India and China. "Iron powerful against fairies," Motif F384.3, is believed from Ireland to India. In Europe this legend could take the form of a fairy tale about an Enchanted Princess.

Text from Reisen Naniwa, "A Trip to Rankei," Tabi to Densetsu, II (July, 1929), pp. 37–39.

Note: Amo-ga-ike is a pond in Niigata-ken.

PEOPLE PRAY for rain at this pond and they believe that there is a goddess in the pond, that it is a big snake, and that this snake goddess dislikes anything made of metal. So the people cannot use iron hooks when they fish here.

A long time ago a brave samurai of the Muramatsu clan went into the pond to see the big serpent with his own eyes. He found a splendid palace at the bottom of the pond. There was a noble lady wearing a gorgeous dress and dancing, her embroidered sleeves swinging. She must have been surprised to see the fine samurai suddenly appear. He told her the reason why he had come there. When the princess heard it she said: "This is not a place where you should come. Please go away immediately." Her bright, pretty face instantly became sorrowful, and she burst into tears. For a while the samurai gazed at her beautiful figure, and then he asked her politely why she was crying. The lady looked up at his face wistfully and answered: "I am sorrowful because, since you have seen me, I cannot live in the pond any more. So I cry." She stood up and taking the samurai's hand led him into the palace. After she had entertained him with splendid foods from land and sea, she sent him off.

That evening the neighboring villagers were overtaken by a sudden storm. They thought that it was caused by the offended serpent and they were very much afraid. Late at night a beautiful girl visited Sakai in Kasabori-mura. She entered his room, sat by his pillow, and said: "I am the daughter of a woodcutter who lived in the mountain. My father was taken away by somebody and I am in trouble now. Please help me."

As he was a gallant man, he granted the girl's request on the spot. Afterwards they loved each other and married. Of course this girl was the big serpent who was afraid of the samurai whom she had met in the pond, so she came and visited Sakai to ask his help.

From that time on all the heirs of the Sakai family have had three scales under their armpits.

THE SERPENT OF MT. UNZEN

This is an unrelated tradition also explaining why a serpent caused the great earth-quake at Shimabara.

Text from Shimabara-hanto Minwa Shu, *pp. 134–37. Told by Kumakatsu Nakagawa in Shimabara-machi.*

ONCE THE LORD OF SHIMABARA had a hunting entertainment with many retainers around the foot of Mt. Unzen. Not getting any big game on the first day, they stopped hunting and started on their way back. One of the retainers glimpsed some large creature passing through a bamboo thicket, and he told the other people about it. As it seemed of great size, they carefully surrounded it from a distance and began to attack the monster. When they drew near, they saw two big snakes coiling about. They shot one of them to death with an arrow, but missed the other.

After that incident the crops of the fields in Shimabara district were damaged by some creature every night, and the farmers had practically no harvest. So the villagers gathered together and talked the matter over and decided to ask the lord to let them hunt the marauder in the mountains. In the beginning there seemed to be no effect from the hunting, for they could not even get a glimpse of what they were looking for, and every night the crops were damaged worse than before. However, they continued hunting every day without taking a rest, and one day they saw a big snake. Recognizing it as the evil creature that had done damage to their fields, they tried many shots, but could only wound it without reaching its vital spot. The wounded monster hid itself in the depths of the mountains and came out to do evil.

At that time there was a famous doctor in Tahira. He was visited by patients from the villages near and far. Not long after the hunting expedition in the mountains, a woman visited the doctor to receive treatment for a wound she had received while cutting firewood in the mountains. She came every day after that. Although the doctor har-

bored a slight suspicion that she was no ordinary woman, he treated her like a regular patient. After some days her wound was healed and she was told by the doctor that she needed no more treatments.

Nevertheless, she visited the doctor the next day and thanked him for his treatment and said: "As I am too poor to pay you, I beg you to excuse me from payment. But I could not go without doing something in return for your kindness. I shall not be able to pay you even in the future, but now I have something to tell in lieu of giving money. However humble a woman I may be, I pray you to believe what I am going to say now. I advise you to leave this place, because in the near future a great earthquake will occur here in Shimabara, and if you stay here, you may be killed by it. Believe me. I want to reward you by foretelling you of that event." Having said this, she went away.

Although the doctor listened to her half in doubt, he felt there might be something serious in her words. He moved to his relative's home in Higo on her advice, for she had seemed to him from their first meeting to be a woman of mystery. Strange to say, not long after that, a great earthquake did occur with the eruption of Mt. Unzen, and it was followed by a great tidal wave which destroyed the castle town of Shimabara and all the villages around and killed a vast number of people. That is said to be the memorable calamity called Bizan's Collapse.

The woman was the female serpent whose mate had been killed by the retainers of the Lord of Shimabara and who had done harm to the fields in revenge for her husband's death. She visited the doctor of Tahira in the form of a woman to receive treatment for the wounds she had been given by the village farmers.

The great earthquake of Shimabara is said to have been caused by that serpent.

TWO DAUGHTERS WHO BECAME SERPENTS

Motif Q551.3.2, "Punishment: transformation into animal," applies here, although the punishment is visited on the daughters for their father's sin.

Told by Mrs. Hitoshi K. Saito to her granddaughter Kayoko Saito in Tokyo, April 8, 1957.

Notes: Sanshu, i.e. Sanuki Province, now Kagawa-ken. Yasuda, a village about 7.5 miles from the informant's home.

ONCE UPON A TIME there lived a merchant in a town of Tosa. He was very greedy and used two methods of measuring, one for buying and the other for selling things, so that he would make the greatest unfair profit out of the balances.

He had two daughters who were pretty and sweet. They were much worried by their father's unjust deeds and implored him not to do such things. But the merchant was too greedy and obstinate to listen to their pleas.

Gradually the daughters realized that they would be transformed into serpents as a punishment for their father's misdeeds. At last the elder sister plunged into the pond of Manno in the province of Sanuki [Kagawa-ken] and became a serpent. On the other hand, the younger sister left the home crushed with sorrow and came to an inn at Yasuda to stay the night there. Before she went to bed, she requested the maid of the inn under no circumstances ever to look into her room while she was asleep.

But as is typical of human nature, the maid grew so curious that she secretly peeped into the room where the younger daughter of the merchant was sleeping. And she was frightened to see that a serpent, so huge as to fill the eight-mat room, was sleeping coiled up. The serpent-daughter was awakened and said that she could no longer remain a human being since her serpent nature had been detected. She sorrowfully and yet determinedly shook her head once and started out for a deep pool in the Sakase River, which flowed nearby. It is said that she made a tremendous rattle when she was entering the pool. She has made her dwelling there since that time.

Even today, there is a saying in my native town as follows: "The elder sister is in the Pond of Manno in Sanshu, and the younger sister dwells in the Sakase in Yasuda." It seems that this saying is still repeated there as a warning against greediness.

HACHIRO'S TRANSFORMATION

Examples from many parts of the world are cited under Motif D191, "Transformation: man to serpent (snake)."

Text from Tsugaru Kohi Shu, pp. 40–41.

HACHIRO WENT to the mountain on July 27 to cut trees. He was in charge of cooking lunch for the woodcutters. Hachiro caught trout in the stream behind the hut, and he broiled and ate one. It was so delicious that he ate the rest of them as well. As soon as he had eaten the last one, he became very thirsty. He drank all the water in the pail, but it did not satisfy him. He drank the water from the stream. He drank and drank, but he was still thirsty. While he was drinking, the other people saw him. They were surprised to see that Hachiro was no longer a human being.

Hachiro himself knew he had changed to a snake. He made dams in Owani and Kogage and Ikari-ga-seki in order to create a lake for his residence. Fudo, the patron deity of Kogage, was annoyed because his home would be endangered if Hachiro had a lake there, so he turned himself into a crab and made a hole in a dam. So Hachiro was not able to realize his desire there.

Then Dainichi-sama, the patron deity of Owani, gave Hachiro a pair of iron sandals, telling him that he should make his home where the straps of the sandals broke. Hachiro put the sandals on and traveled to a place now called Hachiro-gata [Hachiro Cove], where his sandals broke. He secured permission from Sankichi-sama, the patron deity of Akita, to remain there on the condition that he would present the god a thousand loads of fish every day. Then he made a lake to live in.

Up till thirty years ago Hachiro often visited his native home. At such a time he used to bring one bog-rhubarb or one young bamboo sprout as a present, and sometimes he left his footmarks.

People say that his native house remained standing between Kuroishi and Otsuko till recent years.

THE MARSH OF TATSUKO

Suzuki, in "The Ponds and Love-Knots," pp. 43–46, tells of Hinemon who drowned herself in "Love-Knots-Untying Pond" and Den-emon who drowned himself in "Love-Knot-Tying Pond," uniting two ponds amorously, much as Hachiro Pond of the preceding story is here linked with Tatsuko Marsh.

AT SOME DISTANCE from Hachiro Pond is the marsh called Tatsuko-numa. One day in July a girl named Tatsuko drowned while swimming in this marsh. Her parents searched for her when it became dark. They lighted torches and called out: "Tatsuko, Tatsuko!"

Tatsuko, who had been turned into a dragon [*tatsu*], appeared from the water. The parents were grieved to see their daughter in such miserable form, and they threw the torches into the water. Then those torches were turned into trout. Therefore the trout in this marsh have black heads as if they were burned. However stormy the marsh may be in other seasons, on this particular day in July it is strangely calm because Tatsuko meets her husband Hachiro on this day.

Some people say that Hachiro now lives in this marsh with Tatsuko, so Hachiro Pond is now growing shallow and Tatsuko Marsh is growing deep.

THE FOX DEMONS

De Visser begins his extensive study of "The Fox and Badger in Japanese Folk-lore" by saying: "From olden times down to the present day the fox has played the most important part in Japanese animal-lore. This clever brute is considered to be more skillful than any other animal in taking human shape and hunting and possessing men." He goes on to point out the double character of the kitsune, fox, as a benevolent messenger of Inari, God of Rice, in addition to his role as a wicked demon haunting and possessing men. Hearn has a fine chapter on "Kitsune" in Glimpses of Unfamiliar Japan (V, ch. 15, pp. 358–94), concerned with the fox beliefs of Izumo peasantry. They fear goblin foxes for their deceptive enchantments, for quartering themselves upon a family, and worst, for taking diabolic possession of persons (p. 371). Basil Hall Chamberlain speaks to this last point in Things Japanese (5th ed. rev., London, 1905), "Demoniacal Possession," pp. 115–21, where he refers to a phantom train of 1889 traced to a crushed fox, and says that twentieth-century newspapers continue to report fox deviltry. Mock Joya, IV, pp. 13–14, "Foxes that Bewitch," cites a 1922 newspaper account of an old man held up by six robbers a few days after he killed a fox; he thought they had stolen his money, but it turned out to be his food. Other general discussions of foxes can be found in Anesaki, pp. 325–27, in his section on "Revengeful and Malicious Animals"; U. A. Casal, "The Goblin Fox and Badger and Other Witch Animals of Japan," Folklore Studies, XVIII (Tokyo, 1959), pp. 1–94 [section on The Fox, pp. 1–49]; William E. Griffis, "Japanese Fox-Myths," Lippincott's, XIII (1874), pp. 57–64; Joly, "Fox," pp. 69–74; A. H. Krappe, "Far Eastern Fox Lore," California Folklore Quarterly, III (April, 1944), pp. 124–47 [a valuable comparative study].

Mitford's tale, "How a Man was Bewitched and had his Head Shaved by the Foxes," is similar to the legend below in that foxes cruelly handle a scoffer and lead him to commit murder.

Text from Kikimimi Soshi (Tokyo, 1931), pp. 290–92.

ONCE A HUMOROUS MAN named Santaro, while on his way to town, saw several foxes lying in the sun. He drew near the foxes quietly, and then suddenly shouted to surprise them. Taken unaware, the foxes jumped up about ten feet high and immediately ran away to the mountains, looking back and making their tails round. Santa was pleased to see them running away and said to himself laughing: "I've heard that foxes foresee events which will happen even a thousand days later. But now I know it's not true at all. They can't tell what's going to happen right now. They're nothing but animals."

He told this to every person he met in town, heaping ridicule on the fox. He bought some fish and when evening came started home.

Soon night fell, and it grew too dark to walk on. Santa looked around and noticed a light some distance away. He proceeded to the house from which the light came and asked for a night's lodging. There was only a white-haired old woman in the house, who agreed to put him up, and then said: "Now I am going to my neighbor's, so I want you to look after the house while I am away." And she went out.

Santa felt uneasy when he was left alone and waited impatiently for the old woman to come back. In the meantime the fire grew low. Santa looked for something to burn. Then he saw a white object in the corner. "What is it?" he wondered, and looked at it more closely. It was a dead man, and to his surprise the corpse began to get up, groaning the while. Stricken with terror, Santa rushed out of the house. The dead man ran after him uttering sounds with wide-open mouth and outstretched hands. Santa feared that he might be caught by the dead man and, without a moment's thought, climbed a big tree standing near him. The dead man failed to see this and passed by, groaning.

Santa felt relieved. "Thank God!" he thought. "But I wish the morning would come soon."

At last day dawned in the east. As it grew light, Santa perceived that the tree was a persimmon, and that its upper branches bore fruit. He climbed higher up the tree in order to get the persimmons. But the branch broke under his weight and he toppled from the tree. Unhappily, the tree hung over a river bank, and he dropped into the water. However, he suffered no injury, and only felt quite chilly. Then suddenly he became conscious of himself crawling around on the spot where he had surprised the foxes that morning. The fish that he had bought were of course gone.

THE FOX WRESTLER

"Foxes quite frequently rob people of their food," reports Yanagita, Mountain Village Life *(ch. 61, "Foxes and Badgers," p. 426), and gives a case of an old man*

in Kamisanji-mura who was bewitched by a fox while on his way home with wine and sardines and was found worshiping the bottle, in which he had placed a sprig; the sardines had disappeared. Stories of evil foxes who impersonate people are in Yanagita-Mayer, Japanese Folk Tales, nos. 35–37, pp. 108–14. Cases where the disguise of the fox is imperfect and lead to his undoing appear in nos. 38, 39, 43, pp. 115–18, 127–28.

This legend was turned in to me in his term paper by a student of mine, Nobusada Kawasaki, at the University of Tokyo in March, 1957. The events it relates transpired in his home town, Funabashi-shi, Chiba-ken, in 1912.

Notes: Shichi-go-san, a national festival honoring children of seven, five, and three. Orizume, a box of food given to guests to take home from a party. Yokan, a sweet jelly of red beans. Kinton, boiled beans mashed and sweetened.

In MY CHILDHOOD, my storyteller was a window-sill library which my father, a Buddhist priest, had made for the convenience of the children in the neighborhood. It contained many books, almost all of them recommended by Mrs. Carl Schultz, a specialist in juvenile literature.

One Thursday recently I returned home after your lecture wondering whether or not I knew something that could be called a folk tale. The only tales I seemed able to remember were those of Grimm or Andersen, or some famous Japanese animal tales. I racked my brains. "Don't I know *any* unique folk tale that was told me directly?" After a while I recalled a tale related by my grandmother. And I have decided to set it down here because I know my grandmother believed the story. This is what she said.

"When your mother was a child, the graveyard at the back of this temple was thickly covered with bamboo grass. And it was said that foxes were living there.

"The autumn that your mother reached the age of seven (she is now fifty-two), we celebrated her *shichi-go-san,* inviting our neighbors in to dinner. The guests returned to their homes in high good spirits, each carrying an *orizume* in his hand. Genbe-san, a farmer, took a short cut back to his house through the overgrown graveyard, in spite of our warning not to. He was a tall, powerful man, and on that evening, he was fairly drunk.

"Next morning he was back at our house with a thoroughly sober

appearance, and told us of an astonishing experience he had had the previous night on his way home. As he was hurrying through the bamboo grove he was stopped by a strange man who appeared to be about his age. 'Hey, you! Let's have a *sumo* match,' the stranger said to Genbe-san. Since Genbe-san was big and strong and had been boasting of his strength, he immediately agreed. It was a close contest and neither man could emerge victor. When both became tired, they stopped to take a rest. A few moments later, Genbe-san discovered that the stranger had disappeared without his having noticed. Feeling totally bewildered, he returned to his home. When he opened the *orizume* with his family, he received a further surprise. Broiled bream, lobster fritters, chicken en casserole, all were gone. Only two dishes—*yokan* and *kinton*—remained in the box.

"It was surely a fox that had done such mischief," concluded my grandmother, nodding sagely. Then she added: "Of course it was quite natural that there should be foxes living there, since brush had grown so thickly on that graveyard."

After I returned home, I brought this story into our dinner table conversation. Pretending to be a folklorist, I concealed my real intent from my family. I talked on as if I were merely retelling a reminiscence of my late grandmother. But I was surprised to find my father and mother apparently believing this story. Father even told me of another man who was tricked by a fox and made to walk all night in the woods.

So I am convinced that folklore can be found nowadays just as in olden times. It will last at least another generation!

THE FOX WIFE

Foxes often appear as beautiful women. Yanagita, Mountain Village Life, *pp. 426–27, tells of a girl-fox who accosts a flutist in Hippo-mura and gives him food for playing; the food later disappears from a wedding party. In the story of "Sanuki Vixen," the storyteller describes chasing a fox out of a strawberry bed and finding a beautiful girl with foxlike features, whom he rebuffs; next morning she is introduced to him by his host as his kinswoman from Kyoto (W. Alexander, "Legends of Shi-*

koku," *New Japan, V, 1952, p. 579*). *Fox-wife stories are summarized in Krappe, pp. 130–31. The idea of gratitude appears in Mitford, "The Grateful Foxes," pp. 213–19, where foxes kill their own cub to provide a fox's liver, prescribed as the only cure for the ailing son of a tradesman who has rescued the cub from a trap. A variant in Yanagita-Mayer of the present tale, no. 61, pp. 178–79, "The Fox-Wife," begins with a married farmer's finding two identical wives on his return from the privy and arbitrarily driving one out.*

Text from Aichi-ken Densetsu Shu, *pp. 263–64.*

ONCE THERE LIVED on a hill on the way to Kido a farmer named Narinobu. The road started from Nishihara in Ichinomiya, passed the Narinobu Bridge and Bonji Pond, and led to Kido. One night a beautiful woman came to his home and asked him to make her his wife. He granted her request and married her. Not long after that she bore a boy whom they named Morime and whom they loved.

One year the boy fell ill in bed, and the parents tended him day and night. It was May, but Narinobu's wet rice field alone lay waste and unplanted. He was worrying about it in his heart. Then one morning when he went out, he beheld his rice field completely planted. However, he discovered that all the rice plants were planted upside down. Astonished, he ran into the house to tell his wife. But he saw there a fox's tail hanging out of his wife's bed. His wife awakened and realized that her real form, that of a fox, was now discovered. When her husband told her that the rice plants were planted upside down, she took the child in her arms and went out into the rice field. There she repeated the following poem three times:

> "Be fruitful.
> My child shall eat plenty.
> The inspector shall pass over.
> Bear fruit in the husk."

No sooner had she finished the last word than the rice plants turned over erectly and grew high and thick before her eyes. Leaving her child to her husband, she waved her hand to the sky. Then a black cloud appeared and, with a gust of wind, turned day into night. In the darkness the fox-wife disappeared, rolling up the arrowroot leaves scattered nearby. For that reason arrowroot leaves always show their undersides.

The autumn came, but nevertheless the rice plants of Narinobu's field did not come into ears. The officer who inspected the field therefore exempted Narinobu from rice taxes. However, the ears ripened in the husk and the harvest was plentiful.

THE BADGER THAT WAS A SHAMISEN PLAYER

As De Visser points out in his study "The Fox and the Badger in Japanese Folklore," the badger is a less complicated figure than the fox. Of the three kinds of badgers—tanuki, mujina, and mami—it is the first that figures principally in folklore and is often linked with the fox in the word kori, *meaning "foxes and badgers." The tanuki is first reported in the thirteenth century as a mischievous shapeshifter. Bruno Taut writes in* Houses and People of Japan *(tr. from the German by Estille Balk: Tokyo, 1937), p. 101: "The Japanese badger, which figures largely in superstitious jokes, has been mixed up with Buddhism by the people, who like to dress him up as a Buddhist priest. They also accentuate his round belly which he has probably filled during the winter time, exaggerate the size of his testicles and put a wine-bottle on his back." Joly, p. 14, under "Badger," says: "Standing by the roadside on its hind legs it distends its belly (or rather scrotum) and striking it with its forepaws uses it as a drum . . . wrapped in a kimono, it begs like an itinerant monk, waylays folks at night across paddy fields, causes fishermen to draw up their nets empty, and only laughs at their misfortune."*

Like the fox, the badger plays several roles. He is a roguish transformer as in the present tale; he is a foolish dupe; and he is a grateful friend. The badger as rogue is indicated in Yanagita, Mountain Village Life, *p. 427: ". . . in Yamagata-mura, Iwate-ken, they believe that when a badger wishes to dupe a man it puts its moustached mouth between its thighs to make them look like a woman's thighs." An evil badger disguised as a beautiful girl and as Buddha is discovered and slain, in Mitford, pp. 224–26, "The Prince and the Badger," and Hearn,* Kotto, *"Common Sense," XI, pp. 11–15, respectively. Foolish badgers appear in Yanagita-Mayer,* Japanese Folk Tales, *no. 10, p. 43, and nos. 40–42, pp. 119–26. Grateful badgers are found in Mitford, pp. 220–23, "The Badger's Money," and Suzuki, pp. 109–12, "Shirahage Daimyojin." The several types are discussed in U. A. Casal, "The Goblin Fox and Badger and Other Witch Animals of Japan,"* Folklore Studies, *XVIII (Tokyo, 1959), pp. 49–58 [section on The Badger].*

Text from Satoshi Sakakigi, Tabi to Densetsu, *II (June, 1929), "Legends of Shimabara," no. 6, pp. 16–17.*

Note: Shamisen, a three-stringed musical instrument.

THIS STORY IS TOLD at Sakashita in Kita Arima-mura. One day a man went out to do some shopping at Tanigawa, a little distance from this village. When he was about to cross the Arima River on the way, a badger appeared and began to wade the river. The man looked at him, counting the number of stepping-stones. When the badger reached the other side he looked back at the man, and then looked at the surface of the water. He picked up a log which came floating by. Then he put some weeds on the log and made it into a *shamisen*. He picked up another log and put some weeds on it again. Then it became a little girl. The man was pleased to see the badger doing such things. At last the badger put the weeds on his own head. Immediately he turned into a blind woman. After he finished disguising himself, the blind woman walked on with the *shamisen* in her arms, led by the girl. They looked like a true party of traveling *shamisen* players.

The men followed after them to see what the woman would do. She went into a temple at Tanigawa and began to play the *shamisen*. The persons in the temple entertained the party very well, and the neighboring people gathered together to listen to the *shamisen*. In the meantime the man thought how foolish the people were to be pleased, when all

the time they were being fooled. He went in back of the temple and poked a hole in a paper door, through which he peeped. The listeners increased and created a great hubbub. Then someone patted the man's shoulder. "What are you doing here?" "The badger disguised himself as a *shamisen*-player," he answered. "I am waiting for a good time to expose him."

But he heard a loud laugh. And he realized he was peeping into the buttocks of a horse.

DANKURO BADGER

This is a variant of the bowl-lender legend. See "The Kappa of Koda Pond,"
p. 61–62.
    Text from Densetsu no Echigo to Sado, *I, pp. 67–68. Collected in Tagami-mura, Minamikambara-gun, Niigata-ken.*

A LONG TIME AGO a vassal of Abe Sadato fled to the mountain called Gomado-yama following a defeat in battle, and he built a castle there. He maintained his power for a long time, but eventually his castle was captured.

In the woods near the castle was a cave in which a badger lived. The villagers called this badger Dankuro. This badger was a queer fellow. When the castle fell, he stole into the castle and secured valuable utensils and treasures, carrying them to his cave. So he became the owner of abundant treasures beyond compare with any in the neighborhood. When the people of the neighboring villages were in need of utensils and the like on the occasion of weddings, funerals, or memorial services, they went to Dankuro Badger to borrow such things. And the badger was ready to lend them. But it was said that if they did not return what they had borrowed, he would refuse to lend any more.

Once a mischievous villager borrowed some things and did not return them all. The badger was offended. Not only did he stop lending; he also did much damage to the fields of the villagers. He piled up firewood in his cave and, setting it alight, vanished from view.

But one can still see the cave in which Dankuro Badger lived.

SEVENTY-FIVE BADGERS

In this legend the badger is a fearsome creature. As happens here, a strong dog is often used to destroy such evil beasts, for instance Hayataro in "A Heroic Dog of the Ko-zenji Temple," Murai, pp. 88–93, who killed and was killed by three huge monkeys.

Text from Kamekichi Nagata, Impaku Mintan, I (January, 1936), pp. 69–70. Collected in Yashiro-mura, Yazu-gun, Tottori-ken.

ABOUT 1,500 YEARS AGO an old man and woman lived in Shimo Yamaguchi. One day the old man went to the mountains to cut trees, and the old woman stayed at home pounding soy-bean paste. In the afternoon their red cow suddenly shied at something and, breaking down the door, rushed out of the stable. The old woman ran after the cow trying to catch it, but when she was about to overtake the beast, it sped away and when it had traversed some distance it stopped a while. In such a manner the old woman was led to Otaki-ga-naru in Miyahara, and there was killed by a badger. In those days seventy-five badgers lived at Otaki-ga-naru and they troubled the villagers sorely.

When the old man came home in the evening he learned what had happened to the old woman. Determined to get revenge on the badgers, he made a petition to the god of Ashio Shrine. Every day for twenty-one days he visited the shrine. On the last day the god appeared in his dream and said:

"Todarabo Dog of Tsukidani is the only creature that can destroy the badgers of Otaki-ga-naru. Go to the village of Saji tomorrow to borrow the dog, bring him back with you, and make him fight against the badgers."

The old man was glad to hear this. Early the next morning he went to Tsukidani and borrowed the dog. On the way back when they entered Enami Pass, the big dog found it difficult to pass through the rocks. Therefore the rock at that place was called Inubasami [Catching the Dog].

The next morning the old man rose very early and made seventy-five rice balls and went out to Otaki-ga-naru with the dog. There he let Todarabo enter the badger's den. Soon the dog came out with a badger in his mouth. The old man gave him one rice ball. They repeated the same action seventy-four times. At last when there was only one badger left, the old man became so hungry that he ate the rice ball himself instead of giving it to the dog. The tired dog was at last defeated by the last badger. The old man felt sorry for the dog and enshrined him at Shimo Yamaguchi. This is the origin of the present Inu-yama [Dog-mountain] Shrine.

Because this seventy-fifth badger was not killed, there are badgers nowadays.

KOIKE'S BABA

This tale is found in northern Europe and has been assigned Type 121, "Wolves Climb on Top of One Another to Tree" (Motif J2133.6). Ikeda comments, p. 48: "In the European tales it is a woman who turns into a cat, but in Japan it is a cat that eats an old woman, usually the mother of a village blacksmith, and assumes her shape. At night she sneaks out from the house to harm travelers. In this story she usually appears in the capacity of an adviser to a group of wolves. . . . It is told widely in Japan as an actual happening in various localities."

Text from Shimane-ken Kohi Densetsu Shu, pp. 41–42.

Note: Baba, an old woman.

AMONG THE VASSALS of the Lord of Matsue there was a man named Koike. One of his servants named Tobizo went on an errand to a distant village and it became dark on his way back. As he was walking along the path under the moonlight, some wolves came out from the thick woods and jumped at him. Tobizo could not find a way to escape, so he climbed a tree beside the path. He guarded himself with a sword. The wolves were howling around the tree. After a while one of the wolves stood firmly at the foot of the tree, and another one jumped on its back, and another on the second one's back, and thus they reached to a height of four or five feet. Then one of the wolves said: "Bring Koike's *baba* immediately." Then another wolf ran away as fast as lightning. Soon it came back with a big cat, as big as a dog. The cat jumped up on top of the wolves and was about to bite at Tobizo. In desperation he threw the sword at the cat. The sword hit the cat's forehead, and it fell to the ground; the wolves also all fell down. In the meantime the day dawned and Tobizo went home, having barely escaped with his life.

When he arrived at his home he was told that the night before, while in the toilet, Koike's mother had been injured on her forehead. Tobizo had a suspicion when he heard this, so he told his master all that had happened the night before. Koike himself had been suspecting his mother, for she always took her food alone; she never ate with other people. As he wanted to find out the truth, he secretly peeped into the mother's room that evening. The mother was sitting down upon her heels and eating the food by lowering her mouth to the dish. After a while she lifted up her face and looked around. Her face was just like a cat's face. Koike pushed down the door and jumped into the room. He killed the creature with one cut of the sword. When he examined the mother's bed, he found the bones and flesh of his real mother under the bed.

THE GOD AKIBA REVEALED AS A BEGGAR

Motif K1811.1, "Gods (spirits) disguised as beggars. Test hospitality" enters here. Anesaki, pp. 250–51, tells of the god Susa-no-wo traveling as a beggar and rewarding a hospitable home with a charm against evil spirits. Akiba is a Shinto god of fire prevention, and Akiba shrines issued charms against fire. Curiously, a Southern-born Negro told me of angels disguised as beggars who ascended to Heaven in a puff of smoke (R.M. Dorson, Negro Folktales in Michigan, *Cambridge, 1956, pp. 156–57, "Mangelizing").*

Text from Shimane-ken Kohi Densetsu Shu, Yatsuka-gun, *p. 14.*

Note: Banta, eta, members of the outcast caste.

DURING THE TIME of the sixth chief priest of Entsu-ji in Ino-mura, a beggar came to the temple one day and told the servant at the gate that he wanted to see the chief priest. As the chief priest was not in the temple at that time, the servant said: "Come again later because the priest has gone away on business." But the beggar did not move away, saying: "I will not leave until I see the priest." The servant was vexed and said: "I will call *banta* and have them tie you up." The *banta* came and were about to tie the beggar up when he turned into a big glittering fireball and flew up into the sky.

All the servants and the *banta* lost their senses from the shock. When the chief priest came back and heard of that he said: "It is an awful thing. It must be the revelation of the god Akiba. I cannot know what punishment we shall receive for such an impious deed." From that night on he offered prayers for seven days. On the last night he was so tired that he slept a while. In his dream the god revealed himself and told him to make an image of him and to worship it. When the priest was awakened, he saw something shining by his pillow. He looked at it. It was a small statue of Akiba. Encouraged by this miracle, the priest devoted himself to his religious services. Consequently the mountain shrine was built and many people came to believe in Akiba.

THE HUNTERS TURNED TO RATS

Light on this legend is thrown by a similar version from the opposite end of Japan reported by Kunio Yanagita in the valuable essay on "Yamadachi and Yamabushi" that he appends to Mountain Village Life. *He found the legend preserved in an old manuscript on hunting owned by an ancient family in the mountain village of Oka-*

wachi in southern Kyushu. "Two hunter brothers go into the mountains for hunting and meet with the mountain goddess who has just delivered a baby. She asks them for help. The older brother will not render any help to her, because the blood of childbirth is the veriest taboo for a hunter. But the younger brother takes pity on the goddess and helps her. As a reward, he and his posterity are granted prosperity in their occupation of hunting, while the older brother is changed into a small fish in a mountain stream. In this story there is no blending of Buddhism" (p. 460). In the present legend the two brothers are replaced by two groups of hunters.

Text from Toö Ibun, pp. 86–90.

ARASE-MURA in Kita Akita-gun is a village in the deep mountains, and most of the villagers live by hunting. In the mountains of this village lived so-called *kodama* rats, which are smaller than ordinary rats and have brown fur. In the bitter cold of winter these rats often burst to death on the trees, with pitiful sounds. The hunters frequently hear such sounds and find the dead rats. The name *kodama* may be derived from that sound. Why do these small creatures alone among the wild beasts have such a miserable existence? A tradition gives the reason as follows:

A long time ago two groups of hunters were in the mountains where each group had a hut. One numbered six men who called themselves the Sugi Group. And the other numbered seven and called themselves the Kodama Group. One night a young woman came to the hut of the Kodama Group and asked the men to let her stay that night, because she was going to have a baby. The hunters had a taboo against women in general, not to mention pregnant women. So of course those hunters did not allow this woman to come into their hut. They thought she must be an evil creature, and the head man held his gun point-blank against her. Then the woman went away regretfully.

After that the woman visited the hut of the Sugi Group and approached the men there in the same way. The hunters of that hut kindly let her in, saying: "You must have had troubles. Please come in and warm yourself by the fire." They took care of her and helped her to give birth to the baby. The woman thanked them and said to the head man: "I am not an ordinary woman. I am a mountain spirit. In reward for your kindness I will make you catch three bears tomorrow morning. When the morning comes, go to the ravine below this mountain. You

141

will find there three big bears in a hollow log. You can shoot them in this way." And she taught them how to shoot. She also told them to go to see the hut of the other group, who had treated her badly. After she uttered those words she went away.

The hunters of the Sugi Group went to the ravine as the woman had told them and found three big bears in the hollow of the big tree. After they had shot all the bears they went over the mountain to the hut of the Kodama Group. There were only guns and other tools, but no men to be seen anywhere around. When the hunters looked up, they saw on the beam of the hut seven little rats with strange colored fur. They knew that the seven hunters of the Kodama Group had been turned into rats.

So nowadays the hunters have a taboo against making a group of seven.

THE MYSTERY OF THE BULL-TROUT

The Minzokugaku Jiten, under the entry "Kawaryo" (River-fishing), comments that in many places a legend is told of how a huge eel or catfish appeared in the shape of a man and begged people to cease from poison-fishing.

Text from Hida no Densetsu to Minyo, pp. 115–16.

THE POOL IN YAMANOKUCHI-MURA, Ono-gun, in the province of Hida (Gifu-ken), is called Dango-buchi. In former days it was a deep, gruesome pool, full of water, but now it is known as a beauty spot with a waterfall.

A long, long time ago a villager planned to catch fish by putting *ne* into this pool. (*Ne* is a strong poison made by boiling the bark of the Japanese pepper tree with ashes. They say if one puts this *ne* into the river, fish are poisoned to death.) While the villager was boiling the poison in a big pot over the hearth in his home, a strange bonze suddenly came by and said to the master of the house: "You are making *ne* in the pot for the purpose of putting it into the pool up the river. Since this is not a good thing to do, I advise you to give up your plan." The people of the house gave him a dumpling which they were making just at that time. The bonze ate it and went away.

Feeling suspicious of the bonze, the master followed after him. The bonze disappeared when he came to the pool in which the master was going to put the *ne*.

After the *ne* was prepared, the villager dropped it in the pool despite the bonze's advice. Then an exceedingly big bull-trout came up to the surface of the water. The man caught it and, when he put it on his shoulder, its tail touched his heels. He took it home and cut it open. A dumpling rolled out from inside the fish. So it was realized that this fish had visited the house disguised as a bonze. Thereafter the pool has been called Dango-buchi [Dumpling Pool] because the bonze ate the dumpling.

It is believed not only in this region but also in the province of Hida in general that an old bull-trout has power to change himself into a human being.

THE BLACKSMITH'S WIFE

From China comes a tale with a motif very close to the present, "Tiger grateful for woman assisting tigress as midwife" (Motif B387). Anesaki has a legend of a grateful crane who takes the form of a fine young lady and marries the man who saved her life, then finally returns to her bird life (pp. 323–24).

Told by Mrs. Hitoshi Kawashima Saito to her granddaughter Kayoko Saito in Tokyo on April 8, 1957.

ONCE UPON A TIME, at Yasuda in Aki, there lived a blacksmith. One day this blacksmith went to Awa, a neighboring province, on business. In order to reach Awa, he had to go across None-yama, an isolated mountain infested with wolves. If a traveler could not cross the mountain before sunset, he had to sleep at night in a tree, and many wolves with glaring eyes would gather under the tree and roar at him.

When the blacksmith was walking in great haste along the mountain path to Awa, he was surprised to see a wolf beside the path. Approaching the wolf, however, he found that it was suffering in the throes of birth. He felt sorry for the wolf and helped it deliver its cubs.

The sun was going to set, so he hurried to reach Awa. It grew dark, and yet he met no more wolves on the way. He reached Awa and returned again safe and sound.

Several days had passed after he came back from Awa, when a pretty and well-built woman came to his house and asked him to marry her. Since he had no wife, he married her. The bride was a hard worker and helped the blacksmith forge iron very ably. She bore many children for him, and they led a happy life. She was called Kajigakaka, which meant "a wife of a blacksmith," and she was loved by her neighbors as well as by her husband.

One day, Kajigakaka confided to the blacksmith the story of her origin. She was the wolf whom he had helped on None-yama! Thanking him, she expressed her desire to go back to her old den on None-yama since she had helped make him happy. She left the amazed blacksmith and disappeared.

Afterwards it was learned that all the children of Kajigakaka had thick hair on the chest. Even today, those who have hair on their chest are called the offspring of Kajigakaka.

THE GIRL WHO TURNED INTO A STONE

Mock Joya, III, 201–2, comments on the numerous legends of women turned into stone. The examples he gives are of grief-stricken women. Suzuki, pp. 58–60, "The Frog Stones," tells of lovers who turned into frog-shaped stones north of Kumamoto-shi.

Text from Bungo Densetsu Shu, *pp. 114–15. Collected by Hideko Akiyoshi from Nishi Kokuto-gun.*

LONG AGO a mother lived with her only daughter. They lived quite comfortably. The daughter was about twelve years old. But she grew spoiled and always bothered the mother. One fine morning the mother said: "Since it is such a lovely day, you may go to the sea."

The daughter answered: "No, I won't. I will go to the mountain."

"Well, then you may go to the mountain," said the mother. But the daughter answered: "No, I will go to the sea."

Thus the daughter was always contrary. In the meantime the mother became seriously ill. When she breathed her last, she said to the daughter: "Please bury me in the river after my death."

She really meant to be buried on the mountain, which had a beautiful view, but she gave her daughter instructions contrary to her own wish because she thought the daughter would act in the opposite way as usual. However, after the mother died, the daughter felt sorry for her disobedience, and she determined for the first time to do as the dying mother had told her. She buried her mother's corpse by the river.

A year later the river was flooded and the mother's tomb was washed away. So it resulted that the daughter did not fulfill the mother's last wish. One day afterwards, while the daughter was going on her way to Hachiman Shrine, she was crushed by a stone that came down from heaven, and was turned into the stone. Thus she was punished by the god for her disobedience to the mother.

Now, in Tokata-machi, by the *torii* that stands in the forest alongside the little stream of Katsura-gawa, there is a stone shaped like a girl but crushed flat as a frog.

THE WOMAN WHO LOVED A TREE-SPIRIT

Anesaki, p. 333, refers to the legend of Oryu, the spirit of an old willow tree, who married a warrior but had to part from him when the tree was cut down. "In the dramatized form of the story, the chief motive is the agony she manifests as each axe stroke cuts deeper and deeper into the tree." Hearn tells of a tree-spirit who had a

child by her lover; when the daimyo *ordered the tree cut down, the woman vanished
inside it, and three hundred men could not budge the fallen tree; then the child pulled
it easily (VI, ch. 16, "In a Japanese Garden," pp. 22–23).*

Text from Toö Ibun, pp. 111–14.

FUJIWARA TOYOMITSU was the governor of the province of Uzen about
1,200 years ago, during the reign of Emperor Mommu. He had a
daughter named Akoya who was endowed with talent and beauty.
One autumn evening as she was playing a *koto* the faint sound of a
flute was heard outside accompanying the tune of her *koto*. Its tone
was sweet and charming and it blended in harmony with the tune of
the lady's *koto* in the serenity of the late autumn night. The player of
the flute was a noble young man in a green dress. His name was Natori
Taro, and he lived at the foot of Mt. Chitose. The two young people
fell in love with each other.

One night the man said to the young lady: "This is the last time I shall
meet you, for my life will end tomorrow. How sad I am to have to
say farewell to you!"

As soon as he finished those words he disappeared, and the shadow of
a pine tree was seen on the sliding paper doors. Struck dumb with surprise, the lady knew not what to do and worried greatly about the
matter.

At that time it happened that a bridge over the Natori River was
swept away by the flood. It was decided to cut down a big pine tree at
the foot of Mt. Chitose to supply the lumber for a new bridge. The
villagers, never guessing that the spirit of the pine tree was the lover of
the governor's daughter, called many woodcutters and had them cut
down the pine tree. But when they attempted to carry the fallen tree
to the Natori River, they found themselves unable to move it an inch,
however hard they tried. When Akoya heard of this, she recalled the
last words of her lover and hastened to the pine tree. She placed her
hand on the tree and pulled the rope with the other people. Then the
tree, which had stood as firm as a great rock, was easily moved and
carried to the river without any difficulty.

Akoya never married and lived the rest of her life alone. Many genera-

tions passed. The pine tree was succeeded by others, several times over, and nowadays an old pine tree called the Pine of Akoya stands at the foot of Mt. Chitose in the suburbs of Yamagata-shi.

OKESA THE DANCER

Motifs C423, "Tabu: revealing the marvelous," and C945, "Person carried off to other world for breaking tabu," appear here.

    This is the legend behind the popular Okesa dance and costume I mentioned in the Introduction. It was told to me by the leading folklore collector of Sado Island, Shunosuke Yamamoto, at his home in Mano-mura on Sado, July 7, 1957. Mrs. Fanny Hagin Mayer interpreted for me. Okesa is said to have lived in Ogi-machi on the southern tip of the island. A text of the legend was published by Mr. Yamamoto in his book Sado no Shima *(The Island of Sado), published at Mano-machi, Sado-gun, Niigata-ken, in 1953. There, on p. 58, he writes: "Okesa was very popular not only because she was a beauty, but also for her beautiful voice. Nobody had ever heard the songs that Okesa sang, so the people of the place called them 'Okesa-bushi'." (Bushi or fushi means an air.) The author comments on the variety of Okesa legends, at least ten being current, and states that the strange-cat form, here given, is the best known.*

THERE IS an Okesa dance commemorating a girl who changed into a cat.

Once upon time there was an old couple and they had one little cat which they cared for very lovingly. The old couple became very, very poor, and their days were full of suffering. Then the cat asked them one day to let her go home for a little while. And the form of the cat vanished. It reappeared after a few days in the form of a very beautiful girl and explained that it had lived with them for a long time and enjoyed their affection, and had returned now in the form of a beautiful girl to help them. She sacrificed her beautiful body to become a geisha, in order to bring in money for the old couple.

Her name was Okie-san, and has become Okesa. She was very popular, and many people went to see her. But once a boatman saw in the next room, where Okesa had been just a moment before, a cat eating, lapping up the oil in which the wick was floating in the lamp. She was aware that she was being spied upon. Okesa said: "I am very worried because you have seen my real form, but I want you to promise never to tell anyone the real truth."

The next day the boatman took a boat to Hokkaido, and right before a great company of passengers he told this story that he had been forbidden to tell. At once the sky became overcast and a black cloud covered the sun. A big black cat reached down from the cloud into the boat and pulled him up into the sky.

PART FIVE

HEROES AND STRONG MEN

SEVERAL different cycles of heroic legends flourish in Japan. One goes back to early myth and tells of demigods who in prehistoric times founded the kingdom where the village now stands. A much fuller spate of tales deals with the exploits of samurai in the Middle Ages, especially those who fought in the twelfth-century wars between the Heike and the Genji clans, which saw the defeat and dispersal of the Heike to remote corners of the islands. In Shimane-ken, for instance, densetsu are still told about Akushichibyoe Kagekiyo, a Heike general appointed governor of Izumo Province. When another lord's servant took away a nightingale from Kagekiyo's district, the bird sorrowfully sang "Ho-ho-koga Kagekiyo, Kagekiyo," and the servant sickened, until he released the bird to fly back to Kagekiyo. One night Kagekiyo shot a white arrow into the air, to locate a shrine for Hachiman, God of War; the arrow lodged in a pine tree and is still preserved in the shrine.

Such bits of legend hark back to stirring ballads and tales that sprang up after the civil wars and were gathered together in the thirteenth-century classic, Heike Monogatari. A truly heroic age existed in the time of the Heike, when samurai devoted their Spartan lives to combats, sieges, and raids, and treasured their swords, dogs, horses, and beautiful women. Renowned warriors like Tametomo and the mighty Benkei emerged as heroes of folk history and linger on today in fragmentary and broken legends.

In more recent times a new stock of heroes has arisen from the peasant class, farmers famed for their prodigious strength and woodsmen for their marvelous hunting. In Japan the sumo wrestler has commanded admiration from the nobility as well as from the common folk from whom he springs, and many village legends celebrate the bulk and might of wrestlers. Similar stories in Europe and the United States centering on phenomenally strong men no longer carry supernatural overtones. (In colonial times, however, George Burroughs of Salem, Massachusetts, was accounted a wizard because he lifted up barrels filled with molasses and cider.) The strong men of Japan are still regarded as more than human and are said to be possessed by a kami. Sumo originated in divine ritual, and the victorious sumo wrestler assured his province fertile crops.

THE CHILD OF THE SUN

This tradition has the quality of an ancient myth. Yanagita in the preface to Fishing Village Life, *pp. iii–iv, notes that sea people relate much older ancestral histories than do mountain people, who customarily ascribe their origins to refugee warriors of the civil wars. "But in many islands the people relate that their ancestors are a god and goddess who came to their island in the remote Age of Gods."*

Text from Kikai-jima Mukashi-banashi Shu, pp. 24–25, reprinted from Shima, *II, 1934, p. 487.*

THE SUN sent his child down to earth. He was brought up by his mother. When he was seven years old he was one day playing outside and his friends mocked at him, saying that he was fatherless. And the child told that to his mother. She told him the story that she had kept secret up to that time. She said: "You are really the son of the sun." When the child heard this he thought he should go up to heaven, and he went up. When he came to the sun and told him why he had come, the sun became angry and said: "I have no child on earth. Take this boy to the demon and let him be eaten up." So the servants took the boy to the demon, and the demon immediately tried to eat the boy. But because he was the son of the sun, and nobly born, the demon could not approach him. And the demon bowed down before the boy. Then the sun realized that the boy was his real child, and he said to the boy: "You may go down to the earth and wait for the time when I will feed you and your mother." And he sent the child back to the earth.

There the child tended the cows. One day when he was feeding a cow in the field, a sheet of paper dropped down from the heavens.

The cow swallowed that paper, and the child kicked the cow's belly. Then the cow vomited up the paper. This paper contained a sacred prophecy. When it came out from the cow's mouth, the letters were colored red from the blood of the cow. The child became a prophet by the command of the sun, and the mother became a priestess. The boy was the first prophet of the island.

Note: This paper is the bible of the island. It is preserved on the island, written in Toki (the dialect of Kikai Island), and some letters are inscribed in red.

THE JEWEL THAT GREW GOLDEN FLOWERS

Legends of a princess who broke wind in public are discussed by Ikeda, pp. 198–99, under "The Gold Bearing Tree" and by Yanagita-Mayer, Nippon Mukashi-banashi Meii, p. 416, no. 26, under "The Golden Eggplant," Motif S411.2. "Wife banished for some small fault," reported from India, is central. This historical tradition incorporates the theme of breaking wind which is very popular in Japanese humorous tales and is often told about an old bamboo-cutter who swallowed a bird. See "The Old Man Who Broke Wind," pp. 207–8.

Text from Okierabu Mukashi-banashi, pp. 176–77.

LONG AGO there was a king. One day when his pregnant wife brought him breakfast she broke wind. The king became angry and exiled her. So the wife departed from the king's house, and gave birth to a boy. The child grew up, and when he was seven years old he asked his mother: "Mother, have I no father?" And the mother said: "You

are so young that I cannot tell you." But the child wished to know the secret. At last his mother told him the story. And she said: "You are the son of the king."

Then the child asked his mother: "Have you a jewel shaped in six squares?" The mother answered: "Yes, I have. The king gave it to me when he drove me out." And the child said: "Give it to me." And he went to the king with that jewel. He stood at the gate of the king's palace and cried aloud: "I have the jewel from which grow golden flowers." The king heard this but at first pretended not to hear. But the boy kept shouting the same words all through the night. At last the king lost patience and ordered a servant to bring in the child. When the child came to the king, he did not use the servants' entrance but the nobles' entrance.

The king asked him: "Have you really the jewel from which golden flowers grow?" And the boy answered: "Yes, I have. But unless it is tended by a woman who does not break wind, the jewel will not bloom with golden flowers."

Then the king said: "There is no woman who does not break wind." The boy said: "Then why did you drive out my mother? I have the jewel that my mother gave me." And he took out the jewel. The king looked at it and said: "I was wrong. I will give you much money. So go back to your mother and live happily with her."

But then the child said: "As I am your first child, I cannot make a branch family. So I must stay here." So the king made him his successor.

THE TALE OF YURIWAKA

Japanese trade with the maritime nations of expanding Europe, beginning in the middle of the sixteenth century, brought an unexpected import in the story of the Odyssey. Adapted to the Japanese scene, the tale has enjoyed strange curves of popularity, both in oral legend and in literary forms: puppet plays, lurid novels, pantomimic chants, and children's readers. Ulysses is replaced by Yuriwaka, a favorite minister of an early emperor. Esther L. Hibbard points out, in her comprehensive study, that the story of Ulysses would appeal to Japanese sympathy for the betrayed, lonely islander, and arouse Japanese admiration for the martial hero. Donald Keene gives the Polyphemus episode as a Japanese scholar heard it at the Dutch trading post in Nagasaki in 1774 (Japanese Literature, New York: 1955, pp. 90–91). Motif K1815.1, "Return home in humble disguise," occurs here.

Text from Bungo Densetsu Shu, pp. 8–10.

IN ANCIENT TIMES there was a governor of Bungo by the name of Yuriwaka. His father was Kimimitsu, Minister of the Left at the imperial court in Kyoto. Yuriwaka possessed great strength and always used iron bows and arrows. By order of the emperor he was appointed Governor of Bungo, and went down to Tsukushi to destroy the Mongolian forces which were attacking Japan at that time. He fought against them at sea near the island of Tsushima and at last gained victory by the aid of the gods. On the return voyage to the homeland Yuriwaka anchored his warboats by the shore of Genkai Island. As soon as he landed on this small island he took a nap, for that was his habit.

Among his retainers there were two brothers, Beppu Taro and Beppu Jiro. The elder brother, Taro, enticed his younger brother into a plot of rebellion against their lord. While Yuriwaka was fast asleep they secretly set sail from the island, leading away all the boats, and left him stranded alone. On returning to the province of Bungo they told Yuriwaka's wife that he had been killed in battle, and they delivered the same report to the imperial court. In consequence they came into possession of all the province of Bungo, and they lived in luxury. Moreover, Beppu Taro's arbitrariness reached such a point that he persecuted in many ways the wife of Yuriwaka, for whom he felt an immoral passion.

The helpless lady was in great distress, but she clung to the hope that her dear husband might be alive somewhere. So she sent Yuriwaka's pet falcon, named Midorimaru, off into the air with a letter from her tied to its leg. When she let it go, she told the bird to fly to her husband if it felt sympathy for her. The falcon flew away into the clouds. In the meantime Beppu Taro treated the lady more bitterly than ever, and when he realized that she would never obey him, he determined to drown her in a pond. However, an old gatekeeper sympathized with her and had his own daughter, Lady Manju, substituted for the lady.

Meanwhile, Yuriwaka woke up after a long sleep and perceived that he had been deserted on the island. There he had to remain without any means of returning to his homeland. One day a falcon flew down beside him. He looked at the bird and saw that it was his pet falcon, Midorimaru. Then he found and read his wife's letter that was tied to its leg. Learning how the Beppu brothers had revolted, he was enraged by their infidelity. He bit his finger and wrote a letter with the blood. Tying the letter to the falcon's leg, he let the bird fly back to the homeland. The falcon flew away high in the sky and safely returned to the lady's hiding place. She was glad to see the letter from her husband, but the blood writing saddened her heart. She tied an ink-stone and a brush to the falcon and sent it back to Yuriwaka again. Those things were too heavy for the falcon to carry, and after barely reaching Genkai Island its energy was entirely exhausted, and it fell into the water to die.

Afterwards Yuriwaka was saved by a fishing boat and returned to his homeland. He secured a position as a servant in the Beppu house, naming himself Kokemaru. One New Year's time when the Beppu brothers held the ceremony of the first shooting of the New Year, Kokemaru, who attended the ceremony as a servant, laughed at Beppu's archery. Beppu grew angry and ordered Kokemaru to shoot with the iron bow and arrow which only Yuriwaka had used. In response to the order, Kokemaru stood up with the iron bow and arrow. He spoke to Beppu, accusing him of infidelity, and revealed himself. "I myself am Yuriwaka, to whom you have done treachery."

No sooner had he said so than he shot Beppu to death.

Yuriwaka explained matters to the imperial court and was reappointed the Governor of Bungo. For the repose of the soul of faithful Lady Manju, who had drowned herself in the pond in place of his wife, Yuriwaka established a temple by the pond and offered donations. The temple was named Manju-ji after the girl. Yuriwaka also built a shrine at the spot where he had buried the corpse of his pet falcon Midorimaru, and erected a temple for the salvation of its spirit.

Yuriwaka passed away in peace in Bungo Province. It is said that he was buried under the mound which bears the name of the Mound of Yuriwaka.

THE STORY OF KIHACHI

This hero-legend has the true folk rawness usually softened by collectors and writers of folk tales. The close identification between the hero Takeiwatatsu-no-mikoto and the spirit of Mt. Ojo is clearly seen. Motif A 972.1, "Indentions on rocks from imprints of gods and saints," occurs.

Text from Aso no Densetsu, pp. 34–36.

Note: Mikoto, a title applied both to Shinto gods and to legendary persons of high rank, here translated as "lord."

TAKEIWATATSU-NO-MIKOTO liked to shoot arrows more than anything else. Sometimes he shot from the heights of Tano, aiming at the stone at Oga-ishi in the west, and sometimes he sat on the peak of Mt. Ojo and shot at the same stone. Mt. Ojo is sometimes called Doben-dake [Buttock Peak] because he sat on top of it. This mountain has several gullies. They are said to be the places where this lord's urine ran down the mountainside.

One day the lord sat on Mt. Ojo as usual, attended by a strong man named Kihachi from Aso, and shot his strong arrows at the stone. His arrow sometimes hit the stone and sometimes missed. The spot where his arrows dropped is now called Ya-buchi [Arrow Abyss]. Kihachi, who possessed supernatural strength, was ordered to retrieve the fallen arrows. Ninety-nine times he brought arrows to Mt. Ojo and returned to the stone called Mato-ishi. But he was so tired by the hundredth

time that he kicked the arrow with his toe toward the lord on Mt. Ojo. The lord became very angry and was going to kill Kihachi when he returned. Kihachi in fear ran away as fast as he could. The lord ran after him. He overtook Kihachi at Yabe and forced Kihachi down with his arrow. Then Kihachi broke wind. The name Yabe originated from this time. [*Be* means "breaking wind."] It is supposed to mean "Arrow Breaking Wind." The other explanation is that Yabe means "Breaking Wind Eight Times."

The lord was confused by Kihachi's breaking wind; he loosened his hold, and Kihachi escaped. Kihachi ran to Madonose at the border of Mitai, and he fought with the lord on opposite sides of the Itsugase River. When the lord broke off a big rock and threw it over to the other side, Kihachi threw it back. When the lord pulled up a big pine tree and threw it at Kihachi, Kihachi threw it back. But finally the lord overcame and caught Kihachi. This time he cut off Kihachi's head at once. But Kihachi's head returned to his body immediately. When the lord cut off Kihachi's hand, it returned to his arm. And when he cut off his foot, it also returned to his leg. Strong as he was, the lord was very much embarrassed by this, but finally he cut off Kihachi's arms and legs and buried each part in a separate place. And at the same time he buried Kihachi's body in Takachiho, which now is called Kihachi's Tomb. Each of the places where his limbs are buried is now called Oni-zuka [Demon Mound]. As for Kihachi's head, it flew up into the sky when it was cut off.

After that time Kihachi's spirit cast a spell on the lord's crops. Every year in the warm season of June he caused a frost to fall from the sky and spoil the crops. All the plants in the fields withered. The lord took pity on the people who were suffering from lack of food, and he spoke to Kihachi's spirit:

"Spirit of Kihachi, please come down to earth, that I may enshrine you in the center of Aso-dani."

So the spirit of Kihachi descended and was enshrined as Shimo-miya—The Frost Shrine.

KOGA SABURO

This local legend of Suwa, Nagano-ken, dealing with the adventures of the hero Koga Saburo, who rescues a princess from another world, has attained considerable fame. When modern printing methods were adopted in Japan at the end of the six-teenth century, the tale was cast into fiction and drama. The Kabuki play Account of Koga Saburo in the Cave *was performed in 1808 (Ikeda, pp. 81–82). There are elements here of a world-wide heroic legend, Type 301, "The Three Stolen Prin-cesses," to which the epic of Beowulf belongs, where a hero descends underground and vanquishes a monster (briefly suggested below by reference to a tengu). As the* Minzokugaku Jiten *points out in its entry on "Koga Saburo," the idea of a man's being metamorphosed into a serpent and deified as a water god is widespread in Japan (e.g., in "Hachiro's Transformation," p. 126–27).*

The notion present here of a male serpent or dragon visiting a female one via an underground passage, as in the legend of Hachiro and Tatsuko, is also thoroughly Japanese. In Suzuki, pp. 58–60, "The Frog Stones," a road was constructed by villagers in Kumamoto-ken to enable a female stone to visit more easily a male stone each night.

The text below was told by Ichino Okabe, 72, a farmer's wife in Sakae-mura, and is printed in Minami Saku-gun Kohi Densetsu, *pp. 82–83. It is obviously frag-mentary, as tales collected directly from the lips of the folk are apt to be.*

ONCE UPON A TIME there were three brothers, Taro, Jiro, and Saburo. One day they set out together to go hunting on Mt. Tadeshina. The beautiful daughter of a certain lord heard of their plans and asked them to take her with them. So the four of them went together. But when they came to the pond called Futago-ike, the princess suddenly dis-

appeared. The brothers looked everywhere for her. Finally they discovered a deep cavern in the earth.

Saburo, the youngest brother, looked down the cavern and called
out: "Is Princess Tokiyo down there?"

The princess answered from the bottom of the cavern: "Is Saburo
there?"

Still peering into the hole, Saburo saw the princess standing beside
a palace. So the three brothers quickly made a basket with some vines
and lowered it into the cavern. They called for the princess to get into
the basket, and then they pulled her up out of the hole. But when she
was safe on the ground she said in a sad voice: "I was in such a hurry that
I forgot the precious book of sutras that my parents gave me and left
it down in the hole."

So Saburo went down into the cavern to get the book for her. In
the palace there was a *tengu,* and he was in trouble because of the sutra.
The brothers waiting up above became impatient when Saburo did
not return and they dropped the vine rope.

The princess was filled with sadness. She said she could not live without Saburo and she threw herself into Lake Suwa.

Meanwhile Saburo walked on and on underground and finally he
came to a beautiful village. Some villagers saw him and hailed him as
a great samurai. Thereafter, Saburo became the son-in-law of a certain
house in the village and had a son. Thus nine years passed.

One day when Saburo was reading a book alone he shed tears.
When his wife questioned him he told her the story and said he still
loved the princess. His wife felt sorry for him and said: "You may go
to search for her with nine rice bowls."

Saburo was glad. He started on the journey and came to the temple
called Shinraku-ji in Onuma-mura. The village children ran from him,
crying: "Here comes a snake." This frightened Saburo, and he began
looking for water in which to hide. Suddenly he saw the princess beck-
oning to him from Lake Suwa. So he too entered the lake.

One day some years after that Saburo's underground wife was
weeping. Her son saw her and asked why she wept. She told him about

159

his father. Then the boy made nine rice bowls for her, and sent her to search for Saburo. After she had looked in many places, she came at last to Lake Suwa.

Ever since then there always appears across the surface of Lake Suwa a streak of upheaved ice. People call this the "God Crossing the Lake" and say it marks Saburo's path down under the lake as he travels back and forth between the homes there of the princess and his wife.

THE HEIKE REFUGEES

The great struggle between the Heike (Taira) and Genji (Minamoto) clans in the second half of the twelfth century is a Japanese epic, which has contributed lavishly to literature, drama, art, and folklore. After twenty years in power the Heike were crushed in 1185 by the Genji, and their samurai dispersed to remote corners of Japan. Hence the legend arose in more than one hundred mountain villages that Heike lords had founded their mura *and procreated their families—although a good many more Heike survivors than history records would be needed to justify their claims (Yanagita,* Mountain Village Life, *pp. 6–8, 455). The inhabitants of some islands south of Kagoshima also claim to be Heike descendants. Near Miyazaki in Kyushu houses were pointed out to me as being of Heike-type construction, with sloping thatched roofs.*

Text from Bungo Densetsu Shu, *pp. 62–63, to which Miss Y. Ishiwara adds a note: "I heard that those people, especially the women, sell fish from pails carried on their heads. They themselves say they are the descendants of the Heike."*

IN KAIBE-MURA, Kita Amabe-gun, live the people called Sha, who are said to be the descendants of Heike refugees. After the splendid days of the Heike, during which they said that all those who did not belong to their clan were not human beings, all the Heike people, oppressed by the rising power of the Genji, were obliged to get out of the capital city. On that occasion they had no time to make rice balls, so they just cooked rice in bags and started out saying "*Sha iko,*" meaning "Well now, let's go." They were driven away by the Genji to the west until at last they arrived at the shore which is the present Kaibe-mura. That they had said "*Sha*" when they ran away was known to other people, and they were called "*Sha*" after that.

In these days they still retain certain old customs such as hanging from their heads bags which contain cooked rice, and carrying things in pails on their heads. According to tradition, these customs originated when they carried rice bags on their heads as they crossed the river when driven away by the Genji.

THE LAST OF THE AKI

Here is a family tradition of refugee-warriors, told by Mrs. Hitoshi Kawashima Saito to her granddaughter Kayoko Saito on June 1, 1957, in Tokyo. Mrs. Saito heard the story from her grandparents in Kochi-ken (formerly Tosa), and learned it in her elementary-school history lessons. The last paragraphs are clearly her own personal comments.

IN THE AGE of the civil wars [1467–1600], Tosa was divided into seven districts and each of them was governed by a feudal lord. Aki, which was one of the seven districts, at the eastern end of Tosa, was ruled over by the lord Aki Kunitora who lived in Doi Castle. It seems that our place was named Aki after his surname.

During that stormy period it was reported that the army of Chosogabe Motochika, a strong feudal general who later reduced and governed all Tosa until 1599, had begun marching on Doi Castle to lay siege and capture it. Aki Kunitora gathered all his forces at Yanagare, which, though at some distance from the castle, was deemed the safest point to make the defense.

However, one of his men betrayed him. The traitor crossed Mt. Myoken secretly and told Chosogabe that if he would take such-and-such a route and attack the castle from behind, it would certainly fall into his hands. Chosogabe followed his advice and set fire to Doi Castle, taking advantage of Kunitora's absence.

When Aki Kunitora perceived that his castle was burning furiously, he realized that it was too late for him to recover his power. So he ordered two of his subjects to take his wife to the home of her birth, and he on his part committed suicide by *hara-kiri* in the yard of Jote-ji. This temple was just above my house, and stood about midway between Yanagare and Doi Castle.

The faithful subjects of Kunitora who had accompanied Aki's wife to her native house returned to find their dead lord at Jote-ji, and they too killed themselves by disembowelment. Now we can see three tombs at the yard of Jote-ji, standing side by side with the tomb of Kunitora in the center. Also there is an old, ruined well in the back yard in which Kunitora's subjects washed the bloody sword with which their lord had cut his stomach.

When peace came, Kunitora's wife visited Jote-ji to see her husband's tomb. On that occasion she secretly brought a small seedling of cedar in her sleeve and planted it in front of Kunitora's tomb. The cedar grew to be a huge big tree, and is called the Sleeve Cedar by the village people even today.

Near the remains of Doi Castle is a pond called the Noblewomen's Pond. Formerly this was a moat which surrounded the castle, and it was so named because all the noblewomen inside plunged into its waters when the army of Chosogabe assaulted and burned the castle. They say that sometimes you can hear the cries of the women from the pond and see the shadows of noblewomen in the dusk. It is prohibited, or rather regarded as despicable, to catch fish there, so you can see many fish swimming in the pond.

The offspring of the traitor now live in Kodai-ji, which is a mile from my house. In my elementary-school days, we called them "the savages of Kodai-ji" when we quarreled with them, and it was, so to speak, an unwritten law that they should not go to nor look at Jote-ji.

By the way, the ancestor of our family, Kawashima, was one of the fugitive warriors who came to Aki from the next country when his lord was defeated by Chosogabe. They settled at Ueno in Aki and began farming, as did most of the fugitive warriors when their lord was defeated.

RELICS OF BENKEI

Benkei is a legendary warrior of astounding strength who served the famous hero Yoshitsune on the side of the Minamoto clan against the Taira in the civil wars of the twelfth century. Joly writes, pp. 20–22, no. 74: "The son of a priest of Kumano, in Kii, he was of so boisterous a nature as to receive the nickname of Oniwaka (young demon); as such, he is depicted fighting with the Yamabushi, or capturing a huge fish in a waterfall. . . . He grew to a height of eight feet and was as strong as one hundred men; a stone is still shown in the gardens of the temple of Yoshino in which he is said to have driven two big iron nails." Anesaki gives the background of the Benkei and Yoshitsune legends, pp. 310–11, in his chapter "Heroic Stories," and plate no. 35 shows their celebrated encounter on the Gojo Bridge. A Noh drama, "Benkei on the Bridge," probably from the fifteenth century, also dealing with this episode in which the stripling conquered the giant soldier-monk, is trans-lated in Arthur Waley, The Nō Plays of Japan (New York, n.d.), pp. 115–20.

Text from Shimane-ken Kohi Densetsu Shu, Yatsuka-gun, p. 23.

THERE IS A HILL called Benkei-mori in Nagami, Honjo-mura, Yatsuka-gun. A small shrine formerly called Benkichi's Shrine, which is now in the precinct of Nagami Shrine, stands there. According to a document kept in the shrine, the woman named Benkichi was the daughter of a samurai in the province of Kii [now Wakayama-ken]. She was born on May 5, in the third year of Taiji [1129]. For some reason she came to Nagami in Honjo-mura in the third year of Kyuan [1147] and stayed there. After three years she met a *tengu* on a mountain path and conceived a child. In the thirteenth month she gave birth to Benkei.

When Benkei was seventeen years old his mother died. He enshrined her as the goddess Benkichi and left this place. These things are written in detail in Benkei's letter, which is said to have been presented to the shrine by Benkei. Near Benkei-mori there is a well. Tradition says that Benkei took his first bath at his birth with water from this well.

A small island called Benkei-jima is in the sea off the coast of Nohara in Honjo-mura. Trees grow thick on its mountain. According to tradition, Benkei was a very naughty boy and in his ninth year he was abandoned on this island. Benkei played the game of fox and geese with the *tengu*. While they were playing, the *tengu* taught Benkei many tactics. The stone base which they used for the game was later carried by boat to another place. But the boat was overthrown by a sudden storm and the stone base sank into the sea.

This island is connected to the mainland by a narrow sand path. It is said that Benkei made this path, by dropping little stones which he carried in his sleeves and skirt, for the purpose of escaping from the island. There is also the place called Benkei's Smithy at Shinjo in the same village, where Benkei is said to have had his sword forged.

BENKEI'S STONE MORTAR

Text from Shimane-ken Kohi Densetsu Shu, *Hikawa-gun, p. 52.*

ON THE BORDER of Kamiyokan and Yao in Yokan-mura there is a place called Ishiusu [Stone Mortar]. There are two big stones there, each in the shape of a mortar. It is not known how long they have been there, but tradition says that when Benkei went to exchange the bell of Wanibuchi Temple for that of Taisen Temple in Hoki Province, he brought them down to this place. Each stone weighs almost sixty pounds. Men who boast of their strength have tried to place one on top of the other, but no one has succeeded.

THE FAMOUS HORSE IKEZUKI

In heroic saga, ballad, romance, and epic, the warrior-hero is customarily accompanied by a horse and dog of matchless powers, whose attainments add to his fame. The steed Ikezuki has achieved legendary renown in his own right. Eiichiro Ishida

in his study of "The Kappa Legend" (Folklore Studies, IX, 1950, pp. 1–152),
refers to various traditions about Ikezuki to show their close connection with rivers
and marshes and dragons who cover mares. He writes: "The legend of the kappa
trying to lure horses into the water, and the idea of setting up pastures by the water-
side so that dragons or water-gods might breed with mares, and the superstition that
famous horses have appeared either out of the water, or some place near the water,
may all be considered to . . . form a part of a common folklore" (p. 3).

 Text from Shimane-ken Kohi Densetsu Shu, *Yuchi-gun, pp. 5–6.*

THE JISHO ERA [1177–81] marked the high point of the horse fair of
Asuma. Horse-dealers from various regions gathered to attend the
fair. Numerous shows and performances were put on, and the people
thronged to see them.

 In that time the famous horse Ikezuki was born near Ryuzu Waterfall in Matsukasa-mura, Iishi-gun. While a young colt, he lost his
mother. Longing for his dead mother, he walked by the basin of the
waterfall and saw his reflection in the water. He took this to be his
mother and jumped into the water to go to her. Of course it was
nothing but a vision, and the colt could not find his mother in the water.
So he came out and looked at the water's surface. There he saw his
mother again and jumped in once more. Almost every day he repeated
the same action. In this way he learned by himself how to swim.

 In the third year of Jisho [1179] Ikezuki was taken from this place
by a horse-dealer. When they came to Tsugahongo, the river was so
high owing to the melting snow that it seemed impossible to cross.

But when Ikezuki saw many horses and cows coming in a row toward Asuma fair, he did not hesitate any more, but jumped into the angry waves and swam straight to the other side. As soon as he got there, he neighed aloud and ran away toward the fair, passing Tsuganishi and Utsui. When he came running at a furious speed, all the people at the fair were frightened. A clever man among them was able to tie the horse to a tree. After a while Ikezuki's owner arrived. He wanted to sell the horse but no one dared buy such a spirited steed. So there was nothing for the horse-dealer to do but start home, taking the horse with him.

However, when they came to Nagata in Kuchiba-mura, he met a buyer. As the buyer showed six fingers, the dealer thought that he meant six hundred copper coins and they struck a bargain. But on payment the buyer handed him six hundred pieces of silver. The dealer was astonished and asked him why he paid so much money. The buyer answered that it was really a fine horse worth more than six hundred pieces of silver.

Just as he said, this horse was finally bought by the Shogun Yoritome in Kamakura.

THE FAITHFUL DOG OF TAMETOMO

A similar legend, elaborately told, is in Suzuki, pp. 80–85, "Kuro, the Faithful Dog," save that the hero ignores the dog's warning and is killed by a small snake which turns into a great monster. De Visser in "The Dog and the Cat in Japanese Superstition," pp. 23–24, recounts faithful-dog legends from the eighteenth century. The Welsh tale of "Llewellyn and His Dog" (Motif B331.2), famous in Western tradition and known in India with the mongoose replacing the dog, differs from the Japanese form in that the loyal animal kills a snake threatening its master's child and is then slain by its master when he sees it smeared with blood.

Tametomo is a celebrated hero, uncle of the still more celebrated Yoshitsune, who fought a losing struggle with the Minamoto clan against the Tairas in the civil war of 1157–59. He was a renowned archer and sank a ship with his bow. Anesaki discusses the legends of Tametomo, pp. 307–9.

Text from Bungo Densetsu Shu, pp. 88–89. Collected by Toshiko Iwao.

AKAIWA IS SITUATED between Mt. Kibaru and Mt. Miyake, astride an important road which since olden times has connected Kuchizuna and Takeda.

The ancient hero Minamoto Tametomo, an heir of the Genji clan who lived in the twelfth century, displayed from early childhood the marks of an unusually strong and violent disposition. His father Tame-yoshi worried about him and decided to send the youth to the province of Bungo, with a samurai servant named Hatano Jiro, and entrust him to the care of the Ogata family who lived there. The master and the servant set out on their journey with a pet dog and eventually reached Bungo. They traversed mountains and fields and came to Akaiwa Pass. The view from that point was so beautiful that they decided to rest under a big pine tree and admire it the longer. Tametomo was entirely charmed with the splendid scenery all about.

Then the dog, which had been squatting down quietly beside Tame-tomo, suddenly burst out barking and sprang violently at Tametomo. Rough and quick-tempered, Tametomo impulsively unsheathed the sword he wore at his waist and in a moment cut off the dog's head. But it did not drop to the ground. Instead, it flew up into the pine tree and bit the throat of a big snake glaring down at them with fierce mien from the tree. The unexpected attack of the dog's head gave the snake a mortal injury. Writhing in agony, it breathed its last and fell down to the ground as the great tree itself toppled and fell.

The master and the servant were dumfounded at this event. When they had recovered, they looked at each other sorrowfully. Tametomo regretted the imprudence that had led him to kill his faithful dog. They buried the dog's corpse carefully and left there in mourning.

BANJI AND MANJI

This is a version of the legend quoted from Yanagita, ch. 4, in the headnote to ''The Hunters Turned to Rats.'' It crosses with a popular Japanese theme of rivalry be-tween mountain deities; Ichiro Kurata gives variants from different parts of Japan, told on specific mountains, in ''Yama-No-Kami (Mountain Deities),'' Contem-

porary Japan, *X* (September, 1941), pp. 1304–12. *Where in one form, as the present, the hunter who befriends the mountain spirit prospers and the unfriendly hunter suffers, in reverse a hospitable mountain goddess is rewarded and a surly one punished; hence Mt. Fuji has snow while Mt. Tsukuba remains vernal. As Mock Joya writes, IV, p. 2: "Kami-sama is almighty, but there are many tales of mere humans helping and saving kami (gods). The story of Banzaburo of Nikko is one of the most widely known of such stories" ("Banzaburo of Nikko," pp. 2–3. Banzaburo and Banji are interchangeable).*

Text from Toö Ibun, pp. 54–55.

IN THE MOUNTAIN VILLAGE called Oide in Tsukumoushi-mura, Hei-gun, there were two hunters named Manji and Banji. Manji was a skillful hunter and shot much game. On the other hand, Banji was often without a single deer even though he tramped around the mountains all day. One day when Manji went to the mountains hunting, he met a beautiful woman suffering in labor. As he passed by, she asked him for his help. But he went on, refusing to aid her because the hunters held severe taboos against childbirth. Some time after that Banji came along. When he was asked for help by the woman, he was willing to assist and take care of her. The woman gave birth to twelve babies. She was very glad and thanked Banji, promising to give him the blessings of the mountain. She said: "If you call out your name 'Banji,' you will have good luck in the mountains hereafter."

From that time on Banji shot much game every day. To commemorate the bounty of the mountain goddess, he observed a holiday on the twelfth of every month. Later the hunters came to observe a holiday only on the twelfth of December. On that day not only the hunters

but the farmers in general do not go into the mountain. For they say if they do, they will meet some evil.

That woman was really the mountain goddess. When a hunter shouts "Banji, Banji, Banji," he will have good luck, and if he wishes to curse another hunter he shouts "Manji, Manji, Manji." Then that man's bullet will not hit any animals.

This is because Manji was cursed by the goddess and deprived of luck in the mountain.

NUE THE HUNTER OF HATOYA

The world of difference between two cultures can be seen in comparing the mountain hunter Nue with American frontier heroes like backwoodsman Davy Crockett or mountain-man Kit Carson. The American legends are naturalistic and humorous-exaggerative; the Japanese are supernatural-magical. The animals that Nue hunts turn out to be demons or genii, and the mountain itself is a zone of occult mysteries fraught with taboos. The motifs in the first and third episodes below, "Magic charm catches fish," and "Magic treasure ball catches game," do not appear as such in the Motif-Index, but could be placed under Motif S1327, "Magic object locates fish (game)." The main motif of the second episode, D1385.4, "Silver bullet protects against giants, ghosts, and witches" (a gold bullet here), is widely known in Europe and the United States.

Text from Toö Ibun, pp. 151–56.

Note: Saru-no-futtachi, a kind of legendary monkey resembling a human being. He likes women and often steals them from villages. He varnishes himself with resin and sand, so that his fur is as hard as iron and a bullet cannot penetrate it. (Kunio Yanagita, Tono Monogatari, new ed., Tokyo, 1948, p. 26, from a statement by the present storyteller, Kizen Sasaki.) This creature seems to be known only in Iwate-ken.

A LONG TIME AGO a skillful hunter called Nue lived at Hatoya in Kamigo-mura. He had an only daughter. One day as she was weaving by the window, she stopped moving the shuttle and began muttering and laughing to herself. When Nue saw that, he wondered what was caus-ing the girl to behave so. Looking around carefully, he spied a little snake clinging to the window. Whenever the snake shook its tail the girl laughed and murmured. Nue realized that the snake was tempting the girl to do these things, so he shot it with his gun and threw the dead snake into the stream that flowed in front of his house.

The next year when the season for the melting of snow came, a great many strange small fish gathered in the stream. Nue had never seen such fish before. He caught them, uttering the charm which had been handed down from his ancestors, and stirred them with grass sticks. Then the fish all turned into small snakes. At this Nue became fearful and took all the snakes to the field near his house and threw them away. When summer came, a strange grass grew thickly and luxuriantly there, and the cows and horses that ate the grass all died.

2. Once Nue went to the mountain on a huntiug trip and decided to stay overnight. Suddenly a light shone from a big tree nearby, and he saw a woman spinning at a spinning-wheel. Guessing she must be a fox or a badger, he fired at her, but the woman only laughed and would not go away. Nue shot again and again, but the woman kept on laughing. He gave up shooting and went home that night.

Next morning when he told his father about the woman of the previous night, his father said: "Such a creature cannot be shot to death by an ordinary iron bullet in the ordinary way. If the bullet is covered with mugwort and iris grass such as are used at the May Festival, and if the gun barrel is stuffed with grass or the leaves of trees, the bullet will hit such an enchanted creature. But if the creature still suffers no harm, then a gold bullet must be used to kill it."

In addition to these instructions, his father taught Nue many other hunting secrets. Nue went to the mountain again that night. Again he saw the same light coming from the big tree and the same woman with the spinning-wheel. He fired the bullet covered with the mugwort and iris grass used at the May Festival, but the woman only laughed at him in the same teasing manner. He thought there was no recourse but to use the precious gold bullet. He stuffed it into his gun and fired it straight at the woman. With a shriek the woman and the light were gone in a trice.

When day broke Nue followed the blood drops on the ground until they led to a strange dead creature in a rock cave. He carried the creature back to his home. When his father saw it he said that it was a so-called *saru-no-futtachi*. Nue presented its fur to the feudal lord and was rewarded and given the name Nue by the lord.

3. One day Nue was hunting near the swamp of Fukasawa on Mt. Kataha. He shot and killed a big white deer. When he skinned one side of the deer, the skin continued to stick to the carcass of its own accord; and when he skinned the other side, the skin stuck to the carcass again, and the deer was restored to life. As soon as it came to life it ran away. Nue pursued the deer to the mountain peak where now stands the shrine of Shisuke Gongen. There the deer was finally destroyed. One of the deer's eyeballs proved to be a magic treasure ball. At the moment that Nue seized this ball in his hand, a gray horse appeared before him. He mounted the steed and rode back home. When he dismounted from the horse it ran away back to the mountain.

Thereafter, everything came to pass as Nue wished on his hunting expeditions. The magic ball was handed down from generation to generation as a precious treasure of his house. But on the occasion of the fire in 1916 that consumed the ancestral home, the ball vanished from sight, and in consequence the house of Nue has not enjoyed such good fortune as was its wont in the past.

So say the villagers.

THE STRONGEST WRESTLER IN JAPAN

Joly explains one theme that enters this legend, in connection with an ubume, *the spirit of a woman who has died in pregnancy and cannot rest in the underworld; she travels about with her baby in her arms begging a passerby to hold it; when he does so, the baby becomes heavy as lead and (unlike the present tradition) drops to the ground in the form of a boulder (pp. 32–33, "Ubume," and p. 16, "Bakemono"). Two versions, in which the holder of the baby is rewarded with great strength, are in Yanagita-Mayer,* Japanese Folk Tales, *pp. 245–47, no. 83, "The Strong Man and the Woman in Travail." The idea expressed there is that the baby's weight is*

171

equivalent to the pains of childbirth; the woman with the baby is a mountain deity, and the prayer of the samurai holding the heavy baby enabled her to assure its birth. The same volume has a series of tales about strong men, strong women, and wrestlers, pp. 245–61, nos. 83–89.

Text from Toö Ibun, pp. 133–38.

THERE WAS a wrestler named Yokoguruma Daihachi who was born in Gojonome-machi in Minami Akita-gun. According to the local tradition, this man was the strongest wrestler in Japan, but as he was born in a poor family, he took service in a certain rich house in the vicinity. One day he was ordered by his master to carry the rice to be paid as land tax to the lord in the town of Akita. He started off pulling a cart full of rice, and when he came to the slope near the castle he felt too tired to go any further. He stood in the middle of the slope holding the shafts, pale-faced, sweating, and out of breath.

A little child had been walking along the path beside the cart. When he saw Daihachi stand still in the middle of the road, he mocked him: "What a weak fellow you are!" Daihachi was angered. "You naughty boy! If you say such a thing, pull this cart yourself."

The boy said: "I can pull ten such carts at a time. I will show you how." And putting his little finger on the shaft, he pulled the cart up the slope as if it were completely empty. Taken by surprise, Daihachi thought this was no ordinary child and politely asked him his name.

Then the boy said: "Listen to me, Daihachi. Because you are proud of your strength you always go in the wrestling matches at festival time. But you must not be satisfied with such a small accomplishment. If you want really great strength, come secretly at night to Mt. Taihei where I am." At those words Daihachi knew that the boy was actually the famous deity Sankichi. And he threw himself at the feet of the child, who forthwith disappeared.

Subsequently Daihachi went to Mt. Taihei at midnight and stayed in the Sankichi Shrine for seven days and nights, praying to the god. But no sign of the god appeared to him. On the seventh night when he began to feel doubts and was unable to stand the piercing cold, he saw a young woman with a baby at her bosom come to the front of

the shrine and worship earnestly. Daihachi watched her, wondering how and why she came there on such a cold night. The woman stood up and asked him to hold the baby for a while. Daihachi willingly received the baby. The woman went away somewhere and did not soon return. While Daihachi was holding the baby in his arms, strangely the baby grew heavier and heavier. Finally, as it became too heavy to hold, Daihachi supported it on his knees. Then he felt as if his knees were broken. But Daihachi endured the pain with all his might. His face reddened all over, sweat ran down his forehead, and he clenched his teeth grimly. He tried with all his strength not to be overwhelmed by the baby, but at last he could no longer bear the pressure.

At that moment the woman came back and thanked him, saying: "I am sorry to have kept you waiting for such a long time." She took the baby effortlessly from Daihachi and stood up straight before him. Suddenly a bright light issued from the bodies of the mother and child and shone all around. Amid the brilliance of the light she announced aloud: "Daihachi, listen to me. I am the highest protecting god of this region, Sankichi Daimyojin. You have well endured the trial of holding this baby. I will give you strength to do that. It will be boundless strength."

Daihachi impulsively threw himself at the feet of the god and gave thanks to her. When he looked up to see her again, her figure had vanished. The next morning when Daihachi stepped out of the shrine onto the bare ground, his feet sank into the earth from the weight of his strength.

Afterwards, he came up to Edo and became the strongest wrestler of that time.

THE MIGHTY WRESTLER USODAGAWA

A close text is in Yanagita-Mayer, Japanese Folk Tales, pp. 260–61, no. 89, "The Wrestler from Awa and the Wrestler of Kumano." Their preceding tale, no. 88, p. 259, also deals with a strong man, "Fujinuki Kinai," who points out his own

home to a samurai seeking a contest with Kinai by raising up a Chinese plow and
horse. Discouraged at this strength in a mere servant of Kinai, as he thinks, the
samurai hastily leaves. This strong-man motif is universal, and I have heard it from
American college students who say that Minnesota's football coach would recruit
husky farm lads who pointed directions by lifting a plow. In the present tradition the
mother of the strong man overawes the challenger by lifting a great weight. Pertinent
motifs are F617, "Mighty wrestler," reported only from Africa, and F631, "Strong
man carries giant load."

Text from Muro Kohi Shu, *pp. 54–55.*

ON THE PASS which leads to Tagawa in Inari-mura there lived long ago
a wrestler called Usodagawa. His strength was immeasurable, and
he was said to be the strongest man in Japan. In those days there was
also a strong wrestler at Awa in Shikoku. No one in the neighboring
districts could equal him in strength. That man came to visit Usodagawa to have a match with him and to gain for himself the reputation
of being the strongest man in Japan. When he arrived, Usodagawa was
away from home gathering firewood, and his mother met the wrestler
from Awa. She carried a big brazier in one hand, and she told him to
wait for her son to come back from the mountain. She said that she
would be able to tell when her son was returning because he would
be carrying a heap of firewood on his back and it would cut off the
sunlight. The wrestler from Awa tried to move the brazier which the
old woman had held with one hand, but it was too heavy for him to
move. In a short time it became dark and Usodagawa appeared with
a heap of wood on his back.

The wrestler from Awa thought it was beyond his power to defeat
him. But as he had come on purpose to have a match with Usodagawa,
he agreed to wrestle him on the bank of the river called Egawa in
Tanabe-machi. The wrestler from Awa put on a very thick loincloth,
and Usodagawa crushed a bamboo stick and used it as his waistband.
Usodagawa grasped the wrestler from Awa with his hands and, lifting
him on high, asked: "Heaven or earth?" The wrestler from Awa answered: "Earth." And he was thrown down into the sand.

The wrestler from Awa went back to his country, but before going
he secretly prayed to the shrine in Tanabe at night that there might

never be another strong wrestler like Usodagawa in Tanabe. He presented a couple of stone lanterns to the shrine.

Those lanterns are still at the shrine.

NASU KOZAHARA THE STRONG MAN

While local legends like the present embodying Motifs F632, "Mighty eater," and F624.2, "Strong man lifts large stone," are universal, the Japanese form characteristically associates the strong man with a god. In chapter 24 on "Figures Prominent in Oral Tradition," in Yanagita, Mountain Village Life, *the statement is made that most villages investigated had legends of strong men and heavy eaters.*

Text from Bungo Densetsu Shu, *pp. 24–25. Told by Shika Hori.*

LONG AGO there lived a man named Nasu Kozahara at Fuchi, Shonai-mura, Oita-gun. He was a very strong man and his name was known to all the villagers. They said of him that he must be possessed by a god.

Once there was a trial opened in the town of Hida. Nasu Kozahara had to go to stay there for seven days. In the morning before he set out for Hida, he ate all the rice cooked in a big pot and crammed himself with food for seven days all at one time. Having done so, he spent seven days without eating anything. Such was his marvelous capacity.

On another occasion he needed a stone and went out to look for a suitable one. He found a stone about two feet wide and four yards long which filled his need. He picked up another stone one and a half feet square which lay by the big stone, and put it in his sleeve. Then he easily lifted the big stone in his arms and set out for his home. The landowner, who saw him carrying the stone away, grew very angry and ran after him. Nasu Kozahara ran away as fast as he could, carrying the big stone in his arms. He ran on and on almost four miles, when he became a little tired. So he threw away the big stone. It still remains standing erect in the same position it landed in when it was thrown away. The smaller stone which he put in his sleeve was used as the tombstone for Nasu himself.

A RICH peasant is called a choja *and a story about such a person is a* chojatan. *The general theme of such stories concerns an impoverished rice farmer's rise to riches or the decline in fortune of an arrogant wealthy villager. In a society where an insurmountable boundary divided the warrior-samurai from the peasant class, we might expect such wish-fulfillment tales of sudden shifts in status. There is, however, another, Buddhistic element here, the conception of change in the stream of life, from high station to low and from low to high, a conception to humble the lofty and reprove the fainthearted. The Buddhist terms for this idea are* mujo *(impermanence) and* ruten *(transmigration). A curious but close relationship links* chojatan *to Buddhism. Buddhist monks compiled folk tales, especially* choja *legends connected with blacksmiths or charcoal makers; the most famous* chojatan *deals with a charcoal maker who became wealthy. Before charcoal was used in braziers for heating, blacksmiths were the principal utilizers of charcoal, and in their work frequently moved from one isolated mountain village to another, as did the monks. These blacksmiths were carriers of tales, which they transmitted from generation to generation, and transported from village to village. They were much influenced by popular Buddhism, sometimes fashioning bronze Buddhist statues and even becoming lower-class Buddhist priests. In mountain districts where monk and charcoal maker met, nature also contributed to* chojatan, *with natural formations in the rocks readily interpreted as the remains of houses of legendary* choja. *And yet, while the* choja *is a particularly Japanese figure, familiar European tales turn up as* chojatan, *for dreams and envy of riches are universal.*

178

THE CHARCOAL BURNER WHO BECAME A CHOJA

This is an oft-told legend localized in different prefectures to which the noble lady from Kyoto travels in obedience to a dream, oracle, or fortuneteller. Variants are in Murai, pp. 15–17, "Kaneuri Kichiji"; Suzuki, pp. 24–26, "Kichiji, the Charcoal Burner"; Yanagita-Mayer, Japanese Folk Tales, pp. 143–45, no. 48, "Kogoro, the Charcoal Maker." Sometimes this tale is combined with another which tells of the origin of the hearth deity. In his study of the legend Professor Yanagita thought it connected with the guild of foot-bellows workers and their belief in the god Hachiman.

Text from Tosa no Densetsu, II, pp. 1–7.

Note: Hatsu-uma, an annual festival honoring Inari, the god of vegetables and grains.

IF YOU GO about eight miles up the Kamo River as it runs through Ushirogawa Village (now included in the city of Nakamura), situated in the northeast part of the township of Nakamura in Hata-gun, you will find about a hundred farmhouses scattered here and there in deep valleys and mountains. These houses form the two lonely villages of Naka Kamogawa and Oku Kamogawa. Some of the villagers there still believe that their ancestor was that noted strong man, Asahina Yoshide Saburo, who rang the Unringable Bell of Shitenno Temple in Osaka for seven days and nights; and there are still many families whose surname is Asahina.

If you cross the stream at a neat elementary school which stands in the valley of Naka Kamogawa and climb a mountain path about a mile beyond, you will find the small shrine named Tokiwa. This is known throughout Hata-gun as Sumi-no-kura-sama [Charcoal Treasury Shrine]. It stands on a hillside which commands the view of lofty Mt.

Shiraishi beyond a deep valley to the north. On the festival day of Hatsu-uma in February of the old calendar several thousand people from not only Nakamura but from Shimoda, Irino, and far western Sukumo come to worship at this shrine. If they take home with them pieces of charcoal from the precinct of the shrine and from a rock cave behind it, and offer them on their household altars, good luck will attend them, so they say. Concerning the origin of this belief the following legend is still told.

Once upon a time there lived deep within these mountains a charcoal burner, Matajuro. He was so poor that no one would come to marry him. He lived a lonely life on the mountain, burning charcoal and taking it to the faraway harbor of Shimoda to sell, and so sustained himself from hand to mouth.

At this time, there was a famous *choja* in Kyoto who had a beautiful daughter named Ofuji. Her parents were worried because there had been no talk of marriage for her, although she had come of age. They could not tell the reason why she had no opportunity to marry. One day they consulted a fortuneteller, and he told them that it had been decided in her previous existence that a charcoal burner named Mata-

juro who lived deep in the mountains of Kamogawa in Hata in Tosa should become her husband.

So Ofuji was persuaded by her parents to make a trip all by herself over sea and mountain from Kyoto to the recesses of Mt. Shiraishi. She arrived at a place called Deai [Encounter], a lonely spot where no one was likely to pass by. Then there came along a man, blackened with charcoal dust from tip to toe, carrying on his shoulder a straw bag filled with charcoal. Ofuji was so glad to see anybody that she asked him if he knew the charcoal burner Matajuro of Kamogawa. To her great surprise, he answered that he was that very Matajuro and that he was going down to the harbor of Shimoda to sell the bag of charcoal. Ofuji told him the reason behind her long trip from Kyoto and asked Matajuro to take her as his wife. Matajuro was quite embarrassed at her sudden request and refused it, since he had no place to lodge such a beautiful lady. However, Ofuji's determination was firm and she insisted. At last Matajuro yielded and led her to his cottage in the mountain. When they reached it, Ofuji found that the poverty in which he lived was almost beyond description.

As soon as they got to Matajuro's cottage, Ofuji took two gold

coins out of the money she had brought from home and asked Matajuro to buy things with these coins at the town of Nakamura. Matajuro was seeing coins for the first time in his life, so he did not know how precious they were.

When he came to Kamoda at the lower village, Iwata, he saw a wild duck playing in the rice field. He wanted to catch it, and threw one of his coins at the bird in lieu of a stone. The coin did not hit the bird but making a curve in the air, dropped into the swamp. Matajuro took the other coin with him down to the town of Nakamura and tried to buy many things just for trial. The shopkeepers there sold him goods with unexpected pleasure.

Shortly after Matajuro returned home to the mountain, he told his wife how he had cast away one of the coins into the swamp. Ofuji was amazed at this story, and told him that such a gold piece was a precious treasure and that the people of the world would toil greatly to get just one such. Then Matajuro said that there were plenty of such things behind the cottage where he made charcoal and that ashes produced by burning were just like these gold pieces. So Ofuji and Matajuro together went to the place where he had made charcoal, and found, as Matajuro had said, that all the heaps of ashes there were glittering with gold.

From that day forward, the two burned almost daily the *ko* trees which grew in the mountain. They packed the gold thus produced in the charcoal bags under the disguise of charcoal and kept sending them to Ofuji's parents in Kyoto, who were greatly astonished. Before long, this couple went to Kyoto and became millionaires by the name of Konoike. Later, the village people in Naka Kamogawa built a shrine on the former site of the charcoal furnace.

This is commonly known among the local people as the Charcoal Treasury Shrine.

Also, they say that the place now called Deai in this village was named for the meeting there between Matajuro and Ofuji. The place-name "Wakafuji" [Young Ofuji] originated from the feeling of renewed youth in Matajuro when he made his decision to take Ofuji with him to his cottage in the mountain. And the reason for the ashes around the charcoal furnace changing into gold is explained on the ground that since he kept burning *ko* trees for three years, the smoke went up to heaven, from where gold poured down in heaps to the earth.

The villagers also say that if you keep burning *ko* trees for three years, you will become a millionaire.

ASAHI CHOJA

Two traditions of retribution on rich landowners who stop the sun so they can finish their rice planting in one day are in Mock Joya, IV, pp. 40–41, "Stopping the Sun," and in Yanagita-Mayer, Japanese Folk Tales, pp. 150–52, no. 52, "Koyama Lake." None has the ending of the first text below. The folk-Biblical legend of Joshua stopping the sun and the moon for thirty hours to enable the Israelites to defeat the Canaanites is in Joseph Gaer, The Lore of the Old Testament (Boston, 1951), pp. 191–93, "The Longest Day in the World."

The second text gives an entirely independent account of the decline of the same choja, involving Motif C55.2, "Tabu: shooting at consecrated water."

Texts from Bungo Densetsu Shu, pp. 115–16. The first was collected by Tomi Ninomiya and the second by Hiroko Yoshimura, both in Kuzu-gun, Iida-mura.

Note: Cho, 2.45 acre.

1. A LONG TIME AGO Asahi *Choja* lived at Sencho-muden. He had three pretty daughters whom he loved very much. This *choja* owned a thousand-*cho* rice field behind and a thousand-*cho* rice field in front.

One year, during the reign of Emperor Keiko, little rain fell when the season of rice planting came round. The rice fields dried up and the people were not able to plant rice. So the *choja* prayed for rain to the dragon god of the old pond at Takatsuhara in Asono-mura, making a promise that he would give one of his daughters to the god if the god would grant his request. Thereupon the rice fields became wet and the people commenced the work of rice planting.

While they were so engaged, a monkey trainer passed along the nearby road. The people stopped planting for a while to look at the monkey trainer's show. So they were not able to finish planting before sunset. Therefore the *choja* took his fan and beckoned the setting sun to come back again. And the sun indeed reascended, and the people were able to finish planting their rice that day. The *choja* was satisfied. "Well, that is very nice," he said.

Then, however, the *choja* remembered his promise to the dragon god. He asked his eldest daughter if she was willing to become the wife of the dragon god, but the eldest daughter refused. The *choja* asked the second daughter, but she also refused. Finally the third daughter answered that she would go to the dragon god if one condition was fulfilled. The condition was that she be placed inside seven wooden tubs. The villagers did as she desired and carried her in the sevenfold tubs to the old pond, from where she was to be taken away by the dragon god during the night. After they left her, she began to recite the sutras with all her heart.

When the day broke, the villagers returned to the pond. They found the girl alive in a tub. She was weeping but safe, perhaps because she

had recited the sutras. The six outside tubs and all but one ring of the seventh tub were broken.

For this reason the ring at the bottom of a tub has ever since been called a *nakiwa* or weeping ring.

When harvest time came, all the rice plants of the *choja's* rice fields were changed into rushes.

2. This *choja* in his best days indulged in luxury. Disdainfully he shot an arrow at the *mochi* given as an offering to the god at New Year's time. The moment the arrow hit the *mochi*, it turned into a white bird and flew away. From that time on the *choja's* fortune steadily dwindled. His rice field, which extended over more than a thousand *cho*, came to produce little or no crop.

Today there remains a shrine dedicated to the white bird and a mound where the bird was buried on the place called Asahi Yashiki [Asahi Estate]. They say a plum tree there bears strange blossoms.

SANYA CHOJA

This legend embodies Motif N531.3, "Dream of treasure bought. Treasure has been seen by man's absent soul in sleep in form of a fly. The purchaser of the dream finds the treasure." Three variations on this theme, all chojatan, are in Yanagita-Mayer, Japanese Folk Tales, nos. 44–46, pp. 129–34, in which a bee, horseflies, and a dragonfly are seen hovering by the sleeper's mouth. Ikeda assigns Type 840A, "A Bee Creeps Out of a Man's Nostril," to her analysis of eighteen Japanese versions (pp. 228–29).

Text from Bungo Densetsu Shu, pp. 12–13. Told by Yasue Sonoda.

LONG AGO there was a peddler called Sanya-no-suke at Hagiwara. He sold ginger and sieves in the district around Takeda. One day he went peddling with a friend, and on their way back they took a rest by the side of Mt. Toroku. The friend fell into a comfortable sleep. Sanya cast a casual glance at him, and just at that moment a mountain-bee came flying up and entered the nose of the sleeping man. After a while it came out and again entered the nose. It repeated this several times.

Sanya shook his friend awake and asked him: "Didn't you feel something strange?"

"Well, a bee flew to me and told me to go to that mountain, because much gold is buried there; but I don't believe in such a dream," answered the friend.

So Sanya said: "Then, won't you sell me that dream?"

The friend consented. So Sanya gave him his ginger and sieves and bought the dream. He went to Mt. Toroku by himself and dug the ground at the place where he thought gold was buried, but he could not find it. Nevertheless, he continued digging very hard, forgetting any other work, so that at last he had to feed himself with only wheat which he managed to buy a little at a time.

At last his labor was rewarded. He found a gold vein. He soon prospered and became one of the richest men in the western part of Japan. He constructed a great mansion in the region now called Ebisu-machi and Manya-cho (in Oita-shi). To such extremes did he carry his love of luxury that he built a room with a glass ceiling in which fish lived and swam about. He entertained himself looking up at the fish.

Hineno Oribe-no-kami, the lord of that district, was often invited by Sanya Choja to his home and spent pleasant times with the *choja's* son. One day when they were together resting easily, the *choja's* son lifted up his leg and pointed with his toe to the goldfish in the ceiling. This act offended the lord, and as a result Sanya and his family and kinsmen were condemned to death. Sanya appealed to the lord saying: "We shall present you with so many coffers containing a thousand gold pieces each that they will make stepping-stones from my house to your castle, if you will pardon us from so cruel a punishment."

But the lord did not accept his plea.

THE CAMELLIA TREE OF TAMAYA

Many references are given to Motif Q272, "Avarice punished," which is central to the following legend.

Text from Densetsu no Echigo to Sado, *I, pp. 23–26.*

GEIHA IS one of the famous beauty spots in Echigo. Especially breathtaking is the view from Tonowa. Below the precipice is a fathomless pool called Zugai-ga-fuchi. According to tradition, there was land all around this place in olden times and the *choja* family called Tamaya lived there.

Tamaya was a merchant family hereditarily dealing in marine products. Tokubei, the head of the family, was an industrious man who worked hard from early in the morning till late at night and amassed much wealth. Many storehouses were built to hold his goods, and he acquired the reputation of being a *choja*. He married a wife as pretty as a flower, and she bore him a lovely child.

Although Tokubei lived in such comfort, yet he was sorely troubled about where to hide his gold and silver. One might say: "In the storehouse," but servants and maids would enter into the storehouse. There was no assurance against a thief's breaking in. Tokubei could not sleep soundly for worrying about the gold and silver which he had secured with such effort. After many sleepless nights he thought of a good plan. There was a bamboo thicket in the back of his house, and a camellia tree grew in that thicket. One dark night Tokubei dug in the ground under the camellia tree, by himself, and buried the box in which he had put his gold and silver. Nevertheless, his heart was not yet at peace. He constantly felt uneasy and in consequence was taken ill.

So Tokubei went with a servant to Matsuno-yama to take the baths. One day, after he had spent about a fortnight there, Tokubei, while in the bathroom, heard someone singing outside:

"The camellia tree of Tamaya at Geiha in Echigo,
The branches are silver and the leaves are gold."

This startled Tokubei. He wondered why in a place so far from his home there should be a person who knew the secret of his burying the gold and silver under the camellia tree. The servant said that the song was sung in admiration of Tamaya's prosperity. But those words did not dispel the fear from Tokubei's mind. He immediately got into a sedan chair and traveled back to Geiha. As soon as he reached his home, he rushed to see the camellia tree in the bamboo thicket. To his astonishment the tree was glittering, with its branches turned to silver and its leaves turned to gold. Tokubei fell into a swoon on the spot.

Through the care of neighbors he came to, but his health was never restored. When his end drew near he told his wife for the first time all about his secret. After his death his wife went out to the bamboo thicket. However, she found the camellia tree appearing as it always had, and she discovered nothing beneath the tree.

THE GOLD OX

The idea of one survivor's being left to tell the story is in De Visser, The Dragon in China and Japan, *p. 195, in an entirely different legend, about a dragon whose curse killed every person in a clan except one blind minstrel.*

Text from Toö Ibun, pp. 20–22.

A CHOJA ONCE LIVED at Otomo-mura in the Tono district of the province of Rikuchu [now Kamihei-gun, Iwate-ken]. A servant in the *choja's* house was a queer fellow. All the year round, during his leisure time, he used to go into the mountains with a spade and dig up the ground here and there to get wild potatoes. People called him a fool. However, one year on New Year's Eve he finally struck a gold deposit in the valley called Hiishi in Otomo-mura. He took a piece of gold to his house and put it in the *tokonoma*. It shone outside through the broken door. So the servant became a rich man like his master and was respected by the people as Komatsu-dono or Komatsu *choja*.

Komatsu-dono directed his workers to dig further along the gold vein, and in the third year, again on the day before New Year's, they struck the main deposits, which lay in the shape of an ox. Komatsu-dono immediately held a great feast outside the pit and spent the night in entertainment. When the New Year's morning sun arose, he performed a ceremony to celebrate the discovery of the main gold deposits. Then he made all the workers pull a brocade rope tied to a horn of the gold ox. With shouts they pulled on the rope, and the horn of the ox broke off with a snap. So they tied the rope around the neck and pulled it, whereupon the ox seemed to move two or three steps ahead; but all at once the pit fell in, killing all seventy-five men.

On that occasion a man in charge of the cooking (whose job it also was to tell the time), who was called Usotoki (False Time) or Osotoki, (Late Time), was also in the pit, having been ordered to help the miners pull the rope. Hearing a call, he let go his hold on the rope and ran out of the pit, but found no one there. Thinking he mistook the voice, he went back into the pit. Then he heard the voice again, and a third time the voice sounded so sharp and urgent that he ran out instantly. The moment he stepped outside the pit it fell in. Therefore Usotoki was the only one who survived the calamity.

People say that this man was very honest, and never served the food before the exact prescribed time. So the workmen ridiculed him by giving him the name False Time.

THE POOR FARMER AND THE RICH FARMER

The popular Motif K1811.1, "Gods (spirits) disguised as beggars. Test hospitality,"
which appeared on pp. 33–36, recurs here, in conjunction with a common theme of
Japanese fictional folk tales, the good old man and bad old man who are neighbors.
This and the next two tales show the close line between fictional and legendary
traditions. The same story can appear in both forms.
Text from Ina no Densetsu, pp. 235–37.

LONG AGO in Yamamoto-mura, a rich farmer and a poor farmer lived
next door to each other. One evening a poor dirty-looking bonze came
along and asked for a night's lodging at the rich man's house. The greedy
old man, on seeing the shabby appearance of the bonze, refused his
request with harsh words. The poor bonze was obliged to go next
door and make the same request. The poor old man of that house readily
gave him a night's lodging, letting him sleep on his only pallet.

The next morning the bonze cordially thanked the old man, saying:
"I am really a Buddha who has come disguised as a poor man in order
to look into people's hearts in this world. I am very much impressed by
your kindheartedness. In appreciation for your goodness I will give
you a tree planted in front of your house. You may make anything you
wish from it."

As soon as the bonze finished these words he disappeared. Filled
with wonder, the old man stood still for a while, without doing anything. Then he beheld a tree rise out from the ground in front of his
house, just as the bonze had promised. It grew into a great tree before
his eyes. The old man cut it down and made a mortar and a pestle from
the wood. When he put rice into the mortar, one quart of rice became
two quarts, and when he pounded it, the two quarts of rice became
a gallon of *mochi*.

The greedy old man next door, observing this, borrowed the mortar
and pestle. He pounded his rice, expecting to get many times more
mochi than there was rice. But strange to say, one gallon of rice in the
mortar decreased to two quarts and two quarts of rice to one quart.
In his anger, the greedy old man broke the mortar into pieces and
threw the pestle away into the brushwood.

When he came to retrieve his mortar, the goodhearted poor man was very sorry to learn of this outcome. Sorrowfully, he collected the pieces of the mortar and made a moneybox from them. In it he dropped the small change from his daily earnings, gained by selling firewood. In the box that money changed into gold pieces, and before long the old man became wealthy.

When the greedy old man heard about this, he forced his neighbor to lend him the moneybox. He took it to his home and put all his money inside it, expecting to take out a heap of gold pieces. To his surprise, however, his money in the box melted into water and, running out as a river, it formed a pool.

So the Hako-gawa [Box River] and Hako-buchi [Box Pool], which still can be seen, gained their names from this story. The place where the greedy old man threw away the pestle is now called Kine-hara [Pestle Meadow].

THE GIRL WHO ATE A BABY

Hearn tells the same basic story as he heard it from Kinjuro, save that the girl who tests the suitors is daughter of a samurai instead of a choja, and the corpse is made not of mochi but of the confectionery kashi (VI, ch. 25, "Of Ghosts and Goblins," pp. 349–51). Motif H331.1.7, "Contest in reaping: best reaper to get beautiful girl as wife," known in Irish tradition, is present here. The suitor test of cannibalism, which also occurs, is not included in the Motif-Index.

Text from N. Hirano, "Folk Tales from Nanbu Province," in Mukashi-banashi Kenkyu, *II (Tokyo, 1937), 224–25.*

ONCE UPON A TIME three young men set out on a journey. They passed fields and mountains and traveled on and on until they came to the gate of a *choja's* house. There they saw a sign which announced that the *choja* wanted the most able youth in the country for the husband of his daughter.

"This is good news for us. Let's go in and apply," they said and went inside the gate.

The *choja* interviewed them. As they all looked like useful young men, he could not decide which one of the three was superior to the others. So he said to them: "I have a thousand-reap rice field to the east, a thousand-reap rice field to the west, and a thousand-reap rice field to the front. Each of you shall cultivate one of these fields. And I will see who is the best worker."

Each of the three men was determined to become the *choja's* son-in-law. They had rice cooked in a pot large enough to supply thirty men, and ate it all up. Then they began cultivating the rice fields to the east, to the west, and to the front. An ordinary man might have spent ten days cultivating one such field. These young men, however, each having two forked hoes in both hands, dug up the land so speedily that they finished the work easily in one day. All three returned from the fields at the same time.

"Well, I am extremely surprised at your work today. You three have the same ability. I cannot rank you. May I ask you to stay here for a while and serve us?" the *choja* said.

The young men willingly agreed to this proposal and stayed on as servants. Quite a few days passed. But to their disappointment, the daughter of the *choja* never appeared to them. They only caught glimpses of her back. So they became very eager to see the girl. One night two of the young men conferred together and then secretly stole into the interior of the house and peeped into the girl's room. There the girl, in white clothes with her hair loosened, had opened the floorboards at one corner. From underneath the floor, she was about to take out a box that looked like a coffin.

Frightened though the young men were, curiosity overcame their fear, and holding their breath, they watched the girl. With a grin on her face, the girl drew a baby's corpse from within the coffin and cut off its arms with a knife. Then she began eating an arm as if it were delicious food. She spoke to the young men, saying: "Will you have some?" And she thrust out toward them an arm dripping blood. The young men were astounded. Far from wishing to become the son-in-law, they could hardly bear to stay a moment longer in such a place, and they took to their heels that same night.

Now the third youth, who was making a fire in the cookstove, heard of this. He said to himself: "Well, I will look and see for myself." And he went to peep into the daughter's room. He saw a she-demon in white costume, with flowing hair, eating the blood-dripping head of a baby. At first glance he was frightened, but when he looked at her carefully, he saw not a demon nor a snake but a girl wearing a demon's mask and eating a doll made of *mochi*. What he had taken for blood was merely rouge. He thought that he could eat it himself.

So he said: "Young lady, please give me one of its legs." So saying he slid open the door and stretched out his hands.

When the girl heard this, she replied: "You have said just what I wanted to hear. Until now, many and many a young man has come here to be my husband. But at the sight of me they became frightened and fled. No one had courage enough to stay. You are the man to be my husband."

She took off the mask and the white garment and revealed herself as a surprisingly beautiful lady. The *choja* was much pleased. He invited all his relatives, acquaintances, and even servants to a great feast, on which occasion he announced the marriage of his daughter to the young man.

In due time a child was born to them. And their offspring prospered.

THE THIEF WHO TOOK THE MONEYBOX

This tale is a Japanese adaptation of a fiction which has traveled around the world, Type 1525 and Motif K301, "The Master Thief." A vast list of its appearances (but without mention of Japan) can be found in J. Bolte and G. Polívka, Anmer-kungen zu den Kinder u. Hausmärchen der Brüder Grimm (vol. III, Leipzig, 1918), "Der Meisterdieb," pp. 379–406. Ikeda, however, lists seventeen versions from Japan. I collected a long text from a Polish immigrant in northern Michigan (printed in Western Folklore, *VIII, 1949, pp. 39–47), which includes almost all the elements in the brief version below.*

Text from Shimabara Hanto Mukashi-banashi Shu, *pp. 116–17.*

Note: Hifuki-dake, *a hollow length of bamboo used for blowing a fire.*

ONCE UPON A TIME there was a *choja*. He had many boxes containing a thousand gold pieces each. Every night he slept with one box under his pillow. Often thieves tried to steal it, but no one could steal the box, because the door was kept locked and the other entrances were carefully guarded. There were two or three gates or entrances, but it was not easy to enter the house. The rich man gave notice that if there was anyone who could steal that box without being detected he would give it to him.

So some boastful thieves tried, but they were detected and caught before they got into the house. One day a man came to the *choja* and said that he would come to steal the box that night. The *choja* replied that if he could enter that room he would give him the box he was sleeping on. And the man went out.

All the people at the *choja's* house guarded the house more carefully than ever before. But the thief prepared three bowls of rice, one bundle of straw, twenty or thirty millet cakes, and string and fruit, and a wooden pillow. At midnight he came to the *choja's* house.

When he entered the first gate there came toward him an ox with his horns lowered. The thief threw him the bundle of straw, and the ox began to eat it. Then the thief passed through the second gate. Three huge dogs as big as calves came out barking, and he gave them three rice balls. Then the dogs began to eat. So he was able to enter the house without difficulty.

In the big room several menservants were sleeping. The thief stealthily tied their hair together. In the next room there were maidservants sleeping. He put the millet cakes up their buttocks. Then he went to the kitchen and put his flute into the *hifuki-dake*.

When the servants woke up, there was a great confusion. "Who's pulling my hair? Don't do that!" A maidservant said: "What's up my buttocks?" Another maid said: "There's something up my buttocks also." In the midst of this confusion the thief easily slipped into the *choja's* room.

The *choja* heard the noise and raised his head. That gave the thief a chance to exchange his wooden pillow for the *choja's* moneybox.

By this time the servants realized that the thief had gotten into the house, and they tried to start the fire by blowing it with the *hifuki-dake*. But when they blew on it, the flute that the thief had hidden inside made a strange noise. In the confusion the thief was able to escape.

He lived very comfortably the rest of his life.

PART SEVEN

KNAVES

FROM INDIA to America tales are told of simple countrymen who make fools of themselves when they come to town, but develop into rustic rogues and outfox their sophisticated tormentors. These stock characters enjoy considerable popularity in Japan and are reported in more than a dozen prefectures under varying names. In Oita-ken the jester is known as Kichigo or Kichiemon, while in neighboring Miyazaki-ken he is called Kitchomu. People in Oita-ken say that he was the son of a village headman and that his descendants are fuel dealers in Tokyo. The famous sculptor Jitsuzo Kinako thought himself connected with Kichiemon's family. Still, there is no firm proof of the existence of Kitchomu or his sundry aliases, and similar sayings and escapades are attributed to each knave. Kunio Yanagita organized a Kitchomu Society in the 1920's to preserve and study the legends of Kichiemon. A newspaperman in Tokyo, Sempo Nakata, collected one hundred Kitchomu banashi from the society and through the columns of his newspaper, since many former residents of Oita-ken had moved to Tokyo. This was thought to be about two-thirds of the total number of stories in the cycle. Subsequently he discovered a number of the same jests in jokebooks of the Tokugawa period (1600–1867). The fact is that witty rogues and villages of fools belong to a common body of Indo-European humorous stories. These take the form of legends when they fasten onto a likely scapegoat in a given community, whether up in the Himalayas or off on the Emerald Isle.

THE ORIGIN OF FOOLISH SAJIYA TALES

This tradition is related to that of "The Heike Refugees" (see pp. 160–61). Ikeda refers (p. 269, n. 1) to several villages of fools—Sajiya, Noma, Akiyama.

Text from Hajime Ueda, Impaku Mintan, I (March, 1936), p. 142. Collected in Saji-mura, Yazu-gun, Tottori-ken.

LONG, LONG AGO the Heike, who were defeated by the Genji, fled to the Sanin district. The Genji warriors pursued them hotly. The refugees of Heike went into the mountains to hide themselves from the Genji warriors. So some of them took refuge in lonely places in the mountain, such as Sajiya.

The Genji searched hard and long for the refugees of Heike. When refugees were discovered, they would be put to death. Therefore, to fool their enemies, the refugees in Sajiya created foolish tales, which have been handed down to the present time. By that means they propagated the idea that only foolish people dwelt in Sajiya, and thus they caused the Genji pursuers to abandon their inquiry concerning the people of Sajiya. In the village of Sajiya are many remains that are said to be tombs of the Heike. The majority of the present inhabitants call themselves the descendants of the refugees of Heike.

THE CROW AND THE PHEASANT

The deceptive bargain based on "Literal payment of debt (not real)," Motif K236, is found here.

Text from Impaku Mintan, I (May, 1936), p. 193. Told by Choka Nakaya of Saji-mura.

ONE DAY a man from Sajiya went shopping in Yogase. As he walked along the street, people mocked at him, saying: "The foolish man of Sajiya has come." The man from Sajiya grew very angry and determined to get revenge. He instructed a hunter to catch him one pheasant and many crows. The next morning the man from Sajiya put the crows in a bag and, carrying the bag on his shoulder and tying the pheasant to a stick, went once more to Yogase. As he walked along the street calling out: "Birds, birds, birds," people whispered to each other: "The foolish man of Sajiya has come again." Then a gentleman came by. He looked at the man from Sajiya and asked him: "How much are your birds?" "Well, they are ten sen apiece." The gentleman was pleased. "I want three birds," he said and paid thirty sen.

So the man from Sajiya took three crows out of his bag and said: "Thank you very much." And the gentleman was surprised. "They are crows!" But the man from Sajiya retorted: "You said you wanted birds." The gentleman was embarrassed and sneaked away.

KICHIGO ASCENDS TO THE SKY

The collector writes: "Tales of Kichigo which are heard from all people in the neighborhood of Nakatsu-shi in Oita-ken and Shikujo-gun in Fukuoka-ken are perhaps similar to the humorous tales in other places." The present story falls within the section K1700 in the Motif-Index, "Deception Through Shame." Text from Shinichi Umebayashi, "Kichigo Banashi," in Tabi to Densetsu, *VI (September, 1933), p. 66.*

ONCE KICHIGO BOUGHT a swampy piece of land at a cheap price. But he could not make use of it. He wanted to make some money by treading down the land. He put up a sign announcing: "Kichigo is going to ascend to the sky at such and such a time on such and such a day, for the reason that he does not want to live in this world any more."

On the appointed day many people in the neighborhood gathered together to see Kichigo's ascent to the sky. The place took on the atmosphere of a festival. Some of the people set up stores and began selling sweets. Kichigo came out and gave greetings to all the people, and then he began to climb up the steps of a ladder which he had prepared. As his figure grew smaller and smaller, the people cried out: "It's dangerous! It's dangerous!"

When Kichigo heard this, he came down step by step and said: "You are so kind to warn me that it is dangerous that I will not ascend to the sky today. I will do it some other day." And he went back to his home.

The people knew that they had been tricked again and they all went away complaining about Kichigo. But as the swampy land had been trodden on by so many people, it turned into good land. So Kichigo made money from it.

KITCHOMU FOOLS HIS NEIGHBOR

Similar trickeries are cited under Motif K330, "Means of hoodwinking the guardian or owner."

Text from Sempo Nakata, "Kitchomu Banashi," Tabi to Densetsu, I (April, 1928), pp. 72–73, no. 35.

KITCHOMU was short of money and went to his neighbor to borrow some. The greedy neighbor said: "I have some money to save, but I have no money to lend." Kitchomu thought he was a nasty fellow, but he did not cry out in anger. He said: "Well then, I want to borrow from you, but how do you make money? You will have trouble to keep it safe. It may be burned by fire or it may be stolen by thieves." The neighbor said: "You don't need to worry about it. I am always thinking about it myself." "I am sorry to have taken your time," said Kitchomu and went out.

Eager to find out where his neighbor kept his money, Kitchomu peeped through the fence when it became dark. The neighbor came out into the garden and dug up the ground and there he buried his money. When he had done this he said: "May the money increase as the sand increases. May the money appear as a snake to the eyes of other people." Kitchomu, who saw this, was pleased. "I've heard a good thing." Next day he went to the mountain and caught many snakes. Late that night he stole into his neighbor's garden and dug up the ground. He dug up all the money that the neighbor had put there and buried the snakes in place of the money.

Two or three days later the neighbor, who did not know this, went there to bury more money which he had accumulated. When he dug up the ground, he found no money but a great many snakes. He cried out in surprise: "It's me. Have you forgotten me?" But the snakes did not turn to money.

WHEW!

Comparable examples of "The forgetful fool" are given under Motif J2671. The collector of the tradition below writes: "There is a hot spring resort called Hinata-

yama in Aira-gun, Kagoshima-ken. Once there lived there a small man named Hikobei Tokuda. However the people did not call him Hikobei-san nor Hiko-san but Shuju-don (Master Dwarf). This Shuju-don lived a very humorous life and left many funny tales behind him. Whether he was a true character or not is a question.''

Text from Sempo Nakata, ''Shuju Banashi at Hinatayama,'' Tabi to Densetsu, I *(June, 1928), pp. 85–86, no. 6.*

Note: Dango is here rendered as ''dumpling,'' and hentokose *as ''whew!'' This latter term is a Kyushu dialect exclamation used when completing a heavy task, similar to Tokyo's* dokkoisho.

ONE DAY Shuju was invited to dinner by his uncle. "Uncle, uncle," said Shuju during the course of the dinner, "this is very delicious. What do you call it?"

"Don't you know?" said the uncle laughing. "That's called a dumpling." Not wanting to forget the name, as Shuju walked home he kept saying: "Dumpling, dumpling." Along the way he came to a steep, difficult slope filled with large boulders. When he was finally at the bottom of the slope, he said: "Whew! Whew!" Then he walked on, saying "Whew, whew" all the way home.

"I'm back, " he called to his wife. "Make me some whews."

His wife was surprised at these sudden words. "What's a whew?" she asked. "I don't know such a thing."

"I ate a whew at Uncle's. It was called a whew, and I want to eat one now. You ought to know about such things as whews. Do you understand?"

"No, I don't. There's no such food as a whew—not in Japan, and not in China, and not in India either."

"What a stupid woman! A woman like this is no good as a wife." And Shuju picked up the bamboo fire-blower that was at his hand and hit his wife's forehead with it.

"Ouch! You hit me too hard," the wife cried, rubbing her forehead. "Look, it's made a lump as big as a dumpling!"

When Shuju heard this, he cried: "That's it!—dumpling, dumpling."

THE WIT OF NIEMONEN

Niemonen here perpetuates various traditional deceptions. Motif K111.1, "Alleged gold-dropping animal sold," is reported from eleven districts of Japan (Ikeda, p. 290). An example is in Yanagita-Mayer, Japanese Folk Tales, pp. 263–64, no. 91, "Tankuro and Takuro." Other motifs present are K1828, "Disguise as deity," reported from Africa; K236, "Literal payment of debt (not real)"; K1950, "Sham prowess."

Text from Shimane-ken Kohi Densetsu Shu, Hikawa-gun, p. 26.

Notes: The Higan Festival, March 18–24, during which people visit the family tombs and hold Buddhist services for the dead. The Bon Festival, customarily August 15, a major Buddhist rite celebrated in each family for the ancestral spirits. The fact that Niemonen dresses in white in the last story causes the people to mistake him for a Buddhist deity.

1. HE OUTWITS A GOD. Niemonen visited a temple one day during the Higan Festival and put some money in the offering box. After he had worshiped the god, he again put his hand in the box. And when he drew his hand forth the money which he had dropped into the box came back to him, because he had tied the money to a string. He said that he might as well do that because the god had no use for money.

Another time he fell sick and visited a shrine to pray for better health. He said to the god: "If I am healed by your mercy, I shall offer a metal torii to your shrine." He recovered soon. Then he made a model of a torii from needles and offered it to the shrine.

2. HE CARRIES A GREAT ROCK. There was a rock so huge that it could not be carried by twenty or thirty men. Niemonen said he would carry it by himself if the people would do as he told them. The young men thought it a joke, but they agreed to humor Niemonen. They secured a big rope, in accordance with Niemonen's instructions, and looped it around the rock. Niemonen grasped the rope's end and said to the young men: "Raise this rock with all your might." The young men said they could not raise it. Then Niemonen declared: "If you don't do as I tell you, I will not carry the rock."

3. HE KNOWS ABOUT A DISTANT FIRE. One time when Niemonen was

visiting in Osaka he cried out: "Oh, my house in the country is burning!" The people said that he could not see a fire at such a distant place, but he insisted that he was sure of it. They argued earnestly and at last decided to wager five hundred gold pieces.

About ten days afterward, a message came from Niemonen's wife in the country. It said that his house and all his belongings had been consumed by fire on such and such a date. The date coincided exactly with that of Niemonen's assertion. So Niemonen won the wager.

The reason he knew about the fire was that, before he left the country, he had told his wife to set the house on fire on that particular day.

4. THE HORSE THAT DROPPED GOLDEN FECES. Niemonen fed his horse hay mixed with coins every day. The horse dropped the coins in his feces. So Niemonen sold the horse for four hundred gold pieces to his greedy brother.

5. THE SECOND BON FESTIVAL. One night while Niemonen was in Osaka he dressed in a white garment and rode a horse around town, ringing a bell and announcing to the people: "I could not visit you during the Bon Festival, but I have come now so you must hold the festival once more, or else you shall meet disaster."

So the people made preparations for a second festival, but they were taken on such short notice that the Bon flowers soon ran out. Then Niemonen sold branches of the flowers which he had brought by boat from his district, and made a great deal of money.

BOASTER'S WIT

The theme of "Lying contests," Motif X905, is known in Italy, India, and the United States.

Text from Sempo Nakata, "Ichibei Banashi," Tabi to Densetsu, III (May, 1930), 75–76, no. 28.

Note: Sorori Shinzaemon, a famous wit who was an adviser to the first Tokugawa shogun.

ONE WINTER EVENING the young men of a certain village met together to have a boasting contest. Each wanted to win the big prize, and they tried hard to think of wonderful boasts. One of them went out on the pretext of urinating. Once outside, he went to Ichibei's house and called out: "Ichibei-san, please lend me your wit." "What do you want?" Ichibei asked, knocking the ashes from his pipe into the palm of his hand and looking up into the young man's face. "I want you to tell me the biggest boast." "The biggest boast? Why, that's easy. When some-one asks 'How is your father?' you just say: 'The people of Suruga have pushed Mt. Fuji so hard that it has bent toward Koshu; so my father has gone to prop it up with an incense stick.'" "Thank you very much," said the young man. "Surely this will be the winning boast."

No sooner had the first young man left than another one came, named Kumako, to borrow Ichibei's wit. "Are you in?" he called. "Here I am," said Ichibei. "I have something to ask you; please tell me a big boast." Ichibei answered with a knowing look: "Yes, yes, that's easy. When someone asks 'How is your father?' you just say: 'It rains too much because there's a hole in the sky; so my father has gone to plug up the hole with the skin of a louse.'" "Thank you indeed," said Kumako, very pleased. "That's a wonderful boast. Sorori Shinzaemon himself could not do better."

No sooner had Kumako gone than Hachiko came in. "Ichibei-san, please tell me a big boast." Ichibei promptly answered: "Yes, yes. When you're asked 'How is your father?' you just say: 'My father sat on Mt. Fuji and put the blue sky over his head, but his ears were left out.'" Hachiko was very happy with this. "That's good! Surely I'll win first prize with it."

After Hachiko had gone, Ichibei laughed and said: "Well, then, who'll decide which of those is the biggest boast?"

BOASTING OF ONE'S OWN REGION

This is another play on the lying contest, where the biggest lie includes the other lies, as in Motif X1423.1, the lie of the great cabbage, which is topped by a lie of a great pot large enough to hold the cabbage. Anesaki, pp. 339–40, relates a serious legend of a giant chestnut tree in Omi-ken whose branches spread such a distance that its nuts fell many miles away.

Text from Mukashi-banashi, pp. 62–63.

ONCE A MAN from Ise, a man from Mino, a man from Mikawa, and a man from Otsu put up at the same lodging. The man from Ise said that the Ise Shrine had eighty branch shrines and that all those small shrines stood under the branches of a single big tree which stretched out one league in every direction.

Then the man from Mino said: "That's a very wonderful story, but in Mino there is a big ox-skin which covers one square league."

The man from Otsu boasted that in his region there was a potato vine which covered a square league.

The man from Mikawa, who had been listening quietly to the others, said: "There's a big drum in my home district. Its body is made from the big tree of Ise which stretches a league in each direction, and it is covered by the ox-skin of Mino that is one league square, and it is tied with the potato vine of Otsu that covers a square league. And when you beat this drum, it sounds all the way to the eighty branch-shrines of Ise."

So the other men were defeated.

THE OLD MAN WHO BROKE WIND

This extremely popular Japanese folk tale has been collected in 101 versions. Some go into comic detail on the old man's choosiness in picking a spot to demonstrate his wind-breaking talent before the lord; he finds a straw mat too slippery, the road too sandy, demands a silk comforter, or climbs upon the lord. Ikeda analyzes the versions, pp. 150–53, under Type 480F, "Fancy Passing of Air." The Minzokugaku Jiten calls this tale-type Take-kiri Jijii (Story of Musical Wind-Breaking). A tremendous wind-breaker who blows down walls and frightens tigers is "General Pumpkin" in Zong In-Sob, Folk Tales from Korea (London, 1952), pp. 66–68.

Text from Mukashi-banashi Kenkyu, I (1935), p. 73. Collected by Eiichiro Iwakura, from Minami Kambara-gun, Niigata-ken.

Note: Goyo no takara matsu, "five-needle treasure pine"; the other sounds are onomatopoetic.

AN OLD MAN went to the mountain to cut some firewood. A pretty yellow bird flew by, and the old man threw his axe at the bird and killed it. He cooked and ate the bird. Then a long hair grew from his navel, so he pulled it, and then he broke wind, making the sounds "Ao-ao-wa, chio-chio, goyo no takara matsu chinchikin." And he returned home and told his old wife: "Old woman, since today I can make beautiful sounds by breaking wind."

Then the old woman said: "Please try to break wind now." So the old man broke wind and made the same sounds: "Ao-ao-wa, chio-chio, goyo no takara matsu chinchikin."

The feudal lord heard of this. He sent word to the old man: "Grandfather Gombei, I hear you make interesting sounds. Try for me."

So the old man went before the lord trembling, and the lord repeated his command: "Gombei, break wind here." So the old man broke wind three or four times. The lord was pleased and said: "You have broken wind very well." And he gave him much money.

The old man came home and showed the money to the old woman. While they were talking happily about this, the old man next door came in and asked: "Where did you get the money?" Then the old man told him the story. And the neighbor said: "I too will go to the lord and get money." He caught a little bird and cooked and ate it. And he went to the lord, but he could not break wind. He just dropped feces.

PART EIGHT

PLACES

ALL LOCAL legends are tied to particular places, but in some the primary interest centers on the place, while in others a person or an event is the chief focus of attention. The rivers and mountains of Japan, whose breathless beauty covers the land, play the leading roles in many legends. Minkan shinko has invested both mountain peaks and river beds with deities, rituals, and taboos. The deity of river and pond, now degenerated into the kappa, has from ancient times demanded a propitiatory human sacrifice to calm its raging waters, and a host of densetsu recall these voluntary and involuntary sacrifices. When I was being driven through a small village in Miyazaki-ken in April, 1957, my guide, a local antiquarian, stopped the car beside a pond and pointed out a tiny shrine across the road with a bronze marker planted alongside. He proudly read its inscription, which he had himself written, relating how a youth of the village eight hundred years ago had allowed himself to be buried alive to pacify the god of the constantly overflowing pond, now still and serene.

Lofty mountains too are the sacred dwelling places of deities, for there the field god retires after the crops are harvested and resides until spring calls him forth. Woodsmen who enter the forest of the mountainside purify themselves before leaving home and speak a different dialect while working in the woods to avoid using words heavy with taboo. Shrines are built on mountain summits, and worshipers climb all night to behold dawn break upon the peak. Hence traditions flourish about yama-no-kami, the mountain gods, who accost woodcutters and quarrel with each other. The whole landscape of Japan indeed pulses with the presence of kami: in that hot spring a god was born; to the spirit of this pine tree a villager was once wed; mother-and-son deities emerged from those two rocks. Legends are graven into the land.

HUMAN SACRIFICE TO THE RIVER GOD

The theme of "Foundation sacrifice" (Motif S261) is known from India to Ireland. In the usual Japanese form, as below, the victim is not immured in the foundation of the bridge or dam, but drowns in the river to placate a river god (Motif S263.3, "Person sacrificed to water spirit to secure water supply," reported from India and Africa). The connection is clearly seen in the present legend, where a foundation stone for the dam appears after the drowning. The Minzokugaku Jiten has relevant entries on Hitobashira (Human sacrifice) and Hashi (Bridges).

Text from Kiki-mimi Soshi, *pp. 426–28.*

AN OLD WISE-WOMAN came from Miyanome in Ayaori-mura and settled at Yazaki in Matsuzaki-mura, Kamihei-gun. She had a daughter whom she cared for lovingly. The girl grew up and was married to a man who came to live with them. The young couple loved each other, but the mother disliked the son-in-law and wanted to get rid of him.

In those days the dam which supplied the villagers with water from the Saru-ga-ishi River would give way several times every year, and people were troubled by floods. It happened again that the dam broke when the villagers were in need of water. Thrown into confusion, they gathered together and talked the matter over. At last they decided to consult the wise-woman. She, on her part, thought this a good opportunity to destroy her son-in-law. Accordingly, she told the people to catch a person who would be dressed in white and riding a gray horse to Tsukumoshi-mura the next morning, and to throw him into the river as a sacrifice. The villagers assembled at the dam and waited from midnight on for a person in white dress to come by on horseback.

Early next morning the old woman's son-in-law, unaware of impending disaster, dressed himself in white, as he had been told to do by the mother, and rode off on his gray horse. When he came to the dam, many villagers stood in his way to catch him. The son-in-law was surprised and asked them: "Why are you all here?"

The villagers were surprised in their turn to see that the person was none other than the wise-woman's son-in-law, whom they all knew well. When the son-in-law heard about the matter he said: "If it is the god's word, I must obey. I will drown myself in the bottom of the river and sacrifice myself for the sake of the villagers. But a human sacrifice cannot be made by one person. A couple, man and woman, are needed to satisfy the god. I will have my wife die with me."

Just then the wise-woman's daughter, who knew of the mother's evil plot, rushed to the scene, riding on a gray horse and dressed in white. The husband and wife rode into the river together and sank down to the bottom. The old wise-woman regretted that her plan had miscarried. She also jumped into the water, weeping.

All at once the sky darkened and a fierce thunderstorm lashed the heavens. For three days and nights it rained ceaselessly, and the river overflowed its banks. After the flood had subsided, the people noticed a big stone that they had never seen before. The villagers used this stone as the foundation in reconstructing the dam. This stone was called the Wise-woman's Stone.

The son-in-law and his wife were deified as gods of the dam [sekigami]. There is also a shrine called Bonari Myojin where the old wise-woman died.

THE PRINCESS WHO BECAME A HUMAN SACRIFICE

The same general theme as in the preceding legend is here treated by a professional writer, Chihei Nakamura, interested in the folk traditions of his locality, Miyazaki-ken in Kyushu.

Text from Hyuga Minwa Shu, *pp. 55–61.*

In September of the second year of the Hogen era [1157], Nobutsuna Tsuchimochi came to Hyuga from Mikawa and built Inoue Castle at Agata [Nobeoka]. After that time, for four hundred years, more than fifteen generations, the Tsuchimochi family wielded their power over that district as feudal lords. But we cannot tell in which generation of the Tsuchimochi family the events of the following story occurred.

In those days, the Gokase was divided into two streams running from the north end of Inoue Castle and encircling Mt. Atago, whence it flowed into the sea. The people called the dividing point of the Gokase Suwa-no-wakeguchi. It occurred to the lord of that period to dam the stream at Suwa-no-wakeguchi, for the double purpose of shortening the distance from the castle to the houses of the warriors and of making new rice fields from the reclaimed land. The lord ordered his subjects to take up the enterprise at once.

The farmers, who had been gathered together by the village headman, tried to stop the flow of water by making a barrier with bamboo baskets filled with stones and with straw bags filled with earth, under the direction of a building magistrate. They kept working day and

213

night, but the dam was always destroyed by strong currents of water before completion.

"Why on earth are you taking so long just to make a dam? When will it be completed?" asked the lord angrily. One of his subjects timidly answered: "We will complete it within ten days without fail. So would you please wait for a while."

The subjects soon gathered about the village headman and the chief farmers, and informed them of their promise to the lord. However, it was clear to everybody that the completion of the dam within ten days would be impossible. No one could think of a good plan for keeping faith with their lord. A gloomy atmosphere prevailed over the group.

Then, the village headman said: "There seems no other way but to ask the water god for help. If anybody in the village will sacrifice himself and sink into the stream, the water god will surely permit us to stop the flow of water."

Everyone agreed with his proposal, saying: "There may be no better way, indeed. Since the water god is fond of young maidens, a young girl should become the human sacrifice."

The matter seemed settled. But when it came to the difficult question of whom they should choose as a human sacrifice, they again bogged down. Some of the assemblage had daughters. But no one dared propose his own daughter for the sacrifice. The conference was once more at a deadlock.

Before long, one of the people reached this conclusion with a decided air: "Let us select the maiden for the human sacrifice by lot. I demand that all the girls in the village come to the shrine of our tutelary god tomorrow morning."

The next morning the precinct of the tutelary god was swept clear, and a plain wood box decorated with a sacred straw rope was placed in front of the shrine. The village girls came there one after another.

Every girl was blindfolded and was brought up to the plain wood box. She had to draw a card out of the box while blindfolded. Soon the turn of the only daughter of the headman came. She had no sooner drawn out a card than an agitation developed among the caretakers who surrounded her. The headman turned pale. The lot had fallen upon the very daughter of the headman.

Before long, there was a fuss throughout the village. "How sorry I am for the headman! He invited the misfortune of his own accord." Everyone expressed his sympathy toward the headman, but no one could change the situation. At the headman's house, all of his family sat around the daughter lamenting bitterly.

The rumor that the sacrificial victim had been chosen reached the castle by and by. There lived a princess, daughter of the Lord Tsuchi-mochi. She was very sweet and fair, but unfortunately crippled since childhood. Feeling intense shame for her deformity, she was wont to confine herself deep within the castle. The rumor of the human sacrifice somehow reached the ears of this princess. She asked the lord, her father: "Please make me the human offering to the Gokase."

At the sudden request of the princess the lord was frightened, and tried to persuade and coax her not to do such a thing. However, the princess was firm in her determination, and spoke as follows: "I have no pleasure in living like this, for I am a cripple. I hear that the daughter of the headman is his only daughter. It is too cruel to make her a human sacrifice; it is like plucking a budding flower. I can imagine how bitterly her family grieves. If you make me the human sacrifice in her place, not only will the headman be delighted, but the village people will be thankful for your deep mercy, from the bottom of their hearts. Such a deed must ensure good for the future of our family. So please accept my plea, Father."

At such sincere words from their daughter, the lord and his wife could do nothing but accede to her request and give her up to death.

When the appointed day came, the princess was beautifully dressed in her best and drowned herself in the waters of the Gokase. The noble act of the princess must have moved the water god, for the strength of the torrents speedily slackened. The farmers lost no time in stopping the current of one branch of the river. So the difficult construction was at last completed.

The villagers cherished the virtue of the princess so much that they later deified her in the Shisha Shrine of Wakamiya Hachiman-gu. It still remains at Suwa-no-wakeguchi.

Every year when the season comes, the village people make it a rule to offer the first catch of saurel to the shrine. It is said that the deified princess was fond of saurel in her lifetime.

A MYSTERY AT MOTOMACHI BRIDGE

Here is the modern form of the foundation sacrifice, in which death occurs to a work-man accidentally, rather than as a deliberate deed. Hearn gives an up-to-date version of the Gensuke Bridge legend, in which it was held that the first man crossing the bridge wearing hakama (divided skirts) without a machi (cardboard stiffener above the tie strings at the back) must be sacrificed. When the bridge was rebuilt, hundreds of aged men cut off their queues. Then a rumor circulated that police would seize the thousandth man to cross, and the town was empty on market day. (V, ch. 1, "The Chief City of the Province of the Gods," pp. 171–74.)

Text from Hyuga Minwa Shu, pp. 157–60.

IN AUGUST of the second year of Showa [1927], a typhoon hit the city of Miyazaki. It kept raining heavily and the waters of the Oyodo River rose steadily day by day. The Tachibana Bridge across the river was built of wood; on the second day of the typhoon, it was broken in the middle and half of it floated away. Thus the city traffic was completely cut in two by the yellowish, swollen Oyodo, which flowed through the middle of the city. As an emergency, they used sailing boats to cross the river, but these served only for transporting people, not horses and wagons.

The leading men of the city and the prefecture came together to discuss this. They decided to rebuild the Tachibana Bridge strong and permanently and, since this would take some time, they decided also to rebuild as temporary substitute the Motomachi Bridge, another wooden structure connecting Moto-machi in Miyazaki City with Zaimoku-machi in Oyodo on the opposite bank. Although this bridge was always only a simple, makeshift affair, it had served the citizens well from the beginning of the Taisho era until only a year earlier, when it had been swept away in a flood. (After being rebuilt, it would again serve them until the end of World War II, a total of twenty years.) It was urgent to rebuild it as soon as possible, pending the completion of a concrete Tachibana Bridge.

It would have taken too long if the rebuilding of Motomachi Bridge had been left in the hands of private contractors. The president of the Miyazaki Reservists Association at the time was Mr. Rokichi Mieno. Through his good offices and in order to speed the work, the city authorities asked the headquarters of the Sixth Division in Kumamoto to send army engineers to rebuild the bridge. And the Division immediately assigned ten engineering units to rebuild the bridge as a practice maneuver.

The construction was so urgent that the soldiers worked night and day, hastening the task by floating barges on the wide surface of the river. During this time the soldiers were quartered in houses around Moto-machi and Kawahara-machi. With the help of about a hundred reservists living in Miyazaki, they were able to finish the work in three weeks.

But two soldiers were sacrificed before the bridge was finished. It was on a day toward the end of the job, and the soldiers were working near the Motomachi bank. Suddenly the scaffold collapsed. In an instant, three soldiers had fallen into the water, which was still at a high level. One soldier was rescued, but the other two never reappeared on the surface. A great commotion ensued, and the other soldiers began searching by boat all over the river, but they found no traces of their two comrades. Thinking the bodies might have been caught on the bottom, they searched the bottom from the point of work to the mouth of the river, but the bodies were never found.

After the bridge was built there were some who proposed changing its name to Engineer Bridge in honor of the soldiers who had worked so hard and the two who had been drowned. But nothing ever came of this proposal, and the bridge continued to be called Motomachi.

Some time later a rumor spread through the town that if one

crossed the bridge late at night he could hear the marching song "Far, Far Away from Our Motherland" and the sound of marching feet going across the bridge, but without being able to tell where the sounds came from. Because of this frightening rumor, no woman or child dared cross the bridge at night.

Some of the townspeople discussed this, and the following year they built a shrine at the northern end of the bridge, dedicating it to the God of Water. There they erected a memorial tablet to the spirits of the two sacrificed soldiers. Toward the end of the war this bridge was again swept away by a flood, and the memorial tablet was destroyed by the war. Today nothing is left except a lonesome fragment of the broken tablet in the underbrush of the wasteland.

A HUMAN SACRIFICE AT KONO STRAND

In this personal recollection of a foundation-sacrifice legend by Kayoko Saito's grandmother appears the buried-alive theme (Motif S261). William H. Erskine comments (pp. 88–90): "The burial of the living in the erection of buildings and bridges is a distinct effort to get the spirits on the side of the community. . . . In the rebuilding of dikes or the building of bridges which, because of the swift current of the stream or heavy rains were always falling down, living people were buried to give strength to the bridge or dike. In the Japanese Encyclopedia *the article on burial says that this practice was kept up until the opening of the country to foreign trade in 1868. Only eighty years ago a man was buried in the pier of the famous Temma bridge in Osaka." Erskine then gives four legends of immolation.*

Hearn tells of a dancing maiden interred in the walls of a castle (V, pp. 189–90). Murai, pp. 94–98, gives the striking legend of "Kumeji-bashi Bridge." A peasant is buried alive under a bridge pier when his daughter unwittingly reveals he has stolen red beans for her supper. She remains dumb the rest of her life, save once when she sees a pheasant reveal itself to a hunter with its cry. Hence the proverb: "If the pheasant cries not, it will not be shot."

Text from Mrs. Hitoshi Kawashima Saito, told to Kayoko Saito in Tokyo, June 1, 1957.

FIVE MILES AWAY from my native house in Aza-mura, there was a cape called Kono-no-iso. It was a rocky place, bordered by a river and the sea. Many pine trees on the shore rustled in the air when the wind blew. The scenery there was very, very beautiful. When I was in primary school, I often went there on school excursions and played with my friends, picking up pebbles here and there.

There was something like a pond or a harbor there, which was surrounded by a ruined stone works. Beside the harbor was an old stone monument. Concerning this stone monument, I heard a story many times from my great-grandmother and my grandparents. The story is as follows:

A long, long time ago, the people tried to make a harbor for fishing boats at Kono Strand. However, the western wind blew so hard and the waves raged so high that they could not complete the task. They got together to consult how to overcome the difficulty and decided to make a human sacrifice.

Now, there came an old pilgrim who had been traveling on foot from shrine to shrine, ringing a bell in his hand. He happened to hear the rumor that a human sacrifice was to be offered and volunteered himself.

In keen appreciation and sorrow, the people dug a hole deep in the ground. The pilgrim sat in it and recited sutras, ringing his bell. The people covered the hole with a board, thrusting a bamboo pipe through the board so that the pilgrim might breathe the outside air.

For three days and nights, the people heard the pilgrim reciting sutras and ringing his bell, but after that, they heard nothing more out of the hole. Realizing that the pilgrim was dead, they filled the hole with earth and built a stone monument on it in honor of the pilgrim. This is the stone that still stands at Kono Strand.

THE BRIDGE WHERE BRIDES ARE TAKEN AWAY

This legend begins like the popular story, drama, and serpent dance of Hidaka-gawa: ". . . a woman pursuing her fleeing lover becomes a large serpent as she crosses over a stream, and then coils around and melts a bronze bell in which the unfaithful lover has concealed himself" (Anesaki, p. 331). Instead of the bell episode, however, it turns to Motif G424, "Bridal party will not pass over bridge for fear of water-demon." Miss Ishiwara tells me that even in Tokyo, near Shinjuku, there is a bridge brides cannot cross; a choja's daughter once threw herself into the water there.

Text from Yamato no Densetsu, pp. 57–58. Collected in Hirahata-mura, Ikoma-gun, Nara-ken.

Note: Narihira, an ancient courtier and poet renowned for his beauty.

IN ANCIENT TIMES there was a teahouse in Tsutsui-mura. A daughter, aged eighteen, whose name was Kimano lived there. She loved a young

messenger who passed this place almost every day on his way to Osaka. He was as handsome a young man as Narihira. One day the messenger passed there late in the evening. The girl advised him to stay at her house that night, telling him the difficulties of his way. At midnight the girl stole into his room with a strange appearance. The surprised messenger fled from the room. To help his parents recover from illness, he had sworn an oath that he would not love a woman for three years. He was afraid to break his word and ran away. The girl ran after him. When the man came to a big pool, he climbed up a pine tree. The girl running behind lost sight of him but found his *geta*. She was startled and looked toward the pool. By the moonlight she could see a man's form in the water. She thought it was the messenger in the water and threw herself in after him. Then she was changed into a big serpent. After that, whenever the serpent saw a girl it caught and killed her, for fear that she might take her lover away.

Once when a bride in a sedan chair passed by, a sudden rain fell and the porter went away to borrow a rain cloth, putting the chair under a tree. When he came back, he couldn't find the bride anywhere. She had been taken away by the big serpent, who had caused the sudden rain. Thereafter the bridge over the stream before the pool was called Yometori-bashi [Bridge Where Brides Are Taken Away].

And still nowadays brides are forbidden to cross this bridge.

GOJO BRIDGE IN KYOTO

This wandering legend has fastened onto many bridges. Examples are cited under Motif N531.1, "Dream of treasure on the bridge," and Type 1645, "The Treasure at Home." Ikeda mentions five Japanese versions, p. 298. In Ireland I heard the legend attached to the Bald Bridge of Limerick (Journal of American Folklore, LXVI, 1953, pp. 33–34). G. L. Gomme discusses the legend at length in connection with London Bridge (Folklore as an Historical Science, London, 1908, pp. 13–33).

Text from Nishi Sanuki Mukashi-banashi Shu, p. 35.

A POOR FARMER named Kasaku dreamed a dream that if he should go to the Gojo Bridge in Kyoto, he would become rich. Immediately he started out for Kyoto and at length arrived there. While he was waiting at the bridge, a man came by and asked him what he was doing. So he told him about his dream. Then the other said that five days earlier he too had a dream, and in the dream he was told that in the yard of the farmer called Kasaku there was an oak tree, and at the foot of that tree money was buried. But he said he did not believe in such a foolish dream, and he advised Kasaku to return to his home without believing in his dreams. Kasaku hastily returned home and dug a hole at the foot of the oak tree. He found an old bottle there, filled with many gold coins, enough to make Kasaku a very rich man.

THE MOUNTAIN OF ABANDONED OLD PEOPLE

A short story entitled "The Oak Mountain Song" (Narayama-bushi-ko) won a prize offered to new authors by the literary review Chuo Koron, in whose pages it appeared in November, 1956. The author, Shichiro Fukazawa, was a professional guitar player. His story created a sensation in Japanese literary circles and was promptly and skillfully translated into English by John Bester (Japan Quarterly, IV, April–June, 1957, pp. 200–32). Fukazawa built his grim and terrifying piece upon the Japanese legend of Ubasute-yama, a mountain peak where an impoverished village that could not support unproductive members abandoned its aged when they reached the age of sixty. The short story in turn was adapted into a powerful naturalistic Kabuki play, which I saw at the Kabuki-za in Tokyo in June, 1957, and which was subsequently made into a highly acclaimed movie. The family with

*the mother of sixty is pictured in Tobacco Road style, feverishly devouring the last
stray morsel of rice. At the climax, the filial son who has left his mother on the peak
amidst rotting carcasses and carrion crows breaks the strict edict not to look behind and
rushes back to his mother's side.*

*The legend itself does not take so brutal a form. The parent is brought down the
mountain and hidden under the house; he (or she) gives the children solutions to
enigmatic tasks imposed by the lord, who rescinds the edict when he learns the source
of wisdom. Under Type 981, "The Old Man Hidden Under the Earth," Ikeda,
pp. 254–56, analyzes the tale, which she finds widely distributed in Japan, known
in literary forms going back to the thirteenth century, and present also in China and
Korea. The Type-Index reports it as a medieval European Märchen. Discussion
can be found in the Minzokugaku Jiten under "Obasute-yama," and in Mock
Joya, III, pp. 198–99, "Obasuteyama." Versions appear in Murai, pp. 18–27,
Ubasute (Mother-Abandonment), a full text containing three tasks; Etsu Inagaki
Sugimoto, Daughter of the Samurai (New York, 1926), pp. 101–4 (one task);
Die Wahrheit, IV (December, 1903), 221–23, Kumagai, "Der Berg Obasute"
(one task). The commonest task is making a rope of ashes. Writing in the Asahi
Evening News, Tokyo: July 12, 1957, "A Memo on the 'Oak-Mount Song,'"
Santaro speaks of two early literary appearances of the legend in the tenth-century Yamato Monogatari and the eleventh-century Konjaku Monogatari, of a fifteenth-
century Noh dramatization by Seami, and of reworkings into fairy tales, nursery
rhymes, poems, songs, and rakugo (the stories of professional humorists). He trans-
lates the brief tenth-century tale in which a spiteful daughter-in-law, not a village
edict, causes the son to abandon his aged mother.*

*Important motifs are S140.1, "Abandonment of aged" (chiefly Far Eastern);
J151.1, "Wisdom of hidden old man saves kingdom" (European, Jewish, Far
Eastern).*

Text from Chiisagata-gun Mintan Shu, pp. 109–11.

IN ANCIENT TIMES there prevailed a custom of abandoning old people
when they reached the age of sixty. Once an old man was going to be
abandoned on a mountain. He was carried there in a sedan chair by
his two sons. On the way the old man broke the branches of the trees.
"Why do you do such a thing? Do you break the branches in order
to recognize the way to come back after we leave you on the mountain?" asked the sons. The old father just recited a poem!

> "To break branches in the mountain
> Is for the dear children
> For whom I am ready to sacrifice myself."

The brothers did not think much about their father's poem, and took him up the mountain and abandoned him. "We shall go another way to return home," they said, and started on the way back.

The sun set in the west, but they could not find the way home. Meanwhile the moon came up and shone on the mountain. The two sons had no recourse but to return to their father. "What have you been doing until now?" he asked. "We tried to go back by a different way, but we could not get home. Please kindly tell us the way." So they carried the father again and went down the mountain, following their father's instructions, according to where he had broken the branches. When the brothers returned home, they hid their father under the floor. They gave him food every day and showed their gratitude for his love.

Some time afterward the lord issued a notice to the people to make a rope with ashes and present it to him. The people tried to make a rope by mixing ashes and water but no one could do it. Then the two brothers talked about this to the old father. The father said: "Moisten straw with salty water and make a rope of the straw; then after it is dried, burn it and present the ashes to the lord in the shape of a rope."

The brothers did just as he told them and presented the ash-rope to

the lord. The lord was much pleased and said: "I feel very secure in having such wise men in my country. How is it that you possess such wisdom?" The two brothers explained in detail about their father. The lord heard them out, and then gave notice to all the country that none should abandon old people thereafter. The two brothers returned home with many rewards, which delighted the old father.

The place where the old father was abandoned is said to be Uba-sute-yama, the Mountain of Abandoned Old People.

FEATHER-ROBE STONE MOUNTAIN

Usually in this legend, which is often told as a fairy tale, the celestial maiden swims in a pond and falls into the power of her lover when he steals her magic garment: Motif K1335, "Seduction (or wooing) by stealing clothes of bathing girl (swan maiden)." In the Japanese form she frequently hangs her feather garment on a pine tree, thereafter remembered in local legend (Ikeda, p. 89, note 1). The Noh drama "Hagoromo" contrasts the purity of the maiden with the greed of the fisherman who sees her robe on the tree. Some verses are given in Anesaki, pp. 259–61, from B. H. Chamberlain, The Classical Poetry of the Japanese *(London, 1880). Yasuyo Ishiwara has discussed the tale-type in "Celestial Wife in Japanese Folk Tales,"* University of Manila Journal of East Asiatic Studies, *V (January, 1956), pp. 35–41. She reports fifty-nine versions of* tennin-nyobo *(celestial wife), and indicates that in Japan the story takes on more legendary and mythological elements than in Europe.*

Text from Seiroku Kuramitsu, "A Version of the Feather-Robe Tales," Kyodo Kenkyu, VII (Tokyo, 1933), pp. 8–9, no. 1.

ON THE TOP of Mount Ubeshi in Hanami-mura, Tohaku-gun, in the province of Hoki (Tottori-ken) there is a big stone called the "Feather-Robe Stone" or the "Stone of the Celestial Maiden's Appearance." A long time ago a celestial maiden descended from the sky upon this stone and danced about, fluttering her robe made of feathers. Growing tired after a while, she took off her feather robe and, putting it on the stone, lay down to rest. A farmer who lived at the foot of the mountain happened to climb to the summit that day and saw the strange robe on the stone.

"What a splendid dress this is! I wonder if this might be the feather robe of a celestial lady," he thought. He picked it up and carried it home.

The celestial maiden, who had been fast asleep, awakened after a time. She could not find her feather robe. Wondering if the wind had blown it away, she looked for it here and there, but in vain. She was very sad. As she was weeping she heard a voice from somewhere saying: "You must live in the human world for a while. After some years you will be saved by your child under the vine which bears white flowers."

When the celestial maiden heard this, she forgot all about the heavenly world where she had lived, and became an ordinary human girl. She felt the cold because her clothes were thin, and she also felt pangs of hunger. So she had to go down the mountain to the village and ask a farmer for some food. He looked at her wonderingly and said: "What a pity! She seems to be a fine girl." In a kindly manner he invited her in and gave her shelter.

So the girl stayed in the farmer's house and was married to him. In due time two lovely girls were born to them. They grew to be very diligent, clever young ladies. Especially did they love music and, making good progress in a short time, learned to play on the flute and hand drum by themselves.

One day all the family went on a picnic to Kamisaka (Slope of the Gods) in Kurayoshi. Before going out the father said: "I'll show you a beautiful garment which I have carefully kept for a good long time. This is a fine occasion for you to wear it." He brought out the celestial feather robe and dressed the elder daughter in it. Then they set out, and on arriving at Kamisaka the family all sat down on the grass. To entertain them, the elder girl stood up, saying: "Since I have on this garment today, I will dance."

She danced to the tune of her sister's flute. The mother, who was enjoying her daughter's dance, said to her: "The form of your arms is not good. I'll show you how." So she put on the feather robe in place of the daughter and began to dance. As she did so she lost her human heart. Her body became light and rose up in the air. Astonished at this, the girls shouted: "What's the matter with you, Mother?" The celestial lady spoke to them: "Now I remember everything. I am the woman from the sky. I am going back to the heavens now. I should like to take you with me, but there is no room for human beings in heaven."

She rose up higher and higher and at last soared out of sight. Struck dumb with surprise, the girls glanced wildly about. They saw white gourd flowers at the well close by the torii. The girls thought if they played music on the top of the mountain, their celestial mother might listen to it. They went up the mountain and beat the drum and blew on the flute, yearning for heaven. But the celestial lady never came down to earth again.

Because of this story this mountain is called Uchifuki-yama (Beat and Blow Mountain), and the other mountain is called Ubeshi-yama (Feather-Robe Stone Mouutain).

CONTEST IN HEIGHT BETWEEN TWO MOUNTAINS

The height-matching contest between Mt. Fuji and Mt. Haku or the mountain called Yatsu-ga-take is given in Mock Joya, IV, pp. 39–40, "Stones to Mountain Tops"; Murai, typescript, p. 9, "Quarrel of Mountains"; Suzuki, pp. 1–2, "The Quarrel between the Mountains." Sometimes other mountains are involved. Pilgrims are said to leave their straw sandals on the lower peak to raise its height. The Minzoku-gaku Jiten *discusses this legend type under* Kamiarasoi *(Quarrel Between Two Mountain Deities).*

Text from Kai Densetsu, *pp. 93–94.*

IN ANCIENT TIMES Yatsu-ga-take was higher than Mt. Fuji. Once the female deity of Fuji (Asama-sama) and the male deity of Yatsu-ga-take (Gongen-sama) had a contest to see which was higher. They asked the Buddha Amida to decide which one was loftier. It was a difficult task. Amida ran a water pipe from the summit of Yatsu-ga-take to the summit of Fuji-san and poured water in the pipe. The water flowed to Fuji-san, so Amida decided that Fuji-san was defeated.

Although Fuji-san was a woman, she was too proud to recognize her defeat. She beat the summit of Yatsu-ga-take with a big stick. So his head was split into eight parts, and that is why Yatsu-ga-take [Eight Peaks] now has eight peaks.

THE MOUNDS OF THE MASTER SINGERS

The central motif here, H503.1 "Song duel. Contest in singing," is found in Ireland and among the Eskimo. Eskimo magical song duels of shamans may result in death for the defeated.

Text from Hida no Densetsu to Minyo, *pp. 134–36.*

IT WAS a bright moonlit night. The moon was in the middle of the sky shining over the fields and villages along the Masuda River. A charming song sung by Jinsaku of Shogano-mura on the opposite bank floated across the river.

"Jinsaku is singing tonight again. What a sweet voice he has!" The people of Tsukada-mura thus spoke together when they heard Jinsaku's song. On moonlit nights Jinsaku used to sing his songs to the moon, taking no notice of the passing hours. His voice vibrated through the quiet air of the mountain village and resounded farther and farther, attracting all the people who heard it.

Meanwhile someone or other in Tsukada-mura said: "It would be interesting if some person from our village could compete in singing songs with Jinsaku, who seems to be quite proud of his voice." All the villagers wished that some good singer might appear to surpass Jinsaku in singing songs. Then it happened one night that a sweet voice was heard from the top of a hill in Tsukada-mura. It was fully as sweet as Jinsaku's voice. The singer was none other than a young man by the name of Hikoroku from Tsukada-mura. When Jinsaku heard Hikoroku's song, he realized that he was faced with a strong rival, and he sang and sang at the top of his voice. Thereafter the villagers often heard those two young men on both sides of the Masuda River sing in high voices, competing with each other.

The year was renewed and spring visited the lonely mountain villages of Tsukada-mura and Shogano-mura. In both villages people talked about the songs that were to be sung by the two men at rice-planting season. At last the time came. As had been expected, Jinsaku and Hikoroku competed all day long in singing their songs from each side of the river while the people were planting rice plants. Both sang and sang in their highest tones. They must have spent themselves in their competition; when the rice planting finished, Jinsaku took sick and Hikoroku, too, fell ill and lay in bed from the same day on. Strange to say, they both died about the same time.

The villagers felt very sorry for them. "They really exhausted themselves singing songs." The villagers built two burial mounds on the opposite sides of the river, east and west, for the two young men. Those mounds remain even now and go by the name of Utanosuke-zuka [Mounds of the Master Singers].

Townspeople say that on moonlit nights they hear clear voices singing rice-planting songs from under the mounds.

THE VILLAGE BOUNDARY MOUND

The boundary of a village was of considerable importance to its inhabitants, marking off the known from the outside, occult world, and natives returning from the outside were ritually purified when they crossed the boundary. The Minzokugaku Jiten *discusses these ideas under* Murazaka *(Village Boundary), and* Dosojin *(God of the Boundary).*

Text from Aichi-ken Densetsu Shu, p. 156.

ON THE BOUNDARY of Nagura-mura and Kamitsugu-mura there is a mound called Sakai-zuka, by a little stream at the foot of a mountain. In the olden times when the boundary of the two villages was not clear, the people of the two villages talked together about setting the boundary. They decided to set it at the point where persons who started from Nagura-mura and Kamitsugu-mura would meet. The man from Nagura-mura should lead a cow, and the man from Kamitsugu-mura should lead a horse.

When the appointed day came, the man from Nagura started early in the morning and hastened the cow along by whipping her, in order to make her go faster than the horse. So he went over the mountain to a place where he could see the village of Kamitsugu. On the other hand, the lazy man from Kamitsugu woke up late in the morning. He started riding the horse in a hurry. The man of Nagura, seeing this, waited for him by a stream at the foot of the mountain. So therefore it was decided to set the boundary there.

This is the reason why Nagura-mura's boundary is peculiarly shaped, and bigger than it should be.

OKA CASTLE

Under "Hakumai-jo" (Rice Castle), the Minzokugaku Jiten *mentions forty variants of this legend. European counterparts are indicated under Motif K2365.1, "Enemy induced to give up siege by pretending to have plenty of food." Herodotus and Ovid employed the theme, and the Grimms have examples in their collection of German Sagen. Usually the ruse of substituting rice for water is not discovered, but Murai, pp. 3–6, "Another Version of the Origin of Hime-gana," has a spy report the deception, as does the traitor in the present instance.*

Text from Bungo Densetsu Shu, *pp. 91–92. From Naori-gun.*

A LONG, LONG TIME AGO Oka-jo [Oka Castle] stood in Takeba-machi. A river encircled the castle. Had the river contained much water, no force however strong could have destroyed this castle. But in those days the river had little water. When the soldiers of Satsuma invaded the province of Bungo, the people inside Oka-jo were worried about the lack of water in this river. In consequence, they decided to make the river seem full of water by filling it with rice. To put rice in the entire river was not an easy task, but they accomplished it in four days. The following evening the soldiers of Satsuma marched against the castle with shouts. But after a while no sound was heard. It was because they had withdrawn, giving up the attack on seeing the river full of water.

The people within the castle were exceedingly pleased and relieved.

The next day they held a feast. As they were besieged, they had only some sardines and a few appetizers with which to celebrate. So two sardines were given to each man. It happened that two sardines were lacking to supply one foot-soldier. When the lord of the castle heard this, he said: "Never mind about that one foot-soldier. He can do without any sardines." The soldier was mortified at these words. "It is too insulting. I am a human being just like the others. Since the lord has such a hard heart, I have an idea how to humble him."

That night the soldier was missing from the castle. All the other soldiers in the castle slept in peace. But suddenly they were alarmed by terrible shouts from the outside. Being totally unprepared for battle, they were thrown into a tumult. In the meantime the soldiers of Satsuma poured into the castle, and the castle was easily overthrown.

It is said that Oka-jo was destroyed because the lord did not love his servants and was blinded by greed.

THE LAUGHTER OF A MAIDENHAIR TREE

The motifs of "Dying man's curse" (M411.3), "Murder by hanging" (S113.1), "Punishment: choking with smoke" (Q469.5), and "Hanging as punishment for murder" (Q413.4) are present.

Text from Tosa Fuzoku to Densetsu, *pp. 81–82.*

ABOUT A HUNDRED and seventy years ago there was a greedy village headman named Hattori Goemon at Makinoyama in Kami-gun. He dealt harshly with the villagers. When men failed to bring him the rice tax, he hung them upside down from a big maidenhair tree in his yard and killed them with smoke from a fire of green pine leaves. So cruel was he that everyone hated him.

One year when the villagers had suffered a bad harvest, a man named Heiroku went to Goemon on their behalf to ask for remission of the tax. Goemon would not listen to their suit. He seized Heiroku, hung him from the maidenhair tree, and killed him with smoke. Heiroku died crying out in pain: "Kill me at once if you are going to kill me.

232

My grudge will cast a spell on your family to the seventh generation."

After that, many strange things happened in Goemon's house, and Goemon himself went mad. At last he hanged himself from the same maidenhair tree. It was said that horrible laughter was heard from that tree on rainy evenings. This Hattori family died out after seven more generations.

This tree was called Heiroku Maidenhair Tree. A little shrine was built under the tree for the dead spirit.

THE DISCOVERY OF YUDAIRA HOT SPRING

This legend is a thoroughly Japanese variation on Motif B155.1, "Building site determined by halting of animals," well known throughout Europe. A holy hot spring replaces the building.

Text from Bungo Densetsu Shu, *pp. 52–53, from Oita-gun.*

ACCORDING to tradition, Yudaira Hot Spring was first discovered by Fujiwara Hidekatsu during the reign of the Emperor Kameyama. After he had traveled through many countries, he came to this place and named it Nakayama, as he thought it resembled a famous place called Sayo-no-nakayama. He built a temple there and devoted himself to converting the villagers. One day he saw a strange thing on his way back from a villager's home. There were two monkeys in a hollow a little distance from the road. They looked like mother and child. The mother monkey seemed to be wounded. The child monkey was chafing at the mother monkey's bosom, wondering what was the matter. Hidekatsu returned to the temple and the incident passed from his mind. Five or six days after that he saw the same monkeys again in the evening. The mother monkey seemed to be better than before. He looked at them and thought it over. Then an idea came to his mind.

The next morning he went with two villagers to the same spot where he had seen the monkeys. He had the villagers dig in the ground with their hoes. Then they found a hole from which the steam was rising. As they dug deeper, the steam rose more intensely. When the men put their hands down in the hole they cried: "Hot! Hot!" So Hidekatsu told the villagers what he had seen. They were glad to hear his word and according to his instruction they made baths in many places.

Hundreds of years passed. About one hundred and eighty years ago the priest of Myoshin-ji in Kyoto came to this place, having been inspired by a dream, and he established the present bath with the aid of the villagers.

THE SPRING OF SAKE

"Monkey released: grateful" (Motif B375.5) is known in India. Anesaki discusses "Grateful Animals," pp. 318–24. A spring of wine appears in the story of "Dam-buri-Choja," in Yanagita-Mayer, Japanese Folk Tales, pp. 133–34, no. 46, as part of the treasure seen by a sleeping man's soul (Motif N531.3). Under Izumi, "Springs," the Minzokugaku Jiten suggests a connection between legends of springs turning to sake and festival rites held at springs, whose water may have been used in making holy sake.

Text from Bungo Densetsu Shu, pp. 50–51. Collected by Hanako Yoshinaga.

MANY MONKEYS abounded on Mt. Takasaki. Long ago a man named Nakao Kantsu lived near this mountain. As he was very poor, he prayed to the god Sanno every day for wealth. One day he set out for

Tanoura to sell *sake*. As he was walking along the seashore of Takasaki, he saw a hapless monkey, crying piteously by a rock. Kantsu approached the creature and examined it. The monkey was being painfully pinched by a crab. He released the monkey from the scissorlike grip of the crab, and the monkey ran off gladly.

On his way back home that day, as Kantsu passed the same place with a load on his back, the monkey came out to meet him. It took hold of Kantsu by his clothes and guided him up the mountain. After walking about two hundred steps, they approached a spot where a beautiful spring gushed forth between the rocks. The monkey drank from the spring and seemed to be asking Kantsu to take a drink himself. So he drank the liquid from his hands. Indeed! It was a most delicious *sake*. He took this liquid to the village and sold it. In due time he made a fortune from the spring and eventually became the wealthiest man in the neighborhood.

BLOOD-RED POOL

Legends of the ineradicable blood stain that attests a crime (Motif D1654.3, "Indelible blood") are widely dispersed; some New England instances are in my Jonathan Draws the Long Bow, *Cambridge, 1946, pp. 171–73. Three Japanese examples are found in Murai, pp. 38–48, where primroses, grass by the side of a pond, and azalea bushes remain permanently reddened with the blood of slain victims ("Primroses on Shirouma-ga-take," "Princess' Stone on Motodori Hill" and "Azalea Girl"). The earlier story in this book, "Fish Salad Mingled with Blood," p. 105, contains a food-bloodied curse as in the present tale. The curse here is from a golden cock, a central figure in certain legends, discussed in the* Minzokugaku Jiten *under "Kinkei-densetsu."*

Text from Nihon Densetsu Shu, *pp, 92–93. Reported by Yasuhito Yoshikawa.*

A RIVER about ninety feet wide runs through Kuwano-mura, Naka-gun, Tokushima-ken, in Shikoku. Once a Buddhist pilgrim came to this village and asked for a night's lodging at a rich man's house. He carried with him a golden cock and a mosquito net, kept in a small box one inch square. The master of the house heard about those things after they had talked on various matters. He had an evil desire to take those things. Early the next morning the pilgrim left the house. The master followed after him, and when he came to a pool of the river, the master killed the pilgrim with his sword and threw him down into the pool. At that moment the golden cock flew away, flapping his wings, and the master obtained the mosquito net only. The water of this pool became red with the blood of this pilgrim and the pool gained the name of Nigori-ga-fuchi [Blood-red Pool].

At the house of the man who killed this pilgrim, they do not pound *mochi*, because if they do, blood is mingled with the *mochi*. It is said that the mosquito net is still kept in this house.

OTOWA POND

The powerful taboos on women during the menstrual period, which persisted in Japan until recent times, are illustrated in the following tradition. Mrs. Kiyoko Segawa has written an article on menstrual taboos for the forthcoming Studies in Japanese Folklore, describing how formerly women lived in isolated huts during menstruation. The pertinent motif is C141, "Tabu: going forth during menses," and particularly C141.3, "Tabu: not to enter water during menses." The deities of mountain and pond appear conjoined here.

Text from Sado no Shima, pp. 51–52.

OTOWA POND lies about ten kilometers northwest of Kawarada-machi, near Mt. Myoken, at an altitude of five hundred and sixty meters. It is surrounded with trees bearing thick green foliage and contains deep blue water. A famous legend is connected with the pond.

Once upon a time, there came to Chofuku-ji which stands beside this pond a beautiful lady, humbly clad but bearing herself nobly. She asked for lodging there. The priest of the temple pitied her and let her stay in the temple, half as a guest and half as a servant. She kept her origin secret, but told her name, Otowa.

One day in the rice-planting season, Otowa, at the bidding of the villagers, went gathering bracken. Before she knew it, she approached

Mt. Kinhoku, which abominated the presence of women. As it was growing dark, she made haste to descend the mountain. On the way, without much thought, she washed her underwear, which she had stained, in the pond by the wayside.

Then, strangely enough, the pond rapidly enlarged, leaving a spot where Otowa stood in the center like a floating island. From the heavy evening haze came a voice: "I am *kami* of this pond. I have been waiting for you to come as my successor for a long time. Please, for pity's sake, become *kami* of the pond in my place. This is the fate that has been determined since the foreworld. I will not let you return to the village."

Otowa, in utmost astonishment and sorrow, asked for his pardon. But he would not pardon her. At the end of innumerable pleas, the voice said: "Well, I will give you three days' grace. I will send for you on the appointed day without fail." And it faded away.

Otowa came home dazed.

When she reached the temple, she withdrew into a trance. Next day, the priest in great worry consoled her and asked the reason for her sickness. She told him the events of the previous day, weeping bitterly all the while. The priest preached to Otowa the way of Buddha until she conceived firm faith as if she had been reborn.

The three days passed. At dawn, a voice called Otowa outside her door. Otowa, realizing that the time had come, bade the priest her last farewell, and prepared herself to leave the temple, giving the people, in her memory, her comb, clothes, and other possessions. The village folk thronged around her and grieved over her departure to become the *kami* of the pond in the mountain. Otowa then mounted on a palanquin, had the torch lighted, and rode toward the mountain while praying to Amida Buddha.

By and by, they came to an open field covered with tall grasses in front of a *jizo* shrine. There she said good-by to the village people. Before long, a sound of hoofs approached from afar, accompanied by a sudden gust of a strange wind, and a bitter rain. The village people all prostrated themselves on the ground. At this moment, a noble man on a white horse, clothed in white and wearing a gold sword, appeared, picked Otowa up on the front seat of the saddle, and disappeared into the morning mist. He was the *kami* of the pond.

For seven days, the mountain was covered with fog. On the seventh day a heavy rain fell, which covered heaven and earth with darkness. The village people say that during that rain the *kami* of the pond ascended to heaven, and Otowa became the *kami* in his place.

Even today, on the twenty-third of June in the old calendar, the village people give offerings to the pond, commemorating it as the day when Otowa wed the former *kami* of the pond.

SOURCES, BIBLIOGRAPHY, INDEX

SOURCES OF THE LEGENDS

COLLECTIONS

Aichi-ken Densetsu Shu (Collection of Legends of Aichi Prefecture). Compiled by the Committee of Education, Aichi-ken. Tokyo, 1937.

Aso no Densetsu (Legends of Aso). By Seishi Araki. Kumamoto-shi, 1953.

Bungo Densetsu Shu (Collection of Legends of Bungo). Compiled by the Research Group on Local Historical Places and Legends of Oita-shi. Oita-shi, 1931.

Chiisagata-gun Mintan Shu (Collection of Folk Tales from Chiisagata District). By Masao Koyama. Tokyo, 1933.

Densetsu no Echigo to Sado (Echigo and Sado in Legend). By Shogo Nakano. 2 vols., Niigata-shi, 1923–24.

Edo no Kohi to Densetsu (Traditions and Legends of Old Tokyo). By Ryuzo Sato. Tokyo, 1931.

Hida no Densetsu to Minyo (Legends and Folk Songs of Hida). Compiled by the Study Group in Nakayama Nishi Primary School. Takayama-shi, 1933.

Hyuga Minwa Shu (Collection of Folk Tales of Hyuga). By Chihei Nakamura. Miyazaki-shi, 1954.

Ina no Densetsu (Legends of Ina). By Kiyomi Iwasaki. Iida-shi, 1933.

Kai Densetsu (Legends of Kai). By Riboku Dobashi. Kofu-shi, 1953.

Kikai-jima Mukashi-banashi Shu (Collection of Fairy Tales of Kikai Island). By Eiichiro Iwakura. Tokyo, 1943.

Kiki-mimi Soshi (Listening-Ear Storybook). By Kizen Sasaki. Tokyo, 1931.

Minami Saku-gun Kohi Densetsu (Traditions and Legends of Minami Saku District). Collected by teachers and school children of Usuda-machi, Minami Saku-gun. Nagano-shi, 1939.

Mukashi-banashi (Fairy Tales). Collected by the Folklore Group of Ina. Iida-machi, 1934.

Miyazawa Kenji Meisaku Sen (Selected Masterpieces of Kenji Miyazawa).

Edited by Jinjiro Matsuda. Tokyo, 7th ed., 1941; first published 1939. Not a folklore collection.

Muro Kohi Shu (Collection of Traditions of Muro). By Teijiro Saiga. Tokyo, 1927.

Nihon Densetsu Shu (Collection of Japanese Legends). By Toshio Takagi. Tokyo, 1913; 2nd edition, 1924.

Nishi Sanuki Mukashi-banashi Shu (Collection of Fairy Tales of Nishi Sanuki). Compiled by Akira Takeda, for the Marugame Girls High School Local Study Group. Marugame-shi, 1941.

Okierabu Mukashi-banashi (Folk Tales from Okierabu). By Eiichiro Iwakura. Tokyo, 1940.

Sado no Shima (The Island of Sado). By Shunosuke Yamamoto. Sado-gun, Niigata-ken, 1953.

Shimabara-hanto Minwa Shu (Collection of Folk Tales from the Shimabara Peninsula). By Keigo Seki. Tokyo, 1935.

Shimane-ken Kohi Densetsu Shu (Collection of Traditions and Legends of Shimane Prefecture). Compiled by the Committee on Education of Shimane-ken. Matsue-shi, 1927.

Shintatsu Mintan Shu (Collection of Folk Tales of Shintatsu). By Kiichi Kondo. Tokyo, 1928.

Shizuoka-ken Densetsu Meguri (Tour of Legends of Shizuoka Prefecture), Vol. 2. By Kiyoshi Mitarai. Hamamatsu-shi, 1956.

Too Ibun (Strange Things Heard from the Eastern Districts of Oshu). By Kizen Sasaki. Tokyo, 1926.

Tosa Fuzoku to Densetsu (Customs and Legends of Tosa). By Masamichi Teraishi. Tokyo, 1925.

Tosa no Densetsu (Legends of Tosa), Vol. 2. By Kazuo Katsurai. Kochi-shi, 1951.

Tsugaru Kohi Shu (Collections of Traditions of Tsugaru). By Kunihiko Uchida. Tokyo, 1929.

Yamato no Densetsu (Legends of Yamato). By Juro Takata, of the Yamato Historical Places Study Group. Nara-shi, 1933.

Zoku Kai Mukashi-banashi Shu (Second Collection of Fairy Tales of Kai). By Riboku Dobashi. Tokyo, 1936.

JOURNALS

Impaku Mintan (Folk Tales of Im and Paku). Vol. I, nos. 1, 3, 4 (1936).

Kyodo Kenkyu (Local-Life Studies). Vol. VII, no. 1 (1933).

Mukashi-banashi Kenkyu (Studies in Fairy Tales). Vols. I–II (May, 1935–December, 1937).

Tabi to Densetsu (Travels and Legends). Vol. I, nos. 4, 6, 10 (1928); Vol. II, no. 7 (1929); Vol. V, no. 8 (1932).

INFORMANTS

Kawasaki, Nobusada, my student at the University of Tokyo, then 24, son of a Buddhist priest, born in Funabashi-shi, Chiba-ken.

Miyasaki, Masaaki, born in Hokkaido, 1923, grandson of a samurai; on the staff of the American Cultural Center in Kanazawa when I met him.

Saito, Mrs. Hitoshi Kawashima, born in 1888 in Ueno, Aki-machi, a small village on the outskirts of Kochi-shi in Shikoku. She had heard many tales while sitting on the laps of her grandmother and great-grandmother. She herself is the grandmother of my student at the University of Tokyo, Kayoko Saito.

Yamamoto, Shunosuke, then 53, president of the Sado Folklore Society, whom I met at his home in Mano-mura on Sado Island.

BIBLIOGRAPHY AND ABBREVIATIONS FOR NOTES

Anesaki = Masaharu Anesaki: "Japanese Mythology," in *The Mythology of All Races*; Vol. VIII, *Chinese, Japanese* (Boston, 1928), pp. 207–387. An excellent discussion of various kinds of Japanese traditional tales.

Brauns, David: *Japanische Märchen und Sagen* (Leipzig, 1885). 489+xxiv pp. An important translation, even though too early to draw upon field collections, but giving recognition to the variety of Japanese legends, of heroes, specters, saints, localities, and changelings. No sources or notes.

Casal, U. A.: "The Goblin Fox and Badger and Other Witch Animals of Japan," *Folklore Studies*, XVIII (Tokyo, 1959), 1–94 (section on the fox, pp. 1–49; section on the badger, pp. 49–58).

———: "The Saintly Kobo Daishi in Popular Lore (A.D. 774–835)," *Folklore Studies*, XVIII (Tokyo, 1959), 95–144.

Chamberlain, Basil Hall: "Demoniacal Possession," *Things Japanese*, 5th ed., rev. (London, 1905), pp. 115–21.

De Visser, M. W.: "The Dog and the Cat in Japanese Superstition," *Transactions of the Asiatic Society of Japan*, XXXVII, part 1 (1909), 1–78.

———: *The Dragon in China and Japan* (Amsterdam, 1913). Book II deals with "The Dragon in Japan," pp. 135–237.

———: "The Fox and Badger in Japanese Folklore," *Transactions of the Asiatic Society of Japan*, XXXVI, part 3 (1908), 1–159.

———: "Fire and Ignes Fatui in China and Japan," *Mitteilungen des Seminars für Orientalische Sprachen an der Königlichen Friedrich-Wilhelms-Universität zu Berlin*, XVII, part 1 (Berlin, 1914), 97–193.

———: "The Snake in Japanese Superstition," *Mitteilungen des Seminars für Orientalische Sprachen an der Königlichen Friedrich-Wilhelms-Universität zu Berlin*, XIV, part 1 (Berlin, 1911), 267–322.

———: "The Tengu," *Transactions of the Asiatic Society of Japan*, XXXVI, part 2 (1908), 25–99.

Elisséev, Serge: "Une collection de folklore japonais," *Japan et Extrême-*

Orient, no. 10 (October, 1924), 279–92. A review article of Japanese field-collected folklore books.

Erskine, William H.: *Japanese Customs: Their Origin and Value* (Tokyo, 5th ed., n.d., originally published 1925). Ch. 6 on "Old Burial Customs" discusses human-sacrifice legends.

Griffis, William E.: "Japanese Fox-Myths," *Lippincott's Magazine,* XIII (1874), 57–64.

Hearn = *The Writings of Lafcadio Hearn* (large-paper ed., Boston and New York, 1922), 16 vols. The important volumes for Japanese folklore are V–VI, *Glimpses of Unfamiliar Japan;* VII, *Out of the East* and *Kokoro;* VIII, *Gleanings in Buddha-fields* and *The Romance of the Milky Way;* IX, *Exotics and Retrospectives* and *In Ghostly Japan;* X, *Shadowings* and *A Japanese Miscellany;* XI, *Kotto* and *Kwaidan.*

Hibbard, Esther L.: "The Ulysses Motif in Japanese Literature," *Journal of American Folklore,* LIX (1946), 222–46.

Ikeda = Hiroko Ikeda: *A Type and Motif Index of Japanese Folk-Literature.* Doctoral dissertation, Indiana University, 1955.

Ishida, Eiichiro: "The Kappa Legend," *Folklore Studies,* IX (Tokyo, 1950), 1–152.

Ishiwara, Yasuyo: "Celestial Wife in Japanese Folk Tales," *University of Manila Journal of East Asiatic Studies,* V (1956), 35–41.

Joly = Henri L. Joly: *Legend in Japanese Art: A Description of Historical Episodes, Legendary Characters, Folk-Lore, Myths, Religious Symbolism. Illustrated in the Arts of Old Japan* (London and New York, 1908). A valuable reference work for the folklorist.

Krappe, Alexander H.: "Far Eastern Fox Lore," *California Folklore Quarterly,* III (1944), 124–47.

Kurata, Ichiro, "Yama-No-Kami (Mountain Deities)," *Contemporary Japan,* X (September, 1941), 1304–12. Contains the legend of the archer Manzaburo assisting the god of Mt. Nikko.

Minzokugaku Jiten (Japanese Folklore Dictionary), compiled by the Folklore Institute of Japan under the supervision of Kunio Yanagita (Tokyo, 1951). I had access to a manuscript translation by Masanori Takatsuka at the Institute's Tokyo library. This has since been edited for publication by George K. Brady, and is now available in the University of Kentucky Press microcards, Series A, *Modern Language Series 18, 1958* (17 cards).

Mitford = Lord Redesdale (A.B. Mitford): *Tales of Old Japan* (London, 1915). A standard older work, first published in 1871, containing some legendary traditions, particularly in the section "Concerning Certain Superstitions," pp. 199–226.

Mock Joya = Mock Joya: *Quaint Customs and Manners of Japan*, Vols. I–IV (Tokyo, 1951–55). Brief popularized description of Japanese cultural traditions by a journalist. Vol. IV has a section, "Legends and Folk Tales," pp. 1–48. Mock Joya continues to write on folk customs in the *Japan Times*.

Motif(s) = Stith Thompson: *Motif-Index of Folk-Literature*, 6 vols. (Bloomington, Indiana, and Copenhagen, Denmark, 1955–58).

Murai = Masaharu Murai: *Legends and Folktales of Shinshu* (Shinano Mainichi Press, [1949]. 98 pp. Twenty-one legends translated from *Shinshu no Densetsu* (Legends of Nagano), 1929. I met Mr. Murai, an English teacher in a Nagano high school, in June, 1957 in Nagano, and he kindly gave me a copy of this locally printed booklet.

Murai typescript = Masaharu Murai: "Legends and Folk Tales of Shinshu," a twenty-page typed copy of thirty legends, "Prepared for English Study Association of Nagano North Upper Secondary School, Nagano City." These are additional translations from *Shinshu no Densetsu.*

Nippon Mukashi-banashi Meii (A Classification of Japanese Folk Tales), compiled by Nippon Hoso Kyokai under the supervision of Kunio Yanagita (Tokyo, 1948). A 4-volume manuscript translation by Fanny Hagin Mayer, "A Study of the Japanese Folk Tale" (Tokyo University, Graduate School, Department of Japanese Literature, March, 1955) was at the Japanese Folklore Institute.

Opler, Marvin K.: "Japanese Folk Beliefs and Practices, Tule Lake, California," *Journal of American Folklore*, LXIII (1950), 385–97. Section II deals with "Fox, Cat, and Badger Legends" and III with "Perceptive Swordsmen and Sorcerers' Apprentices" (pp. 389–92).

Rumpf, Fritz: *Japanische Volksmärchen* (Jena, 1938). 340 pp. Some legendary traditions are included, e.g., no. 52, "Obasute Yama"; no. 59, "Asahi chōja"; no. 114, "Die Steinkartoffeln" : all variants of texts in the present volume. Sources and notes are given.

Shiojiri, Seiichi: "The Kappa in the Japanese Folklore," in Ryunosuke Akutagawa, *Kappa*, translated by Seiichi Shiojiri, new ed. rev. (Tokyo, 1949), pp. 12–23.

Suzuki = Yoshimatsu Suzuki: *Japanese Legends and Folk-Tales* (Tokyo, 1949). 144 pp. Forty-three legends, with no sources or notes.

Type(s) = Antti Aarne and Stith Thompson: *The Types of the Folk-Tale* (Helsinki, 1928).

Yanagita, Kunio: *Japanese Folk Tales*, translated by Fanny Hagin Mayer (Tokyo, 1954), from *Nippon no Mukashi-banashi*, rev. ed., 1942 (1st ed., 1930). 299 pp. One hundred and eight tales rewritten for children; a number of legends are included.

————: "The Japanese Atlantis," *Contemporary Japan*, III (June, 1934), 34–39. Discusses the legend of the image whose face turns red to warn of disaster.

————: *Studies in Fishing Village Life*, translated from the Japanese publication of 1948, by Masanori Takatsuka, edited by George K. Brady. I had access to the manuscript translation at the Japanese Folklore Institute. It is now available in the University of Kentucky Press microcards, Series A, *Modern Language Series 1*, 1954 (7 cards). Because of the interruption caused by the war, the research on this cooperative investigation by the Japanese Folklore Institute is less complete than the companion study on mountain-village folklore.

————: *Studies in Mountain Village Life*, translated from the Japanese publication of 1937, by Masanori Takatsuka, edited by George K. Brady. I had access to the manuscript translation at the Japanese Folklore Institute. It is now available in the University of Kentucky Press microcards, Series A, *Modern Language Series 2*, 1954 (11 cards).

INDEX

PLACES